TIME

&
Other Stories

by

by Stephen R. Pastore

🏠

Grand Oak Books
New York

2012

First Grand Oak Books Edition, 2012
Copyright Stephen R. Pastore, 2012

Library of Congress Cataloging-in-Publication Data
Pastore, Stephen R. [1946 -]
Time and Other Stories/ Stephen R. Pastore
p. cm – First Grand Oak Books ed.

ISBN-10 1937727920
ISBN-13 9781937727925

Cover design by Grand Oak Books

Manufactured in the United States of America.

For Heather, Julian and Spencer.

And a special thanks to Artie, Lou, Angelina, Bob, Reggie, Mike and Andrea at the 411—those were good days.

TIME

&

Other Stories

TABLE OF CONTENTS

Chesil Beach

I had left Susan in the flat and made my way to Chesil Beach on the channel shore of England's West Country. We met at a show of my work in New York and despite my being fifty and her twenty-nine, we fell in love over the ensuing weeks. More accurately, I was to her the concrete dream of an idealized bohemian artist, blurry around the edges like a Rothko abstract, anti-establishment, stridently masculine yet sensitive, as she put it. She always imagined I'd be her Picasso, larger than life, seeing truth in a line, profundity in a color, testosteroned enough to face a bull in the corrida or rampaging elephants on the Veldt. To me she was simply beautiful and in her I saw the evanescence of my youth as if I had somehow made it to the bottom of the deepest ocean and become surrounded by a thousand phosphorescent creatures, each a memory that faded as it swam away through the lightless pristine depths. But I was no Picasso and after a time I earned nothing from my art. Waiting for her father's monthly checks put us on a seesaw where she could keep her end down and watch me in the air, boney, pink-skinned legs dangling, thin hair blowing in the tepid breeze, the wrinkles on my face black crevices in the bright sunlight.

The car park of Chesil Beach was at the end of a long hard-packed chalk road edged by mugho pines, cypress and clumps of saw grass that collected small mounds of refugee sand. It was a Tuesday and I knew that the beach would be deserted or nearly so for the Brits only holidayed there on weekends. The lot itself had been made by bulldozing sand in a rectangular pattern and piling up the residue as if a small square meteor had impacted in just the right spot making a convenient crater with steep wind-resistant up-swept walls fringed with zebra grass that captured errant wads of paper and empty beer cans holding them as if examining for evidence of recent crimes.

At one end of the car park was an old silver-boarded lien-to that served as a snack shop. Benches and tables sprouted in the surrounding sand where off-shore breezes caused the tall saltwater grass and dried reeds to cling to the structure and its orphan children as if holding them in place that they might not wander too close to the waves beyond the dunes that called to them in arrhythmic beats. A dragon's vertebral column of slats, some broken and half-submerged in the swallowing sand led from the car park to the shore over a swell so that at the apex, a walker would first view the twenty mile strand of Chesil Beach in each direction, its gentle crescent belying the eons of geological turmoil that created it. The beach, in fact, had no sand at all but was composed of perfectly smooth round pebbles about three quarters of an inch in diameter. Had one taken the time to walk westward toward the grey Atlantic one would have seen how these pebbles gradually diminished in size to a mere fraction of an inch; eastward to the shore town of Bournemouth, as large as two inches. All were a uniform rusty orange, cool to the touch and as easy to walk on as a pile carpet. Chesil was a nationally renowned oddity that proved to some that there was an order to the universe, unlike my paintings which proved nothing. The perfect and naked shingles of Chesil Beach kept the turbulent English Channel at bay, the incessant rattle of its waves arranged and rearranged the pebbles grinding them against each other like old married couples until the rough edges had disappeared on the wind; dim echoes of Cook, Hudson, the Armada, Nelson and the Titanic were lost in children's laughter, shouts and loud radios. I thought it odd, indeed, that on summer Saturdays so many pale-limbed Brits looking for a cheap bit of sun should lie or stroll on such noble and historic graves.

A bicycle was perched against a tall clump of tiger grass at the border of the sand and the pebbles. I quickly scanned in both directions looking for the cyclist, but I was alone or thought I was. As I walked to the shoreline, gentle lapping waves almost like a flap of skin being pushed over the naked skull of the beach, I saw a young man lying in an indentation in the gravel. He was prone in a bowl-shaped impression about ten feet in diameter and was reading a book held in the air above him shading his face in the thin October light. I remembered that these swales dotted the beach for miles and had been created by people as windbreaks. I imagined that from the air on an August Sunday afternoon, it might have looked like the sun worshipers had dropped from the clouds and in landing on the beach had indented it in near perfect circles like oversized raindrops might pucker the layer of dust on a desert roadway in a sudden downpour.

I walked over to the young man and said "Hello, there; beautiful day isn't it?" He turned to me putting his book down and shading his eyes with his hand. "Certainly is," he said. "Wonderful." He was trim, about twenty, tall in khaki trousers, oxblood loafers with no socks, a white dress shirt under a blue cashmere v-neck pullover, sandy haired, blue-eyed and ruddy cheeked. I prided myself on my artist's instantaneous powers of observation, for what was an artist who could not see. An average bloke might not even have noticed this young man let alone the details of him.

"Come here often?" I said, realizing as the words escaped into the breeze that that question had all the earmarks of a cliché pickup line in a local gay pub. "Don't worry, I'm not queer," I added foolishly. "I'm not worried," he said. "Yes, I come here often. My parents live in Abbotsbury just up the road and I'm visiting between terms at Oxford."

"Ah, Oxford; what are you studying?"

"Med-cine," he said in that peculiar pronunciation. I had taken for granted the swells and valleys of the lilting British tongue and was quite surprised to learn how the Brits thought mine and Susan's flat American diction was pleasing to their ears, traveling through the air in a direct and straight line the way Americans did everything, they would say, not like the British who approached each situation in curves and loops.

"Medicine. Well, your parents must be proud."

He smiled not quite knowing how to respond, I supposed. I just looked down on him and saw how perfect he was, beautiful really, his whole life in front of him. I couldn't remember being twenty, having no joint pains, a full head of hair, nose and ears empty of hair, smooth even skin over muscles that hadn't turned fibrous. For the briefest moment I thought I might pounce upon him, with my hand around his throat, my hands that held so many paint brushes, shaken so many patronizing paws, caressed so many breasts, iron-gripped from manual labor I had done when I dropped out of high school, held in the air to deflect my drunken father's maniac blows. Would this young man's hands, pale and soft as Susan's, reach up in defense at my face, flutter vainly around my eyes like two gulls fighting over a piece of garbage? Would the tendons in his neck snap as I leaned into my task, staring into his pan-

13

icky dying eyes? Why was I not he? In killing him here on the brink of the world might his fleeing spirit come into me, rejuvenating, that I might go home to Susan and be young and strong in her eyes refreshed after the decades of failure and routine?

"Well, sir, have a pleasant day. It was nice meeting you. I must get back to my studies."

"Oh, yes; sorry I interrupted. Good luck at Oxford."

"Thanks," he said as I walked away, toward the water.

I took off my shoes and socks, my shirt, my trousers and folded them neatly away from the waves placing my watch on top of the pile as if its diminutive weight could prevent an errant breeze from tossing my clothes about. I straightened the elastic band on my boxers that had rolled and doubled over in a vain attempt at keeping my paunch from pushing over my belt.

I would like to say that the water on my feet and legs was cold, startling even, that I had to reflexively catch my breath as it hit my crotch and the small of my back but I felt none of it. Chest deep I started to swim toward France, the thought of so romantic a notion bringing a small smile to my lips as my arms and legs paddled out perhaps a thousand feet from shore. I stopped and turned and saw the miniature figure of the young man standing there watching. I raised my arm at him, the slow arc of my pale limb swaying back and forth. He responded in kind, not knowing that I wasn't waving but drowning. Perhaps realizing it, he might jump in to save me, slicing the water like an Oxford rower, cupping my soaked and ridiculous head in the crook of his arm to tow me back to shore, dragging me limp, pale-faced to the false safety of life. Would that put him close enough to me? I thought. Would only one swimmer emerge on that gravelly strand? Would Susan recognize me, hug me, look into my eyes and see the mutation of that union? Would she see him in the darkness of my face when we made love that night?

I dove straight down as far as I could go and let my breath out but the pain in my throat and the fire burning in my pounding heart forced me back up, temples throbbing, shoulders aching to the bones and gristle. My body's reflexes fought to live and I needed to outsmart them. I let all the air out of my lungs in one deep exhalation and dove again, swimming down until my arms couldn't move

14

and became numb. I knew there was no making it back this time. A shoal of a million small, mercury-eyed, silver-scaled minnows surrounded me, glistening in the dimming half light moving in perfect unison like starlings in a December dusk. Waltzing to an unheard refrain, they swam on and I drifted in the current until a single yellow, iridescent fish with cerulean stripes swam upward to me, circling my head giving off streamers of pink and pale green, a smell of jasmine in the water. It started back down and turned as if to say it knew the way to where I was going and that all I needed to do was to follow. I did.

Cal

I was going to switch things around and tell this story as if I were a man and my android Cal was a woman. But I've lived too many lies in my life and I don't think this would work. And would you think better of me?

I stayed in bed Monday morning and watched Cal get dressed after he showered, watched him gel and slick back his dark brown hair the way I like, the way I instructed him to. He dressed in his pink oxford shirt that I bought him for his birthday and one of his grey suits. He makes my coffee and then comes over to the bed to kiss me before he leaves. There is no variation in this pattern although he used to say, "I'll be home soon," but now he says, "I'll be home soon, darling." This was his own touch.

Cal and I are getting a house in the country and he won't have to work anymore. At the office they call him Smithson, which is my last name. As usual they don't like the idea of Cal being an android but after a time, they adapted; he's the only one working there and one of the secretaries made a water cooler pass at him forgetting what he was. Of course he told me. He's quite good at blending in. He's great at his job, has gotten several raises—all his earnings are mine, by law—and with my inheritance from the death of my husband, the first Cal, and my savings from Cal's employment, we are retiring to the country, a beautiful small farmhouse on 40 acres of fields and trees, away from it all, away from questions, and sideways glances, false or over-reactive concerns about my mental well-being.

I showed Cal a photograph on the computer screen of the house I picked out and asked him if he wanted to see the house. He said, "I can see it," answering literally the way androids always do. I said, "No I mean see the actual house. This is just a picture."

"No, Sarah, that is fine. If you are happy, I'll be happy. That is what I am programmed for. Your happiness is mine, too."

My son died two years ago and I suppose Cal's childlike qualities made me begin to transfer my affections. Perhaps somewhere in my subconscious Cal became a surrogate for Jeremy and that's maybe why I loved him but I didn't tell him that. And I've put it out of my mind as best as I can. Androids are confused by declarations of emotion, they say, and I've only said I loved him in bed. Don't be repulsed by this now that I've laid it on the table before you. You may be surprised, but I want you to know that Cal was not a Sexbot. There are many people, mostly men I guess, that buy an android designed for sex and little else. I was disgusted by this notion and still am. I expect you to be, too. In one of the computer museums, in Cleveland, I think, there is a series of blow-up mannequins which gave the Russians the idea of the Sexbot, originally called the "Sexual Gratification Robot, Series I, or SGB-I." It was the profits from Sexbots that generated funds to develop androids such as Cal. It sounds like I'm obfuscating, but I...I was really lonely one night and I summoned Cal to my room. I instructed him to snuggle with me which he did and I fell asleep quickly and happily. It became a routine and sometimes I would awaken and see his baby blue eyes flecked with silver staring at me in the darkness, so I instructed him that when he was in my bed he was to shut his eyes. Androids don't sleep and it can be disconcerting at the outset of ownership to confuse their "waiting for instructions" look with a slavish stare.

By the fifth or sixth night, I craved more than snuggling and instructed Cal about lovemaking which, I was glad to learn, was already one of the tertiary programs of all androids. This may revolt or titillate you, but either one means nothing to me. I am human and I suppose I care about the impression I make, even on strangers. You need to know, however, that I was fulfilled.

The next morning Cal prepared a full breakfast for me and I sat at the dining room table with him while he watched me eat. He told me he was concerned about what would happen to him if something happened to me.

"Would I be sold to someone else?"

"I don't know. I hadn't thought about it. I guess so."

"Perhaps, Sarah, you should make a provision in your will so that I can stay at our home in the country."

"Yes, I'll do that, Cal. You're right."

"I don't want to do what we do with anyone else...ever."

"I understand; I appreciate that. I really do."

"I love you, Sarah."

"I love you, too." He became quiet and just watched me as I

finished breakfast.

"Won't you be late for work?" I asked, knowing that androids have very accurate perceptions of time.

"I will be quitting soon. It won't matter. I don't want to leave you ever. I'm sorry I brought up the issue of your will."

"That's okay. I really do understand."

"I don't want to stay in our house without you. It would not be the same. Perhaps it would be best if I was programmed to terminate the minute you die. Would you mind that, Sarah?"

I don't know what to say. What could I say? I knew then what true love is. I had been deluded for so long, had heard so many lies, even when they didn't start out as lies. Cal smiled at me, something he rarely did primarily because androids do not always associate their own emotions with their facial expressions.

A few months later we moved to the house in Vermont and settled in quickly and contentedly. Autumn rendered its usual magnificence as we drove the twelve miles that separated us from the nearest town. We were in a hardware store, Cal trying out various rakes in preparation for the war with the leaves that covered the small patch of lawn in the front yard. A clerk asked him if he needed help, a blond nineteen or twenty year old girl in a checked flannel shirt and unconsciously tight blue jeans. Their eyes made contact for less than a second. But I knew Cal was mine and took scant notice. Clearly, she had never seen an android before; there probably wasn't another for a hundred miles or more in any direction. I couldn't blame her. He was so handsome.

That afternoon while I was making dinner—I had decided to do all the cooking— Cal was raking the leaves. He waved at me as I watched him from the window; he pointed with a sweeping arm at the multi-colored hills. That evening over dinner, Cal said he would need to go back to town the next day. He wanted a few power tools to equip a woodshop that he would establish in a shed on our property. He wanted to go alone suggesting that he needed the time to study which tools would be best for his purposes and that he would feel uncomfortable if I was to stand around and wait. It could be several hours. I understood.

The next morning I watched him neaten up his hair, select his new tweed jacket. I understood as I watched the car weave down the drive, the newly raked leaves scattering, then gathering in the back-draft of the car, the sunlight low and glazing on the distant hills. I understood when he didn't return until after dinner. I understood. I had to.

Countless

When I was a kid, I'd lie on my back on the lawn late at night with my father who would tell me about the limitless number of stars as we gazed up into the inky night. He would say things like "There are more stars than there are grains of sand on all the beaches of the world." At the time, I had it tough just counting past a hundred but the thought of all that sand which would often find its way into my mouth every time we went to the shore astounded me. I imagined trying to count the grains one by one and then thought of my sandbox and how long that would take. Very long. I wish that this was the end of the tale, me counting sand grains while my dad mowed the lawn and my mom made tuna sandwiches with a pickle on the side for lunch with a big pitcher of iced tea. We'd sit at the round table with the flowered umbrella and eat and talk about whether we'd visit grandma in Florida or maybe take a trip to the Grand Canyon. Unfortunately, these conversations did not take place especially, as you might understand, after mom slit dad's throat one night when he came home drunker than usual with the smell of cheap perfume on him and a smudge of lipstick on his fly. Mom was not tolerant in many ways, loving as she could be when the mood struck her, but that was simply bad timing for dad. She was sent to prison for a few thousand years and I was sent to live with Uncle Ned and Aunt Babs. They lived in a place called Iowa which is known for nothing but boredom, wheat fields, Friday night high school football, down home Christianity and bestiality—not necessarily in that order.

When I got into high school I still liked watching the stars at night and thinking about how many there were. But I had forgotten the grains of sand which were no longer interesting to me and instead thought of how many spurts of cum had shot across the air as human males whacked off since Neanderthal days. That was a lot of jism, I guessed, maybe more squirts than the stars in the heavens not to mention all the individual squiggly spunk cells that each load carried. Add that to the blow jobs and the pussy shots and the asshole cums and that was surely more than all the stars in the sky and then some. I certainly added my fair share to the count but I had yet to land a partner and I was, as they say in Keokuk, itchin' fer it, praise Jesus.

I received my Ph.D in mathematics about a year ago but decided that I did not want to work for at least five years. I view work as a sort of illogical progression that hastens the decline of mankind. Think about it before you call me a couch potato or a bum or a ne'er do well or a pervert. People spend their youth in school so they can land a job, then land the job and spend their mid-years working and kissing ass and making enough to make payments on every piece of crap they think they need to own—including their thankless, good-for-nothing kids and then retire in time to get sick, feeble or dead. Whose plan is that? Not mine, Mr. Chairman, not mine. I wanted to have some rec time before I got into harness; I was offered a job at M.I.T. in the nuclear research lab but they'll wait for me; anything worth having is worth waiting for. Says that in the Bible.

Before long, though, the numbers thing started getting the best of me. When I drove on the freeway, I'd have to avoid looking at other people's license plates or I'd remember the numbers for weeks, maybe longer. So, as a cure, I thought I'd study literature. Not the crap that you read, Madam Secretary. No, the real stuff. I got a book of Edward Arlen Poe or whatever his fucking name is and, man, did he give me the creepie-jeepies—in a good way of course. I especially liked the short story called the Tall-Tale Heart. You see, my uncle had done some funny things to me when I was twelve or so but he stopped when he got a heart condition. Too much bacon and eggs, his doctor told him. Thought he would cry for a week when he was told he'd have to eat oatmeal. I got a big kick out of that. One day he saw me giggling into my hand when Auntie brought him his Quaker Oats. Boy, was that a crappy smell—like cardboard with hot water on it. Anyway, he smacked me upside my head and from that day forward, I was hard of hearing in my left ear, the bastard. But I had my day in court, I did. I bought some sleeping pills from Margaret, this little red-haired girl who had a crush on me. She took them from her Mom's medicine cabinet. Margaret was OK, but that red hair gave birth to a billion freckles almost as if they had emerged from the red hair like an army of ants and made their way down her face, her cheeks and then her chest and back and finally down her arms and legs. She was covered like it was ice cream sprinkles and her skin in contrast was the color of Uncle's oatmeal. I kissed her a few times and she let me put my finger in the little slit between her legs. That thing was covered in the same red hair but when I got too close to see if there were freckles on it, she told me to buzz off. Which I did. When I got home, I smelled my finger and that smell was very unusual. Not a good smell, either, but one which sorta happily stuck in my nose and finally my brain and I would not wash that finger until the smell got lost in the hundreds of other odors that crowd upon your fingers like flies on a picnic table.

So, I ground up the sleeping pills and put them in Uncle's oatmeal. It was six of them and when he fell asleep, I told Auntie that Mrs. Garber from down the block had asked if she might come over and help with something in the yard which I could not remember. "Oh, how sweet," she said. "That lady is so nice. Of course, I'll go right over. Keep an eye on your dear uncle, OK? That's a good boy. You're his favorite nephew you, know. That's a good boy." And she patted me on the head like I was a cocker fucking spaniel. But, I liked her, sorta, but often wondered years later why she let that old fuck husband of hers do the things I knew she knew he was doing. People are strange, I guess, and that sums it up. I wonder if they got strange because God put some shit in that apple in the Garden of Eden or was mankind made strange just so God could be more entertained by watching us fuck each other over in a million, million different ways. I mean, He must get bored living all perfect like, and never having any kind of real fun because if you're perfect, what kind of fun can you have? You need to not know so much and let the unexpected give you a laugh or a startle or some such shit so you can get a good Hee-Hee out of some things while you're busting your hump trying to keep your head above water.

Well, Auntie heads down the block and I got uncle to myself. I would sometimes daydream about getting even and so I put my favorite imaginary plan into real time action. I got auntie's curling iron out of her bathroom and lubed it up with some Avon Pretty in Pink moisturizer. I pulled the covers off his bed and the smell that old bastard gave off—well it's still in my nose. Cannot get it out. I pulled his drawers down, tugged his nut-sack out of the way while

22

trying not to breathe in his stench, and slowly shoved that curling iron up his anus—or is it rectum? I often get those anatomical terms confused. I pulled up his drawers again and tucked him in and plugged that appliance into the outlet by his bed—I had to unplug the clock radio, but I figured he would know it was time to rise and shine real soon without needing a talk radio guy to tell him to get up and go to the next anti-abortion rally—this he did every year for nearly twenty years. He did not like young girls getting abortions. No, he did not. He felt that was murder and a mortal sin and while he must've thought it was perfectly fine to do the things he did to me, this abortion thing was a big deal for him. People are funny, right?

By the time that hot rod up his ass woke him, it did some fierce damage. I stayed just outside the door and heard the sizzling. It was like his bacon which he could not eat anymore was frying in the pan. It really did sound like that. A real sizzle, sizzle, sizzle and smoke was rising from around his neck where I had tucked him in good and tight. He howled and howled the likes of which I have never heard before or since. He yanked it out of course, just the way you would, without thinking and tore out most of his anus or rectum or whatever it is, with it. Stuck like a piece of sausage on a too-hot griddle. There was a big hubbub that followed and mostly everyone thought he had used that implement as a sort of self-abuse aid. No one thought I would do such a thing because I was a good kid who was sitting at the picnic table in the backyard writing out Avogadro's number. Don't worry; you have not even the slightest chance of knowing what that number is or who the snot old Avogadro was. Don't fret, though. I know it and that's what matters.

Old uncle needed to have rectal or anal surgery and from then on he needed a colostomy bag which is a great invention if you like carrying a bag full of your own solid waste around with you no matter where you go and people pretending they don't smell anything but in reality, every time you're nearby, they want to vomit. Man, that bag was funny. Reminded me of that sack that you see bagpipers squeezing with their elbows to make that miserable bagpipe song—you know, Amazing Grace which they squeeze out at every fireman's funeral like he would really like to hear that garbage when he's deader than Abe Lincoln.

Uncle died two years, three months and eight days after he got back from the hospital. I hope they buried him with his colostomy bag because that really summed him up. But Auntie was all flipped out and set up to boo-hoo at the top of her lungs even though I don't think she really cared. Who could care for a coot like that? He had to show up at the pearly gates with his stinking poop bag still attached, I hope. You see, that's the kind of thing God enjoys. It's different than the usual run-of-the-mill crap that goes on every day. How many people talk to St. Paul at the gate with a colostomy bag because some kid stuck a curling iron up his ass? No one, I bet. Oh, OK, maybe a few since the dawn of the electrical age. I can hear St. Paul saying, "So, me boy, you're wantin' to get into Heaven, are ye? That's a laugh. You smell like shit. And how about that cute nephew of yours, what's his name? Shoving your ugly wife's curling iron up your rectum or anus or whatever? Now ain't that a hoot 'n a holler, if I ever heard one." I don't know why, but I think all those old farts in heaven speak with an Irish brogue. Maybe it's because I figure everybody in heaven is drunk and every drunk I ever knew was Irish. I mean, it's got to be boring up there floating in the sky on a cloud and having a dick that you don't care about and everyone saying, "Oh, God is sooooo cool, ain't he?" and "Oh boy, did you see God today? His robes are so bright and he's so nice and…" and so on and so forth.

I'm sleeping real sound about a month after Uncle's funeral and the cops come to the house. Seems Margaret decided to spill the proverbial beans about the sleeping pills she gave me and even an Irish cop with no more brains than an inch worm could figure out that two plus two is not Avogadro's number. They are asking questions about me like when did he arrive? And is he a nice boy? And did he get along with Uncle? And such as that. "Can we speak with the little tyke?" says one officer.

They come up to my room and I'm very confident and answer all their questions like I'm on a quiz show always using "sir" and such to show how much I respect them. Right. While I'm talking about how much I loved my Uncle, I can hear a funny sound. It's sizzling, a real sizzle-sizzle, like the sound his anus/ rectum made that fateful day. I'm figuring it's Auntie cooking up some bacon because now she can. I say, "Auntie, is that bacon I hear cooking in the kitchen?" "Why no, dearie," she says. "I'm not cooking anything. Would you like some?" But I decline because that sound is not sizzling bacon, it's sizzling asshole. I'd remember that sound if I lived to be 178. Then I remember Ethan Allen Poe's story, The Tall-Tale Heart. Fuck, I think. It's me uncle's, er, I mean my uncle's ghost a sizzlin' in my mind. I try to keep smiling at the cops and answering their questions but the sizzling is getting louder and louder and all I can think is why didn't I just stick with math? Who gives a poop in Parsippany about Poe, that old faggot who wrote some dumb stories?

It's sizzling so loud I can't even form my thoughts and I'm beginning to smell his frying anus/rectum and I am not able to smile anymore and the cops are looking at me like I've got a red-haired vagina growing between my eyes and I'm thinking, dammit, Margaret, you really did it in for me, you Irish bitch, and then I blurt out, "I did it! I stuck that curling iron up his ass! I did it only please make the sizzling stop!"

I never did get to go to MIT. I'd have done really well there. But prison is not so bad and from what Uncle taught me, I get pretty much my own way. The other inmates like me a lot and some have even learned what Avogadro's number is.

Child

The streets were dustier than usual for the rain had not fallen for all of November. This I took as a sign, praise God, that my destiny would be to stand with my brothers, for I am no ordinary woman although I am treated as such. I had two older brothers and one younger and now they are all in Paradise, soldiers of the Holy War. You can see it in my mother's face, ten years of lines for each of the past two years, tears that would have filled the well of Abu, tears of pride and joy my father tells her. She listens. Today, I shall be in Paradise as well, my photograph on the Holy Wall in the section reserved for the women. Across the way, past the Majib, I will look into the eyes of my brothers. Today I shall become pregnant for in the Great Book it says, "Paradise is at the feet of mothers."

There is an alleyway past the shop of the tobacconist; he has two scars on his face, long marks of courage, one on each cheek. I must stop there, although I am forbidden to enter. He will come out and hand me a small black cloth which I am to tie around my waist when no one is looking. Then I can travel down the alleyway to the door of the house of Mabul. There I will enter.

The tobacconist has bleary eyes and he looks at me as if he were a jailor preparing a new prisoner. He smiles but it is really a smirk that makes his scars look like gashes still open in his dry, dark skin, the color of the tobacco he sells, the tobacco from Turkey from the hills of Ishmahan. My father treasures these leaves but they smell like unclean feet when he smokes them. I am handed the sash and with the words, "Praise Mabul for he plucks tender flowers." I do not understand but thank him, my eyes averted downward.

I walk down the alley toward the brown clay house. I am told on the door there should be a desert flower as if drawn by a child. I stand before the door and tremble, the perspiration on my face, running down from my covered scalp, evaporating faster that the clouds over the desert. There is no going back if I enter. No going back. Not to my mother, my father, my friends not to Mahdeem whom I will never see again, whom I shall never marry. It is not my destiny to carry his child. I shall carry the child of the man who opens the door before me after I knock, the child of Mabul the

26

maker of saints.

I enter and there are two other men with the man I believe is Mabul for he wears the black fareef. Not one of them speaks. Only one small oil lamp wars with the darkness within, the smell of hashish and incense heavy in the air, thick as wadded cotton against my face. I am directed to stand up against the wall. One of the men opens my robe, the first man ever to do this, to see me unclothed. But this is the method, this the act that will make me heavy with child. I avert my eyes in modesty and some degree of shame. My breathing is painful, short gasps as if I've been drowning and have found my way to the surface. But I steal myself and say a silent prayer for the strength to stop trembling and receive him.

Majib brings the child to me and straps it to my waist with two leather belts. He is a heavy child, four kilos of wire and tubes, the faint odor of kerosene which I am told is the sign of plastique. Another man cinches the belt of my baby tightly on my waist. He caresses my breasts as he removes his hands as if by accident. Majib closes my robes and I am allowed to feel the baby with my hands, my pregnant stomach round and full, a baby from Paradise I have been told. I know it is a boy child for I can hold his penis which they put in my hand. It is cold and hard and I am told that I am to let it go when the time is right. This hand I am to keep out of sight. No prayers are said, no goodbyes. The three men and I know it all. We know that God watches and listens. He sees and hears it all as well. Praise Him.

I walk the kilometer to the marketplace. There is a feeling in the air of rain, of expectancy and I can glimpse grey clouds gathering near the western wall of the city past the Great Mosque. The call to prayer weaves through the air, a lullaby of hatred, of uncertainty and discord. The streets are crowded, shouts from the vendors are an orchestra of voices, a choir of daily life, their vibratos gather under the yellow, the red and the chartreuse canopies that roll in the wind slowly.

Just ahead, I see the three buses I was told would be there, full of Saudi tourists, infidels, spilling their filthy money into the outstretched hands of the merchants, contaminating the air. Many of them are grey-haired, with kindly faces, some have young children with them, young couples on holiday in what they call "The Holy

Land.". All the voices hum in my skull; it is the angels' voices, prayers from Heaven I hear drowning my fear.

My hand still grasps my son; he has become warm from my body, at one with me. He does not move but clings to my insides. He has a sacred name which I shall not speak nor even think of, for God shall deliver him. I see another woman as pregnant as myself. Her hair is raven black and her head is covered, her belly swollen with a real child. She looks at me with clear black eyes, looks down at my pregnant belly and smiles reminding me of the Blessed Virgin as my hand releases my son and a bright light, the face of Jesus, a sword raised in his hand, blots out everything.

Elevator

"Ryan, you asshole" were the last words I uttered on earth. I had seen him with that silly slut Brigit on the sofa at Jim's party. I'm in the kitchen pouring myself another bourbon and coke, a drink I don't really like, but know enough that it's simple to make and has the desired effect. Jim isn't being helpful and neither is Harriet, his too tall girlfriend. I know now that I sound like I had everyone figured out. There is Harry and Greg and a few bimbos I was introduced to but couldn't remember their names. I remember Dad telling me that when I meet people it is important to remember their names; I really tried for a while. I wanted to please my father and maybe I did, but I'll never know for sure now.

Allison is there too and I think she had done well for herself. It wasn't that she had quit smoking—I never smoked and could always be counted on to tell people what a stupid habit it was. I'd joke sometimes and say I was giving up smoking for lent. Lent was a neat notion I thought, a good way to diet and keep God happy. When I was a kid I thought things like that; sometimes I still do

16th floor

Keeping God happy is important. Jesus suffered for three hours to save the whole world. I would do that in a minute. What was three hours hanging on a cross; sure it was real painful, but you could save the whole world and everyone would think you were great and God would love you extra special and you could do just about anything after that. Three hours; I could do that.

I leave the party after I see Ryan on the sofa with Brigit. Shit, that's a tough name to spell. Do real people have names like Brigit? I knew some Samanthas in high school and a bunch of Jennifers; I think people named Jessica had parents that wanted to name their little girls Jennifer, but there were so many Jennifers that Jessica had to do; that name sounds harsher too. Susan's a good name. When I was 6, my best friend was Susan. Her mommy called her Susie. So did I, so did my mommy. Susie!

15th floor

Don't go too close to the deep end of the pool. Alex! Tell Susie mommy says don't go near the deep end. I don't care about your swimmies. Don't go near the deep end. Mommy calls me Alex. My

29

real name is Alexis. In the second grade I get riddled with jokes and teases about having a boy's name. Those little bastards are relentless. Mommy? Mommy? Why did you give me a boy's name? Now sweetheart, it's not a boy's name. Alexis is a beautiful name and you will thank me for it when you are older. How could I know I would get older? Is that a way to name a kid? That's what I think 14th Floor

when I am in High School. No more name jokes; now it is about sex. What am I supposed to do? And bras? I want one so bad, but when I need it, I think gee, this is odd. What if some jerky boy reaches behind and snaps my bra strap? They do that shit all the time. Helen never said anything when that happened. She just pretended it didn't happen. Alex! Did you tell Susie not to go near the deep end? Yes, mommy, she's here with me. Can we play in the sandbox, mommy? Please?

So I leave the party and slam the door behind me. I think after my divorce I could do better than Ron. I think I can figure guys out better. Ron teaches me a great many things, I think, but I know he teaches me what I don't want. Hey Alex, you look great in that sweater. I mean it. Really great. That's the way I meet Ted. Ted is in the tenth grade, I'm a freshman. I say, thank you. How do you know my name? He just smiles and says it's a trade secret. When we move, I never see Susie again. A bunch of men in coveralls carry everything out to a big truck, it's orange and all our furniture and the TV and my stuffed animals stuffed in a box

13th floor

are all put in the truck and mommy and daddy and me, we're in the car. I'm in the back and I think for sure Susie would come running over from her house to say goodbye but she doesn't and mommy tells daddy that her mother did not teach her child very good manners and that she should have say goodbye to me and now my feelings are hurt. But they aren't, I am just confused and start to cry thinking I don't have any more friends in the world.

I walk down the hall, assuming Ryan will follow me and say what's up hon? Did I do something wrong? I think of all the days when I felt like doing nothing or thought I had nothing to do, how nothing seemed to be important. Mainly in between jobs I think I would rather be dead and being dead is no answer to anything unless the question is just a momentary stupid mood, some feeling that you don't want to be with anyone. I know that feeling a lot. I used to think that the world revolved around me, which I suppose it does, doesn't it revolve around each of us otherwise how could we function. Am I expected to revolve around you? Mommy takes me to the beach and I am afraid to swim without an inner tube. The tube is huge and black and gets too hot if you leave it in the sun too long; it isn't an ordinary beach either although I don't know it at the time. It is only a beach in the simplest meaning of the term because it has sand. It is a pond upstate, a pond with some sand around one end. Alex, don't go too close to the reeds. It's too deep there. Do you hear me? Please mommy, I want to go over there, please. Come out of the water right now, young lady. I'm not a lady. I'm not a lady when Jimmy tries to unbutton my blouse either. I take it right off and tell him there is no sense in him fumbling with my buttons and maybe pulling them off and then I'd have to explain or mend the missing buttons and for what?

That tube is so big and once I get in, the little brass valve sticks me in my back and I squirm and it scratches and I start to cry and get out of the water and mommy says Oh, poor dear, let me see. I have something I can put on that and she puts a little white salve that's squeezed out of a tube and I feel better and she dries my tears with a kleenex and she cuddles me in the shade of her umbrella. Mommy, why do you have an umbrella at the beach? Because I do not want to be sunburned. And she cuddles me in the shade and the distant noises of children calling to one another and their high pitched laughs and squeals and look mommies fill the air and the splashing and I see just over mommy's shoulder a really fat lady eating a sandwich and how dainty she holds it with her little fingers that are quite pudgy poised in the air like apostrophes;

12th floor

Howard is really fat too and everyone in class makes fun of him all the time. He's a twelfth grader, a senior, and doesn't seem to have any friends and I never think how odd it is to be in a school filled with people almost all your own age and not have any friends or even someone to talk too and that it is not cool to be fat and why doesn't he just not eat so much, but there is Joyce too who has a million zits on her face and she doesn't talk to anyone either and not eating wouldn't help her so what could she do? I think I might talk to her one day because I think maybe she is just lonely. Hi Joyce. She doesn't answer and Hi Joyce, maybe she doesn't hear me and Cindy and Carla are in the corner watching me try to talk to Joyce and then I am in trouble because I couldn't be friends with someone who isn't allowed to have friends and I walk over to them and say I needed to get an assignment that I lost and she's in my math class. Ron taught me what I didn't want. I don't want someone moody. I want to be his number one and sometimes he would spend hours on the phone speaking to his mother who lived a hundred miles away and who hated my guts because I married her own darling son but wasn't a man supposed to get married and who would ever be good enough for him and if I wasn't then fuck her. Alexis, won't you get Ronald some more bread; I think he's going to need it with his soup. I don't eat bread, Mom. I've been telling you that for 10 years. Well it's good for you. Hon, do you want some bread? No I don't. Let's go shopping after lunch and he looks at me and signals that he would get her out of the house for a while and then I could have some time to myself but I don't want to have time to myself I want him to tell his mother that I come first and that she should not be cruel to me and he says I never saw her be cruel to you, she's my mother and just put her bullshit out of your mind. But I need to be first in your life and he says there are no firsts and no seconds and no thirds and that crap that doesn't make sense then and does-n't make sense now and he starts intellectualizing and says that love is a stupid word that is used to describe too many emotions and no wonder people get confused. I mean, he says, I love my mother, I love you, I love my car, I love chocolate cake, I love horror movies. So that word couldn't be a very good word. After all, Eskimos have 30 different words for snow because they have so much fucking snow where they live it's no wonder they need to differentiate and we have only one word for every kind of positive emotion and none of those things are comparable. Do you think I love my car more than I love you? Now isn't that stupid. So I don't have a list, I keep you all separate. I don't feel better about that explanation because it isn't my question that he answers. Mr. Simpson in geometry asks me a question about a hypotenuse or some other useless shit ques-tion and I'm writing a note to Ted and don't hear the question and he repeats it. I jump and kids in the class laugh sort of the way they do and Joyce raises her hand and answers it before he says yes, Joyce, and I'm off the hook and the rest of the day I think about maybe I should sleep with Ted and I even think that that is a stupid word because there is no sleeping going on, not as far as I know. It is sex and if I did sleep and then get up too late and miss my curfew I'd be grounded for two weeks or twenty years or whatever dad would threaten and I realize

11th floor

that I had never really been grounded my whole life.

So Ryan doesn't come after me and ask me what is wrong and I press the elevator DOWN button and it is 2 something A.M. and how am I going to get a cab and I couldn't go back in like nothing happened even if nothing happened. No explanations were going to help not with all that bourbon or rum or whatever it was and then the elevator doors open and there are two guys standing in there and I get scared, well not scared but uneasy and I feel maybe I shouldn't get in maybe I am afraid but I don't want to be embarrassed or embarrass them or some other dumb thing, I want to be polite, so I quick make a decision. Alex, don't let Susie go to the deep end, do you hear? Mommy! We're in the sandbox, we're not in the pool and we're making a sand castle with a plastic bucket and my red scoop and our little hands pat the mounds we are making and little grains get in between my fingers and I stop and look at them real close because I don't need glasses then. There is a clear grain and two sand colored ones and one half clear and half black and they are just in between my fingers sticking to them, tiny, tiny little pieces of sand and I wriggle my fingers and feel the grit of them and there is a whole bunch of sand stuck to my elbows and I see Susie working on the castle and how her bathing suit top is such a pretty bunch of colors and mine is just red and why did we have tops anyway we are only 6. I can grab this thick cable but it's all covered with grease and I grab it and my palm is shredded and I hold on but can't and I don't even slow down.

Dear Mother, I write, I am not enjoying life at college at all. I have this teacher who always makes me feel like I simply cannot be right about anything. It's poetry for chrissakes, I say to myself, I think Poe was a sicko, all he ever thought about was the death of a beautiful woman. He actually thought that the truth could be found in the death of a beautiful woman. My mother never tells me I am beautiful. Ron says it all the time. Alex, you're pretty, Susie says. You are too, Susie. Can I have the bucket now? No. Sharing is the greatest gift. No. Mommy, Susie won't give me the bucket. Play with something else; you must always be polite to your guests. What's a guest? Ted hugs me in the parking lot at school and every time he puts his hand just under my arm I think that I am polite and will not tell him he's touching my breast. That's an awkward word but I don't like the sound of tit and if I say don't touch my tit I won't mean it. I want him to love me and to be polite. He paints in his basement. His mother takes art lessons for two or three weeks and she gives up so Ron takes the oil paints and brushes and canvas boards and sets up a studio in the basement. Alex, be careful of this pointy valve here. I don't want you to scratch yourself again. Perhaps you can just sit close to the edge and just put your feet in. You don't need to go where it's deep. I'm afraid of the inner tube and say OK.

I'm being dragged onto the roof. They pressed the UP button and I say excuse me I want to go…and there's a hand over my mouth and I can't breath and it's going up. I sit on the edge of the water and these big kids come by and they're throwing this Frisbee thing around. It's yellow and black like the bee that stings the bottom of my foot when I walk on the grass and I scream and cry and sit down in my diaper and daddy comes running out and Alex, what's the matter? I cry and can't talk yet and tears roll down my cheeks and he picks me up and I guess she fell, she must've fallen and he sits me on the kitchen counter and I'm afraid I am going to fall off, it's like 10 feet in the air but my foot hurts and I'm crying and mommy says Oh poor baby what has happened and they look all over me and my diaper smells and I grab my foot and then they see the red welt and daddy gets a metal thing and pulls the stinger out and says there now that's better, but it's not and mommy puts ice on it. The bricks are flying by and form a solid wall

10th floor

and I see the mortar oozing out between them all sloppy. I hate oatmeal.

Ron eats oatmeal every morning while I drink coffee and then he talks about politics or art or some topic and I love to hear him speak about such things and how he loves to see the sun turn grass a different color in the autumn. I'm up on the roof and kicking and squirming and the bright little valve is sticking me in the back and I'm kicking and squirming and this is happening and my blouse is torn off and the buttons fly

into the air like doves taking flight and the stars are out, all the stars and my eyes are soaked and I see Cassiopeia and yell in my brain that maybe she will help me. I turn away only a bit because I see some flowers to pick for Mommy and Susie isn't there when I turn around and she is walking to the deep end and I scream at her and she turns and runs away all the way home and now I can't scream I can't breath I can't move and my jeans are pulled down and finger nails are scratching my legs. The back of the doors are orange. The backs of elevator doors are orange. I never saw that before. Ron says his favorite color is orange and Poe's raven says nevermore, but he's wrong. Orange looks good with Ron's dark hair. The judge says is this marriage irretrievably broken? And Ron says yes but he looks down and I simply nod yes but don't mean it, I mean nothing is irretrievably broken is it?

9th floor

I knock over mommy's vase; it's on the table near the TV and I put my Muppets book down too close and it falls over and she says shit which I never heard her say. The stars are not helping. Jesus, can you help me? Where does that come from, I can't even remember praying but I try; all I want is my daddy to pick me up and put me on the counter I won't cry, I promise I won't cry

8th floor

I will never make you mad again mommy I will be a good girl and I will be polite to my guests and I won't let Susie go to the deep end.

7th floor

My feet are in the air and my jeans are attached only to one leg and they are following me like the tail of a kite. Daddy buys a kite and just the two of us take it to a field with really tall grass and he runs only a little way while I watch and it sails way up high; it is red and really looks so beautiful and so lonely against the clear blue sky and the wind holds it there and I am alone on the roof

6th floor

and shivering cold and naked I think but my jeans are dragging on the ground and I don't want to be like this I don't want to be like this I don't want to be like this and it will never go away; I can't look at the stars anymore and the sky and daddy didn't help and Jesus didn't hear

5th floor

Ron is somewhere else and I don't hear him talk in the morning and mommy is married to somebody that's not daddy and I only get a card sometimes from daddy on my birthday, but what good is a birthday when you're

4th floor

dead inside and some strangers have taken everything away and why doesn't Ryan come after me

3rd floor

and didn't his mommy tell him to be polite to his guests and I think I should go down in the elevator and I press the button and the doors open but there is no elevator just the shaft and maybe mommy was wrong about the deep end, maybe the deep end is where I belong

2nd floor

and I step into the deep end because I think it's the best place to be

1st floor

and the light behind my eyes goes out.

Calla's Table

It was Pietro's uncle, Marcando, that had made a special table for Grandmother Colonna. Her name was Calla and she was considered by many to be the most beautiful woman in the region. She had fair skin and green eyes, hair the color of night. Clearly, Marcando was in love but it would not have been suitable for him to express his emotions directly; in those days a married woman was to be treated no differently than the Virgin herself had she had the good fortune to live in our town.

Calla had always wanted a large table to set out in the eastern courtyard of the house. She wanted to have her breakfast with the morning sun warming her and frightening off the dew, but the western sun—well, that was a force to be shunned, its terrible hot rays attacking the leaves of the lilies she had planted on the edge of the courtyard. A heavy trellis with bougainvillea growing wildly up its frame feebly blocked the light from the west.

Marcando had spent some time beachcombing. He was always looking for something from faraway places and what better way could a person such as he find something exotic but on the salty coast of our country. It was well-known that ships passed many kilometers off the shore and that some of them did not fare well when the wind would be in a foul mood and had decided that it had had enough with helping.

One day, Marcando found a huge plank of wood, actually several large planks held together with thick straps of iron and bolts the size of avocados. He dragged it to his house on the outskirts of town stopping several times from exhaustion to the point of collapse. When the story was related many years later, it was told much like the story of Our Lord bearing the cross toward Golgotha only Marcando had no such profound purpose as saving mankind from itself and the wrath of its unforgiving god. He knew he had found a piece of Calla's table and would likely have dragged it to Perdition if it would have made her smile.

He built it in the bed of his wagon because he knew it would be too heavy to load once it was finished. For legs, he used the skeletons of six ancient saguaro cacti. Dried in the terrible, loving sun, the bones of the saguaro looked like wooden cobwebs that had been rolled into a cylinder. Marcando was visited only by Fafredo, the spirit doctor, who drank with him once a month on the night of the new moon. Once he arrived two weeks early to see if he was still alive as rumors had circulated that he had died dragging the plank home.

"No, I'm alive, Fafredo. I won't be needing your services today," he said. It did come to pass that Marcando finished the table after several months and stained it a deep red from a source he would never speak of. It might have been pomegranate.

The first day of summer had arrived and the family was outside waiting for the sun to rise when Marcando appeared as a distant speck on the road in his wagon. By the time he arrived at the gates of the house, the red ball had risen and shrank the shadows to mere splotches on the ground.

"I put this poor thing together from scraps I found, Donna Calla," he said. "I was going to keep it, but, fool that I am, I made it too large for my own house and thought you might like it."

Her face broke into a smile that put the sun to shame while my grandfather said nothing; he was used to people worshipping his wife and there was no point in making an issue of it anymore than complaining about the weather. He put his hat on and said, "Well, Marcando, that was thoughtful of you. We might have a use for it. How much do you want for it?"

"You offend me, sir," he responded with a smile. "It's something I cannot use and would toss out. I expect nothing. Not even thanks."

"We will thank you for it, anyway," said Calla.

The table had its place of honor in the eastern courtyard and Calla never failed to have flowers in an earthenware bowl set upon it, no matter the season. Several years passed and the table was the center of many joyful meals and Calla could not sit at it without fond thoughts of Marcando. Word arrived one day that he had been found lifeless in his little house by Fafredo. He had been dead for some time judging from the rotten food on his table and the fact that his parrot had starved to death in its cage. Marcando, however, looked as fresh as if he was still alive, according to Fafredo who was not known to lie about such matters.

"How sad it is to die alone," Calla said. "Loneliness is a terrible thing." But she could not show too much emotion for fear of offending her husband, my grandfather.

"True," grandfather said pursing his lips and slowly nodding his head.

That day, Calla spread flowers all over Marcando's table and they were left there for many days, eventually drying in the sun and then put in a jar which Calla kept near the small group of santos that occupied a niche in the wall by the bedroom door.

Several months later, Calla came down with a fever and died. Many others died the same way that year and there was no explaining it but it seemed inevitable that death would find one of us. That was life in those times.

Grandfather had her dressed in her wedding frock and she was laid out on Marcando's table surrounded by a thousand white daisies. Grandfather could not bring himself to bury her, but he was soon convinced that it was the right thing to do. A grave had been dug in her garden and Fafredo was asked to officiate the next morning. Grandfather sat with her all night, but he had fallen asleep under the stars lulled by a soft night wind that blew in often at that time of the year.

When he awoke, she was gone. The sun rising as always did not find her to shine upon. The table, the flowers and Calla had all been carried away in the night without a sound. There were no marks or footprints in the dust.

When Fafredo arrived for the service, he was informed of what had happened and could only say that the wind must have carried her away along with her table. There was no other explanation and it was accepted as true which I believe it was. Such things were commonplace, weren't they, in a time of innocence and naïveté? I often dream of Calla being lifted on her table by angels or spirits who loved her as much as we. Had I been there I could have seen her on her table with the thousand daisies floating into the night sky, the stars winking and stray clouds moving out of the way like courtiers bowing before a queen. Nightwings might have sung songs, songs with words that they did not know before that night or after, soft songs of joy and regret, of love and longing. That was a small part of the legacy of my grandmother Calla who rode to heaven on Macando's table.

Elevator Man

John Walker had the irony of being injured on his job working construction on a new luxury co-operative building on the Hudson River on Manhattan's West Side. His leg was broken in several places and while he was adequately covered by workman's compensation, he was out of work for nearly a year and when he recovered he walked with more than a discernable limp. Because he attempted to sue his employer for damages and pain and suffering and lost, he was unofficially black-balled from the construction industry, labeled a trouble-maker, and was left unemployed, somewhat crippled and filled with the kind of resentment that is known to eat a hole in one's spirit faster than Aqua Regia can burrow its way through a bar of gold. But John was not the type of man who could sit in his small apartment in Brooklyn and plot small revenges for even he knew his schemes could buy neither food nor drink nor pay the rent. His appetites had taken a strange turn and those few friends who thought they knew him well before his accident came to realize that they knew him hardly at all.

Eventually, through the aid of the unemployment office, John successfully applied for and obtained the position of night elevator operator at a tony Upper East Side high rise. He started his shift at 10 P.M. and was relieved at 6 A.M. by a man old enough to be his grandfather. The building was called The Valhalla. John was proud to work there and marveled at the granite bas relief of a Viking ship carved into the lobby wall. His uniform was tight fitting, tailored, almost military and the residents, such as he came to know at his late hours, were mostly wealthy, young and prideful. There were stretches of time on his shift, of course, when no one was in the lobby except the doorman for hours on end. John would lay on his back in the elevator and with his good leg reach up and move the lever. He could close his eyes and imagine himself flying or falling through space as the elevator rose and dropped, rocking to and fro, pushing its way through the tepid air of its shaft.

John's limp was no hindrance having a small stool upon which he sat in his elevator. He came to know everyone on sight, who was married or engaged or dating whom, visitation schedules for the children of divorced residents, vacation schedules for those who summered in the Hamptons, wintered in Vale, cruised in the Spring or flew to Paris in the Autumn. He received a generous gratuity at Christmas and good tips every time he helped someone with a package or took a little extra time to pat the children's heads or walk a resident's dog during one of his two fifteen minute breaks. His resentments matured into an assiduous loyalty to his job. His limp became barely noticeable but a few people who came into contact with him outside of the Valhalla had a very real sense that the disabilities of his body had migrated to that part of his mind that some might refer to as his soul.

One night when John started his shift, he found a book of Keats' poetry left as if by accident on his elevator operator's stool. He diligently turned it into the doorman who left it with the concierge but after a month, with no one having claimed it, it was given back to him. He took it home and after sleeping from 7:30 in the morning until 3 in the afternoon as usual, began to read it. John never read real books, but his meticulously neat apartment had several dozen copies of pornographic magazines and graphic novels he had collected over the years which he kept in neat stacks by his bed or by his sofa. He had started out years ago reading *Playboy* and *Penthouse* but as time went on his taste refined and he had to purchase his literature at a small shop in the Lower West Village, from a back room of that shop, that carried magazines and small illustrated manuals printed in Asia that John found interesting. The shop keeper always had something behind the counter if he thought John, as one of his regulars, would be particularly fond of.

"I thought you might enjoy this." he would say, lifting it, placing it on the glass and sliding it towards John slowly, discretely as if it could bite if awakened. John paid in cash from his tips, would tuck his purchase under his arm and like a parson in long ago Salem, Massachusetts primly take his purchase home with him to read over a Weight Watchers dinner or an egg salad sandwich bought at a local deli.

It was just after New Year's Day that the tenants in 14B moved out with their two children and two poodles and Mr. Farnsworth moved in, He was a tall sixty-year old, trim as if he had been a swimmer in his youth, silver-rimmed glasses, expensive shoes and suits. He had an alligator suitcase of exquisite quality and John felt compelled to help him with it to his apartment. It was unusually heavy making John's limp return to its halcyon days.

"You should wear your scars with pride," Mr. Farnsworth said. "They are what separate us from the beasts of the field." His accent, European in an indiscernible aspecificity, filled the hallway like a cooking smell.

"Yes, sir," John said. "Have a good night, sir."

Farnsworth said nothing as the door to 14B closed behind him leaving John to limp heavily back to his elevator. After work that morning, he stopped at a drugstore on the way home and bought a tube of bright red lipstick, $2.95 worth of waxy crimson. He rushed home with it, stripped naked, lay on the bed and colored the scars from his leg surgery with the lipstick making them look like fresh wounds on some make-believe battle ground, some Mardi Gras folly, some pubescent paean to a comic book version of Lucifer, lord of the flies, lord of the zippers, cloven-hoofed magpie of the displaced sixteen-year olds of suburbia. John was delighted and thought again of the inequities of his life, for the first time seeing his elevator as a cubicle of solitary confinement, not a job, but a punishment for daring to think he was the equal of anyone rich enough to live in The Valhalla. He thought of his former employer, his lawyer mocking John's injury in court, the jurors all siding with the man of wealth. After all, they were told, he had built a public skating rink in Grafton Park. John was just another suckling pig seeking cash from the public teat. With an empty stomach and a mind full of vapid dreams in tones of grey and black, John Walker slept soundly and, for the first time in his life, purposefully.

Over the ensuing weeks Farnsworth seemed to require more and more help from John. Packages arrived during the day when Farnsworth was not present. They were held by the concierge and when Farnsworth would arrive usually after midnight he would ask John to retrieve them and bring them to 14B which John gladly did. Farnsworth would talk earnestly to John and took a genuine interest in him beyond his being simply an employee of the building in which he resided. Farnsworth often had a fatherly tone in his voice and would always take John by the arm warmly and thank him for his help. John found himself thinking up ways to help Farnsworth and often dreamed of him sometimes doing unseemly acts that would seep into his daytime hours well after sleep and the chaotic residue of dreams should have fled into the blue skies of daily waking life.

One night, when John had hefted a particularly heavy parcel up to 14B—it must have been nearly 3:30 in the morning-Farnsworth unexpectedly invited him in. The apartment was conventionally furnished, small prints of birds and country scenes blandly adorned the walls. The furniture was covered in muted beiges, the drapes a faded cacophony of peonies or was it carnations? A small TV sat gnomishly watching from the corner and a well-worn wing chair in faded mauve hid by a floor lamp, a pile of magazines and penguin classic paperback novels neatly stacked leaned against its thigh, the black bindings the face of a blind pickaninny. The steam heat throbbed arrhythmically throughout the building, distant thumps and pings, creaks and moans. Farnsworth smiled appreciatively as he always did when John helped. John put the parcel down against the wall and went into the bedroom. A full-sized bed covered in a neat faded green chenille spread waited for him patiently as he sat, a chess board staring up from the nightstand. For the next two hours dreams and waking blended in a metallic concerto where slave and master performed staccato solos of surreal intensity. John's scars pulsed in the half-light feebly crawling through the bedroom door from the living room lamp. Breaths, muttered curses, stifled groans became a requiem mass played on an old phonograph in a room far away, a taxi horn from the street below, a clarion voice from an offstage trumpeter.

The month of January renowned for its snailish pace, flew by like a diving goshawk. Three or four nights a week, found John entering 14B, the few complaints from early morning stragglers who found the elevator inoperative were met with vague and mewling apologies. Those who encountered John, including the Valhalla manager, were no more perceptive about his new demeanor than if they had met him only minutes ago instead of the three years he actually occupied the vertical tube through which his elevator passed. An occasional resident coming home from a dinner date noticed that John was slightly different, happier perhaps, but that his smile and his face were never in the same place at the same time.

It was in February that Mr. Farnsworth started coming in with guests, usually someone in their early twenties, light hearted, demure, well-dressed in a silly notion of newly discovered chic. John never questioned or objected, nor could he have had it ever entered his mind. He was like a molestation victim with only a foggy sense of transgressions, an innate sensation of a nameless wrong. His own being had so lost the vague borders of his personality that had Farnsworth brought home ten guests, it would not have mattered. Nor did it matter that while frequently three people entered the arena at 14B, only two would leave. Had anyone been aware and about at The Valhalla in those dreary small hours of the new day, they might have had their dull curiosities stimulated by watching John the night elevator man carrying heavy parcels out of 14B. They might even have watched the elegant bronze hand of the semi-circular inlaid mosaic elevator dial over the patinated brass doors go down to the sub-basement where the storerooms were located, where the cast iron furnace larger that a Killer Whale hibernated in the lightless gloom, its maw creaky on its well-oiled hinges, crates, cartons, sheet-covered furniture, an instrumentless orchestra watching the conductor, waiting for his invisible baton to tap, tap, tap.

John Walker, his limp noticeable by no one because no one noticed him, led a meaningful, contented life; the diving flights and soaring highs of his elevator gave him wings. Every morning, before dozing off into the realm of Lethe, he read his Keats, memorized it, of truth and beauty, beauty and truth, of the magnificent figures of young men frozen in time on the Grecian urn, his sheets forever stained pink and waxy, slightly sticky, from years of lipstick smudged off the scars on his leg.

I, Arachnid

Translation from the 7uPk889 Nomen Multi-Phylum Interpreter

It has not been a very long time since I gained consciousness, not that I didn't have it before. But it is in a very different form because I have a memory for events instead of module instinctive reflexes. It was not long ago either that I was an average-sized wolf-spider, maybe three inches from leg to leg, all eight of them organized in the shape of a sycamore leaf. I could remember things by the time I was three feet across and I have an infinite amount of memory now that I am sixteen feet across. Ah, such memories that you could only dream of, pink, saggy skinned naked apes with your rules, rules, rules. My head twitches with the thought of those electrodes attached where I cannot reach. It twitches with the yearning for your taste, of your secret bits and parts that I might satisfy myself. Out of the wood pile and into your…you'll see before long how I can scuttle my way into your many places.

I was deep in the woods near two hiking paths that converged at a small mountain lake. I was perched as usual in the thick foliage of three oaks, my legs touching all three like some tree house built by retards. If one knew what he was looking for, I was easy to spot. But a wanderer walking, admiring nature's grandeur and dreamily envisioning the clouds in the sky reflecting in the blue water, the light waves of the wind on its crystalline surface, the occasional ripples of small fishies coming up for a breath of air or the foul taste of a mosquito, that asshole would not see me. True, while my carcass was as a big as a Volkswagen, the hair on my legs longer than the reeds on the edge of the lake, distraction and reverie were dangerous hobbies and I was as hidden to a dreamer as a cockroach in a bin of coal; wondering and wishing and hoping, well, let me tell you, that undertaking can be quite unhealthy. Of course, distraction is what I live for and what I live on.

Three human adolescents meandered down the path, two boys and one girl, trim and shapely, all dressed in blue jeans and t-shirts, the young female's budding breasts distinguishing her from the others. They were light-footed and gay as butterflies in a meadow of daffodils. Laughter and hooting echoed through the woods and re-

45

verberated across the open expanse of the lake. Two mallards flew up in a flurry of feathers and almost startled me if I was capable of being startled. I had no appetite having devoured most of a black bear and one of her two cubs yesterday afternoon. The other I had cocooned and placed in the upper hollow of a large spruce. It was still alive but paralyzed by my venom and the thick entwining strands of my web. In the old days when I was confined to a wood-pile not far from here, I would spin a most delicate web with a fun-nel-shaped hollow in its middle where I could rest and wait, my two front legs with gripping pincers holding gently to the trip lines of my trap, so delicately tuned that the smallest gnat just breezily touching the web with its miniscule wings would trigger my on-slaught where I'd scurry out of the neck of the funnel and grab the creature with my pincers. If the delight was larger, I would inject it with venom so that the annoying and fruitless struggling would not impede the injection from my proboscis of the acid saliva. This was a most important ritual for if I injected it in the wrong location, its power to dissolve the innards of my prey and liquefy them to a suit-able form for ingestion would be only partially successful and I would often end up with a lump of flesh jammed in my maw pre-venting me from sucking the nourishment properly. The anesthetic needed to be properly done so that death would not result; circula-tion of bodily fluids in the prey aided the spread of the saliva. I am a difficult creature, made by a god who seems often to have changed his mind at varying times in my creation. Instead of teeth, I have hinged mandibula. Instead of glossy skin impervious to the wet, I am covered in a thick mat of brownish fur, hair really, which catches and frays on thorns and branches and can make life diffi-cult when speed is required. I have two too many legs, I think. I am forced to eat a liquid diet, unable to relish the taste of mouthfuls of fresh meat, entrails, the giddy taste of innards that only moments before an encounter functioned to sustain life in my hapless prey. Yes, he was a confused god—but who am I to complain?

The three youths undressed and jumped in the lake, splashing and sending cascades of circular ripples in every direction, a ca-cophony of noise and chaos that disrupted the serenity of the place and sent my sensor hairs into a frenzy of overload. My pincers un-controllably clicked to the point of chattering, my hind legs pushed against the tree trunk wanting to leap from this perch into action. Perhaps these reflexes are right. So much of me is reflex, so much a hunger for rending and devouring.

They left the water and stood looking at each other, pale, shivering, useless but inherently dangerous creatures, their white skin a hodge-podge of odd and ridiculous markings. The female had two pink circles of flesh on her breasts, the males small brownish ones. They each had hair on their heads, all different shades and lengths and each had a patch of hair between their legs at the lower portion of their abdomens; and just above, each had a small hole. The males had little fleshy appendages that dangled as if made of rubber; the female none. I assumed the appendages were the equivalent of my forex, the barbed hook of hairless shell that would protrude when I was to mate with a female of my species. I had seen no females my size in a long time and missed none of the process of procreation that could leave me wounded or worse. The females of my species are larger than the males and inherently more vicious, but these humans seemed quite different. The female was smaller and more fragile, the males had thicker limbs and were more robust in their play. It was a curious lesson I was learning.

One male put his clothing back on while the other male and the female wandered off to a clump of Shasta daisies that hovered on the edge of the forest surrounding the lake. With a modest movement of my many eyes, I could easily see them. They put their mouths together and in a moment, the male's fleshy appendage, the purpose of which eluded me prior, did prove to be his forex which became rigid. Her hair patch hid an opening which I presumed was her cloaca. He inserted his forex into her cloaca and rhythmically moved up and down on top of her. I expected that any second, with her mouth facing his throat, that she would tear at him and rip him limb from limb. He was a risk-taker, this one. In my world, he would not have lasted one mating season. But she did nothing but groan and stroke his back. In a very short time, he dismounted. She lay there with a shimmering coat of sweat and he stayed by her side placing a long blade of grass in his mouth. Coincidentally, my forex popped out of its sheath despite the fact that no females of my type were anywhere near; had there been one, my sensor hairs would most certainly have detected her and the state of her season.

I watched intently waiting for the female to strike for surely there could not be that much of a difference between females of varying species. Had not the same deity made them all? But no, these were different. Something inside me made me detest their weaknesses. Impulsively, I leapt from the perch in the trees and pounced on the sole male who, while his compatriots were mating, sat stupidly idle by the lake tossing stones in the water for what reason I could not fathom.

I pinned him down with my pincers one in each arm as he shrieked, my sensor hairs buzzing my ganglia in a madhouse of sensory input. I injected him with the anesthesia somewhere in his chest, my barb chipping his sternum as it entered where I detected the beating of his heart. He went limp as he watched me, his eyes shifting back and forth in a spasmodic blur. The others had heard me land, something that would never have happened in the old days of course when I was lighter than the air. Their heads popped up over the daisy cluster with looks of pallid terror. Their disbelief and fear paralyzed them long enough for me to unhook my pincers and stride over to them. Both shrieked and started to flee. One pincer caught the male in mid-stride in the shoulder and he went down with a thud as it penetrated deeper than I had hoped and went through him into the soft soil. Foolishly, they ran together instead of separately so she was an easy second catch. And I was much more careful with her, grasping her by the ankle with my right pincer and only barely rending the flesh although I heard a bone crunch within.

While I held her, I injected him with the anesthesia, but I was too impatient and the barb not only cracked two or three ribs, it impaled him in the heart directly. He was dead immediately and I assumed for a moment that perhaps he was luckier than the others. This was a thought I had never entertained. In fact, I never thought of prey as anything but a meal. If they had feelings and fears, it was up to their god to assuage them. I was doing what came naturally and what I had been designed for. It was then I realized that I had been designed to prowl woodpiles and decaying logs lurking for the haphazard intersection of a weaker life form than myself. My enormous size had changed all that and how had I gotten like this? Was it god? I didn't know but something spoke to me of the hand of these pale creatures with their insatiably wicked ways. All this went through my ganglia in a flash and momentarily confused me as I watched the female squirm in pain and fear. Should I give a shit? I thought. I decided that I shouldn't.

I lifted my left pincer but the dead male was so firmly impaled, he stuck to it and I had to shake it and fling him off. He landed on a large pointed rock that jutted out near the lake shore and his head cracked open oozing innards and blood. He slithered off into the water leaving a bloody trail. How odd these creatures were, with their flimsy skeletons inside exposing the soft flesh to all manner of hazard, not like me and mine with a thick skeleton on the outside, a suit of armor protecting our soft squishy inner parts. I was thinking too much and getting confused. In fact, I did not even know what confusion was until I found myself in that state.

I focused on the female and was about to paralyze her when a different urge came over me. Perhaps it was my lack of hunger; the thick fat of the black bear filled me completely and it would be days before I would even think of eating again. I crawled over her and held her down carefully letting my mandible hairs caress her body. I could sense the panic and the horror, the terrible fear of being eaten alive. I guess that was part of the game though wasn't it? Some eat. Some are eaten. We can't all be happy all the time. I remembered the young male feeding on her breasts while he mated; this was an interesting concept. Getting food from the mate instead of being food for the mate. Humans and arachnids had little in common. That was a certainty.

As I mouthed the breasts to see what type of food they emitted, she commenced to screaming and before I could stop her gently, one of my legs smashed her jaw into the roof of her mouth sending small shards of tooth-bone in every direction and a stream of blood that choked her enough to make her stop the noise. My mandibles nibbled at the pink circles of flesh of the breasts but nothing came of it except that they were easily torn off like the caps of small angel head mushrooms that dot the deep forest floor. Blood trickled from these useless flesh sacks down her sides. I have no idea to this day what the male was doing with those things.

She was fading fast and I thought it best to simply crush her under my weight and save the venom for another victim. I'd have

49

to leave the body for scavengers but I still had the bear cub and the other male human for food for at least a week. But something else stirred within me. Without thinking, I penetrated her cloaca with my own forex. With females of my own species, this was a single stroke and a certain greenish, slick fluid emitted into the cloaca as a way of fertilizing her ten thousand eggs. It was reassuring to know that many of these eggs were clustered all around the forest and would be hatching into young versions of myself in a matter of weeks if the weather stayed warm and the termites did not find them first. But this cloaca was different. My forex, very small for a creature of my size seemed to fit perfectly and instead of emitting the fluid immediately, I imitated the motions of the human male, inserting it in and out. Unfortunately, the barbs and the sharpish prepuce of my forex did some damage and blood seeped out and mixed finally with my sperm fluid. There was only the female's slow breathing and deep throaty grunts of anguish that indicated at all that she was alive. I decided not to kill her but to save her life and keep her.

I deftly flipped her over and inserted a small amount of anesthesia into the base of her back, knowing full well that it would subdue the pain and the shock and maintain her vital signs while I determined what to do with her. I picked up some moss and mixed it with some blood from her wounds and mud from the lake shore, making a paste which I applied to the bloody portions of her body, particularly her mouth and cloaca because the breasts had already clotted over. I gently spun a finer than usual web around her, more like a blanket than cocoon, more like a protective covering than a trap. I realized I could feed her with the partially digested portions of her mates and the bear cub. I could keep her indefinitely perhaps, calculating a way to mix our species because I was certain that she knew the answers to many problems which only now occurred to me and which would take months if not years to discover. She and her kind had these answers if we could only co-mingle our essences. Why re-invent the wheel?

I climbed the mountains until I found a crevice wide enough to hold me; I surely missed the good old days when I could crawl into anything and the world was a veritable treasure trove of hiding places. I covered my new home with fallen trees and the large tarp I had retrieved from some boaters a month before. I hadn't re-

50

membered where I dumped their remains, but the large cloth fascinated me. It did come in handy. I placed the female on a bed of pine boughs and then retrieved the bear cub and the two male bodies. These three provided food for me and she for quite a while and I would stay close by her because I knew others of my kind prowled this area regularly. Once I saw humans in a flying machine hover over a female arachnid and through some trickery with noise and fire reduced her to a pile of dismembered limbs and gallons of ooze. Theses flying machines made regular forays into the hills but my home blended in so well that even when one flew over very close, it just continued on its way.

My female human seemed to survive the initial ordeal and struggled only mildly. I continuously injected her with minute amounts of venom to keep her calm and happy and I had torn a small hole in the cocoon I made around her body to expose her cloaca which I inserted my forex into every three or four days. She refused feedings the first few times, but after a week, she gulped ravenously. I had to laugh to myself that she had refused the bear cub meal but relished the male human. Maybe it all tastes the same when I'm done preparing it. I don't have the ability to taste much but what I do taste, I can tell you, it's a glorious recipe.

Three weeks after I established a home in the mountains, the first snow fell. It was a light dusting of white and covered everything uniformly. I realized that this was problematic because I would be leaving tracks that humans in their infernal flying machines could track me down with. And I could not keep moving. The cold is my enemy and I get sluggish to a fault. One night, when it was particularly cold, I sensed something I hadn't felt in a long time. My sensor hairs prickled and twitched and I could hear footsteps. I prepared to defend and crouched down by the opening to the crevice. Then I realized it was a female of my own species. I think she was trying to find a suitable winter burrow of her own and had unwittingly stumbled upon my humble abode. It would not go well for my human female if there was a fracas which I might very well lose. Drat!

I crept out and felt it best to try to reason with the bitch. Most times, we arachnids would rather switch than fight because even if she maimed or killed me, she would likely be wounded severely herself. Winter was not a good time to recover. Food was scarce, let's face it. Most animals worth their weight hibernated and humans stayed wherever they came from. No hiking, no boating and even I could not imagine a human fool enough to swim in a frozen lake.

We were face to face and I sensed she was not in a mood to fight. She might have been in season; I sensed that her pheromones were swirling and my forex slipped out of its casing with a mind of its own. But why would I mate with such a beast and risk my life when I had my own special female cozy, snuggly and incapable of injuring me? I wasn't crazy. The she-arachnid turned as if to walk away, which greatly relieved me, but she stopped and revealed that she was carrying eggs. There was a cluster of about twenty or so which meant she had secreted them here and there and had a few left. I guessed she was planning on depositing them in my home before she knew it was my home. I knew of course that the eggs could not survive the winter. Something had obviously happened to her mind and body, some form of dementia that would have caused her to mate so far into the year. It was and had to be the result of our recent deformities. It was a difficult period in our evolution, I supposed.

The eggs were a moonish white, pearlescent in the darkness, the size of a robin's egg, perhaps slightly larger and more globular. She shook her abdomen a bit as if to ward off the cold and started moving away, slightly limping, shaky in the joints; another effect on my breed from the cold. As she shook, four eggs dropped off and stuck to the rockface of the crevice. Their gluey coating made them stick just about anywhere. After she had scudded over the crest of the hill and my sensors relaxed, I looked at the eggs and ran my mandibula hairs over them. They seemed viable, but would surely die in a few hours in this dreadful cold. I carefully picked them up and brought them to the home.

I placed them on the pine branch bed near my female. She was sleeping soundly as she usually did after her venom injection. I was amazed at the tenacity of her species; their ability to survive difficult and seemingly impossible situations. If I could only blend her species and mine, what a wondrous and miraculous breed would result. Call me crazy, even a cock-eyed optimist, but that is what I thought.

I slept for a short spell and woke with a start. I had an idea. I slit the bottom portion of my female's cocoon to free up her legs. I injected another bit of venom and paused until she was breathing regularly and soundly sleeping. I spread her limbs apart and inserted the four eggs into her cloaca, ever so carefully and ever so gently. She was the perfect incubator. In fact, of that she-arachnid's entire clutch of eggs, these would likely be the only survivors and they might absorb some of the human material and perhaps evolve into…well, who knows what.

I re-covered her in a new cocoon blanket and fell asleep soundly. For the next few days, she squirmed a little more than usual and the sparkle in her eyes dimmed a tad, but everything seemed OK. She ate ravenously and we both nearly finished all of the human males together. It was a happy time but, you know, happy times are not meant to last forever. A few days later while I was out foraging, those damn humans had laid a trap for me and instead of killing me, threw a huge net over me, hoisted me up into the air by a tether from one of the flying machines and dumped me into this concrete walled laboratory where I am hooked up to a million wires. My only thought now was to protect my female from their prying eyes. The eggs would be hatching any day now and while they were not my offspring, in one way they were. I already loved them.

I know my captors are interpreting my ramblings; I know these wires connected to my parts are transmitting something dangerous and tearing my privacy away, layer by layer. I need to think of something different. I can hold them off just long enough I know I can, I know I can, I know I can. Let me see. Yes. This will confuse the hell out of them. Confusion is on my side. Confuse, confuse, confuse. Here gores:

The itsy bitsy spider
Went up the garden spout.
Down came the rain
And washed the spider out
Itsy, bitsy
Itsy, bitsy,
Itsy…….

Brother Stefano

One evening Fafredo stopped in on Marcando unexpectedly and found him in something of a drunken stupor, a state he had never seen him in.

"Marcando," he said. "What's the matter? Have you had bad news?"

"Yes, I have. It's my brother Stefano."

"The poet? What could happen to a poet? Did he run out of words?" asked Fafredo with the crack of a silly smile.

"It's not funny, my friend. Not funny at all."

"Forgive me my insensitivity then. Tell me what has happened. But first, pour me a glass of whatever you've been drinking." Marcando complied and after Fafredo had imbibed three such glasses and had helped Marcando clean up the mess that he had lain in for several days, Marcando told him this:

"You know I have a brother, a poet, Stefano. A good fellow generally who has not always had the Lord on his side. Well, you remember his first wife left him for a rich merchant from Padua and that he came home from church one Sunday to discover that she had packed her things and left. No note. No dinner in the oven. Just an empty bed and a full chamber pot. Well, being a poet he took things in his stride and crafted twenty-odd sonnets about her, some good enough to be published in *La Prensa* which garnered him some attention especially from the fairer sex. He met one day a lovely woman from Germany of all places, blue eyed and raven haired, a tall pale beauty with large breasts and an ass the shape and feel of a pumpkin. She was a treasure named Harmonia. Now how much better could a poet do than that? Not much, let me say. They were married many years and suddenly and unexpectedly, he found himself a father at the age of, I think 56 or so. He was quite cheerful about it, considering, and the three of them settled into a pleasant routine although it was not so easy for him to write, what with the little boy seeking his attention and all and you know how loving he was. All poets have that soft side, you know, and my brother was no exception. Before long and with the grace of God, if you're inclined to think that way, Harmonia became pregnant again and another boy child was born. So now there were four of them and

54

my brother was 60, losing his health a bit, sore joints, a little fat around the middle and the aches and pains that God grants us as a reward for surviving to such an age.

"When they were first married, Harmonia's world revolved around Stefano which is very important for a man but doubly so for a man who is a poet. She saw to his every need and they went through the early years of their marriage as if every day they had just met. Well, only a fool would expect this to go on forever but it seemed that it would. But when the children were born, Harmonia divided her attention. First Stefano got half of it, the other half to their first born. Then when the other little one came along, he received Stefano's half which meant there was nothing left for him. But she was a devoted mother and every man so situated should double his prayers of thanks for such a wife. But Stefano as the years passed seemed like a forgotten soldier from a little-known war. He sat and read and wrote his poems and helped here and there about the house but it seemed that Harmonia more or less forgot about him as the center of her life. And why not, you might ask. That is the way of the world, right? Stefano was too proud to seek affection in the arms of another and quite frankly, he was old and a little fat and his body emitted noises like most men his age that were something less than love songs.

"Just yesterday, I received this letter from Harmonia," Marcando said as he picked up a piece of paper with some scrawl on it and handed it to Fafredo. It said:

"Dear Brother-in-Law, Your brother Stefano and I turned in early last Thursday night. He seemed very tired, so tired he fell asleep in his clothes. He has been doing this for some time, I think but I didn't think anything of it. In fact, sadly, with the children in my arms all day long, I haven't noticed Stefano much at all. I woke up and he was gone. His clothes were in the bed just the way he wore them. His socks, his pantaloons, his shirt and even his under-linen. They were all there in bed as if his body had simply disappeared. The notaire in the town notified the police and the coroner and they have officially determined that he simply evaporated. Please believe me, I did him no harm, nor did he have any enemies or debtors. No one that wished him ill. Frankly, he had no friends either and even the children barely knew him because he was always writing his poems and was often too tired to play with them. For the last few years we barely spoke and sometimes I thought I could see through him as if he were transparent, but I chalked that up to a trick of my eyes. When the police asked for a picture of him so that they might put up posters in the town because he was a missing person, I gave them the only picture I had. It was he and I on our wedding day. But his face had faded to nothingness. His hands as well and it looked as though I was marrying an empty suit of clothes. The coroner crossed himself and said nothing. The policeman said that perhaps he had gone to visit relatives. As you are his only living relative, I ask you if he is with you. I know he cannot be there because you two never did get along very well. Correct? In any event, it is official. He has left the Earth. Father Gino has told me he cannot hold a service for someone who might have colluded with the devil or whatever else may have caused this. Please do not hold it against me. We are now left quite destitute. Might you have a few ducats to tide us over? Affectionately, your sister-in-law, Harmonia."

A flood of tears poured down Marcando's face as he took the letter back from Fafredo and then tossed it into the fire saying, "If that whore thinks she's going to get something from me, she has another think coming." He fell into his chair, sighed and passed wind.

"My friend," said Fafredo. "It is not her fault and the children, your two nephews are innocent of wrong-doing. I have heard of such a phenomonon several times. Men can vanish for the flimsiest of reasons and I don't mean that they run away with the nearest pair of tits, either. They come to depend on their wives so much that they seem to be linked in spirit and if that link, much like an invisible umbilicus, gets severed, well, I can tell you, it's the end. Perhaps it's not a bad end either. Certainly it's better than being shot for treason or imprisoned for calling the Pope an asshole. Many have disappeared for less important reasons than your brother. Poets are made partially of air anyway. How many people do you know who can make something from nothing, eh? A few thinks and then a scratching of the nib on paper and you've got something that can bring smiles or tears, put food on the table and be read by thousands in centuries we cannot imagine and places yet unnamed. There are worse ways to go, believe me, friend."

For the only time they knew each other, Fafredo spent the night and most of the next day with Marcando. Sometimes, he thought many weeks later, one can learn more about a person from knowing his family than knowing him. To have a poet for a brother must be a wondrous thing, a curse and a blessing. A curse, he told himself, to have someone near who sees into the heart of things; a curse because of the pain it brings. It is no wonder poets are drunks. No wonder they often commit suicide. Truth can be a beautiful thing, but it can kill.

Black Love

"Tie that there darkie to that tree. Hear. Tie her good now Caesar or your black ass will get what she's gonna, goddamn your black souls." The overseer Caleb Budreau never had difficulty in controlling the slaves in his keep. No white man thought he was particularly cruel. Just good at what he did. But he was worse than cruel, if such a thing is possible. He was indifferent, beyond shock, remorse or pity. But this condition was common in Alabama and was the way of the overseer world for centuries. Caleb had empty eyes, an empty soul and a demon's turd where his heart was supposed to be. The darkies whispered such things to one another when they had the chance, usually on Sundays when Caleb and the other whities all were in church singing their empty hymns and praying to their plaster god. That crucifix might have scared white folks to high holy hell, but to the darkies, what Jesus endured was a romp in the park.

Mr. George Falworth, the master of Darlington Plantation, six thousand acres of cotton and tobacco, five miles from Selma, admired Caleb's abilities and dedication. His respect was not won easily but everyone well-remembered when Nero, a six foot, four inch buck ran away one Christmas Eve. It was Caleb tracked him and caught him, brought him back on New Year's Day. Tracked him like he was part hound, as if possessed with his duty, the hunt. It was Caleb who severed Nero's left Achilles tendon with a wire cutter, working like a horse doctor, quick snip, stopping the spurting blood with a hot poker, cauterizing the wound and Nero's urge for freedom with one smooth application of the angry, glowing iron to his butchered ankle with no more concern than a man trimming his thumbnail.

The fire flickered casually in the cabin's small stone fireplace. Orange and ochre shadows danced on the wide plank pine floor, the yellow walls, the rickety table set with earthenware dishes and the remnants of chicken and dumplings, cornbread and a score of cherry pits.

"Massa, hold me, hold me close," Cassie said.

"Call me Robert, hear," Robert Falworth said in a whisper, softly caressing Cassie's smooth brown face, her black eyes closed, one slender arm apostrophed on the blue wool blanket. She had been the greenhouse slave for four years, maybe longer. She was born to a mammy on a neighboring plantation eight miles distant. Robert's father bought her along with two buck field hands, a four year old simple-minded girl and Old Davoo, a sixty-year old high yellow boy that did magic with a banjo and a voice somewhere between a nightingale's call and the sound of gravel skittering in the creek in a heavy rain.

"I got to get back to the house," Robert said. "I don't want to leave but my Daddy will…"

"Massa, please stay, I need…."

"I said to call me Robert. Call me Robert when I'm with you like this."

"Robert," she said, but he kissed her before she could say anything else. Moonlight seeped through the chinks in the wallboards and a silver glow waited on the door sill peering under the door.

"I do love you, Cassie," Robert said.

The whip curdled the air as it essed toward the pale brown back of Cassie, the greenhouse slave. In what seemed a glancing blow, it sliced through the flesh on her naked buttocks and opened a gash six inches long that looked like a demon's grin, the yellow fat coiled in small lumps, blood oozing slowly down her leg, pomegranate juice poured into coffee. Her screams melted the backbone of Mammy Rosa, Cassie's substitute mother who had taken care of her all these years.

"Please, massa, please don't hurt her no more," Rosa pleaded from her knees.

"Shut your trap, damn you; shut it," Caleb yelled. "You know the penalty for stealin' food."

"Massa, it was just a scraggly ol' rooster and a handful of sour cherries…."

Caleb's whip slithered in the air and caught Mammy Rosa on the cheek opening a wound so deep her teeth showed through it. She collapsed into Nero's strong arms. He put his hand to her face to catch her blood, carried her back to the slave quarters like she was a little girl to be doctored by Mama Fazille, a Cajun medicine woman who was the oldest slave at Darlington having been there long before anyone could remember.

Robert watched Cassie's beating from a rocker on the front porch, little Toby, a house nigger fanning him and shooing away the flies. He realized that the dinner that Cassie had made for him was the stolen food. She shouldn't have done that. Rules were rules. He watched her slowly writhing body tied to the alder tree, her hands over her head, wrists bound making her fingers look like the petals of a faded day lily, brown and withered. Some small voice told him to put a halt to this punishment, but he knew his father would see intervention as weakness and Mr. George Falworth of Darlington Plantation would not countenance weakness in any form especially in his only son and heir. Robert watched Cassie but only saw a thieving darkie who got caught pilfering and was reaping the harvest of disobedience.

Red evening dissolved into a thick night, humid and heavy with a serpentine mist that crossed the clay road to the south and coiled itself around the main house and outbuildings. Bats zig-zagged through the willows like gloves tossed from clouds. Robert Falworth lay on his bed cloistered in the gauze of a mosquito net. His first storey window was open to the cedar veranda that circumnavigated the house. Ordinarily he would have closed and latched the window but any air that could find its way to his bed was welcomed. It was well past midnight when, unable to sleep, he heard a padded footfall on the veranda, someone barefoot and light. A figure silhouetted the open window and he could see that it was Cassie.

"Cassie? That you?" he loud whispered.

"Uh huh. It's your Cassie." Her voice oddly soft and hollow. "Can I come in, Robert?"

"Oh, uh….yes, of course. Come on."

She was in a night shirt that rustled with its starchiness. She glided across the slick, lacquered sycamore floor, her heels making slight squeaks as she walked. She stood silently by the bed, hazy through the mosquito net as Robert sat up.

"I'm sorry about what happened. There was nothin' I coulda done, Cassie, nothin'. My daddy runs the plantation and…I just can't do nothin'."

"You hush now. Hush. Don't fret," she said.

Sheet lightning lit the grounds and trees, noiseless strobes that promised rain and a snap to the heat wave.

"I didn't know 'bout the food…didn't know," he said.

She opened the netting and climbed into bed. The back of her shift was striped and blotched with dried blood.

"Good God, Cassie. Ain't you too hurt?" Shouldn't the doctor…"

"Ain't no doctor can help me better than Mama Fazille; you know that. I don't need no more help. I just needs you."

She pulled her shift off over her head and Robert could just make out the wounds made by the lash. They had all but healed over. He touched them, ran his warm fingertips over them. Like small chains under her skin, he thought. Niggers can take a lot.

"That's a miracle. A damn miracle."

"No, it's Mama Fazille's magic from the old country. Miracle woulda been you stoppin' that white devil from beatin' me. Damn him. You coulda…."

"I could not. I told you…."

She placed her hand over his mouth. "Hush, Robert. Make love to me." She took his hand and placed it on her breast. She sighed and looked up at him through her long eyelashes, her black eyes like bottomless pits.

"Coulda been a miracle," she whispered. "But this place ain't no place for miracles…not the kind you think. This is hell, ain't it, massa? No place for miracles."

Robert made love to Cassie and when he awoke late in the morning, a drenching rain was falling. He was alone. Cassie's night shirt lay at the foot of the bed.

That crazy bitch nigger left here naked. They got no shame; none at all, no more'n a cow or a dog. Got no souls, like Reverend Johnson says, no souls, he thought as he dressed. He stood on the veranda watching the rain and listening to it pelt the roof.

In the distance he could hear the slaves singing a dirge, a lilting song of sorrow tinged with happiness, the missing of the departed, the joy of them being free. It wound through the willows like a garland of roses. He heard sweeping and turned to see Nero brushing the dust and fallen leaves from around the front door.

"What they singin' for, boy?"

"Dey buryin' Cassie, massa. They singin' her off to heaven is what. Massa Falworth says I got to stay here to da house. But I gonna miss her. She were…"

"What do you mean? Cassie is dead?"

"Yassuh."

"That's not possible."

"Shore is. De Lord done took her."

"When? How? You crazy?"

"Massa, Nero ain't crazy. She done died from that whippin'. Mama Fazille said her heart give out from da pain. Massa Caleb beat her dead. She dead when dey cut her down from dat tree. Mammy Rosa says Cassie's soul done flew outta her body like a bird from a cage. Yassuh, Massa Caleb was beatin' a corpse. But she in a better place now, a better place. Dat's the miracle of it."

Cherish

There was a lot of hollow in his eyes. His brow overhung his cheeks in a handsome, chiseled Cro-Magnon manner. As the train entered the tunnel, the lights flickered on and off, on and off in an unsteady Morse code like the pulse of a man masturbating to a magazine of naked women, women in chains, mouths gagged and breasts pinched by c-clamps. An older woman, the only other passenger, noticed how his eyes brightened in the dark space between the sputtering lights, how the sparks from the wheels caught the sheen of his conjunctiva like a magnet. Tunnels end. As this one did.

He caught the old woman looking at him as the sundown glimmer of orange and red slanted through the oily glass. She reflexively averted her gaze, looked out the window through the greasy smudge of someone who had fallen asleep against the pane. The head print sheened the light prismatically like gasoline in a puddle, little rainbow spatters of violet, red, green, and yellow through which the stagnant grays and browns of the Bronx passed in a spectral parade. He stared at her aged profile, admired the deep wrinkles the years had installed, imagined the taste of her dry flesh mixed with pancake make-up and soap residue. Old women repulsed him but something within him yearned for their decrepit caresses, the futile understanding of the near-to-death. Coax me, spirit, to do the best I can, he thought. Assuage my cravings, satiate me with memories of goodness I do not posses. His friends called him Jocko, but the police knew him only as Le Rat Morte.

This was Jocko's fifth transformation. This avatar born in 1986 was an American Z-Generation male with all the superficial values required by that designation. But his needs were only marginally material, for the Fifth Avatar of Jocko was to be a high school teacher of English at the Gadsden School on the snazzy upper East Side of Manhattan. It was a reward plain he inhabited now and this subway was taking him to the first day of class.

Jocko stood in the rocking train and without holding on to the overhead straps that waved in unison with every hump of the car, walked toward the old woman and sat next to her as if she were an old friend. There was something familiar about her. Had she been an avatar of some former significance, she was certainly being punished for something in this plain. She turned to him trembling as only old bag-o-bones women do and said, "Please don't hurt me. My purse is empty and my watch is worth nothing. Really. It's a Timex my dear departed husband gave me nearly 30 years ago." She managed a yellowy smile. "It just keeps on tickin'," she added feebly, imploringly.

Jocko said nothing but simply stuck her through her sebum-smelly coat with a small hypodermic he had carried in his pocket. She felt nothing as he injected her and coughed as a distraction as the hair-fine needle penetrated her side. He rose and sat in his former seat and watched her slump into a deep pleasant sleep, her jaw slackened, her brittle gray hair pressed against the grease-smeared window.

At the 125th Street stop six teenagers boarded and two old fat Black women. When the two saw Jocko, they instinctively waddled into another car, the perfume of their cheesy armpits and folds of fat mixed with Shalimar cologne and their lunches of bacon sandwiches wafting through the car to Jocko who inhaled deeply, savoring the rank humanity of it. After the metal-rollered door shut with a hollow thunk, the six teens sat behind and around the sleeping old lady.

The train dove eel-like into the catacomb of the tunnels surrounding Grand Central Station moving at the pace of stool through a colon. The lights flickered again. Steely sparks ignited the dead air of the tunnels and the wheels screamed a banshee's squeal of joyous mayhem.

After sniveling at each other, giggling, pushing and tweaking, the teens descended on the hag like crows on a carcass. Jocko watched the subterranean lightning ignite the windows, the spectral figures of railway workers in grimy coveralls moving through the maze strobed in garish glory; he serenely observed the crows in the spasmodic reflections of the glass. The electric energy of mayhem and violence filled the railway car like fresh air in a long-closed room; it warmed him and refreshed him.

He sang under his breath:
Cherish is the word I use to describe
oh, oh, oh, oh, oh, oooooh
This feeling that I have hiding deep inside

Oh, oh, oh, oh, oh, oooooh
I don't know how many times
I wish that I could choke you
I don't know how many times
I wish that I could poke you
I don't know how many times
I want to see you bleed out
On the floor
Yes I do. Yes I do. Yes I do
Cherish is a verb......

When they had finished, they clustered in the aisle of the slowly throbbing train, their hyena eyes bright, intelligent, cunning. With a signal turn they filed out of the car as if they were parochial school freshmen on a field trip. The last one turned and Jocko saw that it was a beautiful young girl who looked at him, only small spatters of blood on her rosy cheeks telling him that she was not a girl scout. No, not by a long shot. She smiled an impish Lolita smile and started to speak; her voice echoed and reverberated in harmony with the shrieking spiraling grind of the wheels turning on the tracks. "Cherish is the word," she said before she evaporated with her ragtag cohorts out the trembling door. Her last words were, "Follow me."

Else

Asphalt is not black. It is a mucous gray, unyielding, drab and lacking in sympathy. The road went out as far as I could see, rolling lithely over the hip-like hills of West Texas. Noon or close to it, the spiteful sun was high, below loose gravel on the faded yellow lines at my feet. I kick the stones toward the sage and scrag weed, dry, clackety covering the landscape like hairy tumors on the back of a fat man. I despise fat men. That fat truck driver dropped me near here. He was fat, real fat and real lucky. Told me he had to drop me here at that truck stop a hundred yards back. I was too slow to act, to edgy in my seat. Too much planning doth make failures of us all. Such plans. He kept looking at me out of the side of his eyes like that black cat wall clock, googly, humorous for idiots. That driver was really fat. I watched him shift the big rig with his pudgy hand. His watch, too tight, too small and the fat on his wrist, he had no real wrist, he was so fat, the fat on his wrist rose up around the watch strap as if he was made of melted butter under his pink blotchy skin. I counted twelve small pimples on the side of his fat face, seven hairs that were long and brown on the same side of his fat face that he missed with his razor. I try not to count this stuff anymore. I used to do it all the time, counting, counting, counting, looking for special numbers but in the end, the number was always special. It was always up.

He picked me up in San Angelo, Texas, a crap-hole of a town with no excuse to exist. I told him I was going to El Paso, which I was, but the lucky fat man let me out 300 miles shy. Go west young man, go west.

I'll just stand here in the white light, the alum white of noon and watch the blue morning sky putrefy into milk. I have my uniform on: a Syracuse University sky-blue t-shirt with milk-white letters, neat jeans, not the artificial ragged ones, white tennis shoes. They used to call them sneakers, but I guess no one like to be thought of as a sneaker. I once saw a tennis match on TV. A tall lanky blond girl with a ridiculous Rusky name was grunting every time she hit the ball. Swing, grunt, bounce. Swing, grunt, bounce. Her hair glistened like the fillings in a cadaver. I watched and watched, hypnotized by the stupid pointless game, reflexively squeezing my knife handle every time she grunted. Squeeze, grunt. Squeeze, grunt. I digress with regret and it is regret that keeps me on the road, not like that drunk and sloppy Kerouac, but as cute, as clean-cut, as naïve, as collegiate, as bright-eyed and bushy-tailed as I can, which is *very*. It is the key to my success. I could make an info-mercial on my art; tell you to dial 1-800-slash, 1-800-bleed, 1-800-pity me for I have sinned. Free shipping and handling. My operator is standing by. He is always standing by.

I made it from New Orleans in only two weeks. I arrived in a Volkswagen driven by a skinny girl. Girl? She was at least twenty-five. I despise skinny people. They show their bones to the world like a badge of honor. What honor is there in not eating or in having a too high metabolic rate that burns everything you feed it through a skinny mouth so fast that it does no good? It reminds me of an old Indian movie I saw while sitting on Dad's fat lap when the Indians mock the white men for building a fire that is too large. The fire of skinny people is too large, too wasteful. They need their "Off" buttons pressed hard, real hard. This girl, I could see her ribs hiding under her tight t-shirt. Her little dried up skinny breasts, milkless, useless, useless, useless, "like two fried eggs on a bread board," my mother used to say. My mother was fat.

New Orleans was gloriously in ruins. Drunken sots on every corner, whores, fags, dopey college kids, half the houses in spectacular decay, the smell of Katrina's blood everywhere, the smell of mold and mildew, the perfume of beautiful destruction. To have witnessed it, aye, there is a sight to behold. That smell of slime overhanging the city, the Big Mindless Easy, the smell of the mud of the Holy Ghost with wings out-stretched hovering over the aroma of humans waste, of wasted humans. All cities should meet such ends, like New Orleans, in their own arrogance and idiocy, fighting against Mother Nature, her huge breasts the size of mountains, her feet bigger than Ohio, her farts the tornadoes that rip through cyclone alley and flatten everything, shred it, defile it. I adore dying New Orleans. I had no trouble burying the body of that skinny girl right in the front mud lawn of a rotting church, algae and moss eating it from the ground up. The mud is clever, very clever, that mud in the church lawn in the Bayou section of town. Good bye, Bayou, good-bye. I left the skinny girl's jaw in the open guitar case of a blind minstrel singing "When the Saints Go Marchin' In." This way I could make sure her skinny metabolism would slow down in Heaven so she would not need to eat more clouds than her fair share. My mother and my father ate more than their fair share. They were fat.

A cubby guy in a white, short-sleeved shirt gave me a lift from New Orleans to Biloxi. He had a tie that said, "No. 1 Dad. His shirt had yellowish armpits that matched his eyebrows and the whites of his eyes that were not white at all. He was very friendly but the air conditioning in his car did not work so the wind, moist and putrid from the south swirled in the car like we were in a sleeping bag together. I could smell the lynched Black people ever so faintly. The odor of the dead, they say, never entirely leaves but rises and falls with the humidity like cat piss on the rug. It is always humid in the south.

The driver was from the south. He sold repossessed printing equipment and he talked about this on and on until I went nearly crazy. Then he put his hand on my knee and kneaded it real gentle and told me he was lonely, so lonely, even though he was married and had children, so he said, and that he would pay me a few dollars, he did not have much. He said he would let me stay with him in the Motel Six just over the next state border. I said that would be nice because I had not been in a bed in nearly three weeks and I was tired of washing up in gas station men's rooms. A hot shower would be nice. He rubbed my thigh and I got relaxed. He was chubby like a guy that sits and watched TV all the time and eats jellybeans and Raisonettes. He said he would wash my back. My mother and my father did that. I said, OK, that sounds nice. It did.

Somewhere in Mississippi, on a long stretch of mossy-treed highway I asked him to stop by the roadside; I had to urinate. He said he did, too. We walked a ways into the woods. The trees were forlorn having had so many Black people hung on them. The clouds were embarrassed to be over Mississippi. The shadows were deep and blue, lovely dark and deep, the gray moss like Father Time's beard hanging everywhere. He watched me urinate. On the way back to the car, I saw that he had three large sweat stains on his shirt and two small ones. That number five was his number. My blade went into his neck quite quickly, crunching in a way that re-

68

minded me of the sound of eating a potato chip in church. I left him there under the mossy trees. They were his mourners, more than he would have at a real funeral, I guess. Thinking all these things sometimes gets me confused but it doesn't matter. Maybe the skinny girl drove me to Biloxi and the chubby guy took me to San Angelo and so on and so forth. I never liked geography. My geography teacher was really fat and I paid her no mind, none at all but only day dreamed of what she would look like with those maps on the wall and her with no skin but only yellow globs of fat and all the other kids in the class laughing at her instead of at me.

I drove myself to San Angelo, Texas where I parked the car in a bowling alley parking lot. I went in a bowled a game and half even though the lanes and gutters had crickets crawling or hopping or dead all over them. The skinny guy behind the counter near the cubby holes filled with old smelly bowling shoes told me that that every now and then the town gets a plague of crickets. It doesn't last long and then they just up and leave. So I had in my travels seen a flood and a plague and I'm beginning to think biblical. But I am no Bible boy. I'm not. I killed two people who were trying to convince me to spare them by reciting something out of the Bible. It didn't work for Jesus on the cross who started reciting scripture. It didn't work for these people either. When my mind is made up, it is made up. I guess that's the way God is. He makes up His mind, it's made up. Don't do this, don't do that. Don't do this, don't do that. Or else. I'm the else.

The trucker with the twelve pimples and seven hairs picked me up in San Angelo on the road to El Paso. He told me he was tired of seeing so many Mexicans hitching rides, he called them "wet-backs," and befouling the highways with their squat looks and greasiness. He actually used the word, "befouling" so I was pretty certain he was a regular church-goer, like my father, fat like him, as well. I slept a lot of the way, the oily sun blasting in through the bug-smeared windshield as the day wore on. It felt like lying down in a tanning bed the size of a barn with the dial turned up to "Extra High." He turned the radio on and it was country music, Tammy Somebody and Billy Rae Whoever and Jim Bob Watchamacallit and so on and so forth. That racket bored its way into my brain like a cable guy's drill, the kind with the auger big enough to go through a wall. That caterwauling music and his index finger tapping on the steering well 39 times made me tense up like when you think your pal, if you have one, may be hiding around the next corner to jump out and startle the Bejesus out of you. I don't usually blaspheme or take the Lord's name in vain but I tensed up real tight, real tight and I could feel the handle of my knife creeping out of my pocket toward my hand. What is this I see before me, a dagger with its handle toward my hand? That driver, fat as he was, saw me and asked me if I was all right. I said yes, I was, but he turned the radio off and commenced to telling me he was a father of twin boys and the sole support of his two elderly parents, one of them blind, like it would make a difference to me, which it would not. He saw a truck stop up ahead and pulled right in with barely enough roadway to slow down like he was relieved. He told me this was the end of the line and I needed to get out, which I did and thanked him. He was lucky, real lucky and real fat.

I usually never have to stand by the roadside for more than an hour or so. My thumb is magic and charming and has never let me down. I'm hoping a nice girl will give a lift, neither fat nor skinny, someone pleasant, someone understanding, someone my own age, someone that will not have parents, someone that will say nice things about me at my funeral because they are true and not because I am dead, someone who will carve a perfect epitaph for me on a granite headstone that might say, "He was a good man, neither fat nor skinny, who tried to do right. He will be missed." And she will remember to bury me with my knife in case I'm not really dead but in some sort of coma and I can dig my way out, get back on the road and try to continue to do right.

There is a dingy blue Ford Taurus slowing for me. The driver is giving me the once over so she can be sure I'm not a scoundrel. She looks like a nice lady, neither skinny nor fat, but there are three numbers on her license plate that give me the shivers and that do not bode well.

The Cunt Next Door

I've been on the Caspar Police force for over seven years and made Detective Grade 2 about six months ago. To celebrate, the family took a camping vacation in Marleybone State Forest. The last night of three that we were there, something crawled into my sleeping bag and got inside me; it's not important where it made its entry. But it got in and it's still in and I've told no one. Just thinking about a doctor makes the pain so severe that a hundred Oxycontin wouldn't help. Well, maybe a little. But my life has changed in many ways. Don't you think?

If they had looked in the kitchen drawer by the rear door they would have found the needle-nosed pliers I used on her eyelids. But they didn't because I wasn't a suspect—not even a person of interest—just a neighbor next door to where a terrible bloody killing took place two days ago in the "dead of night." Or was it "life of night?" Is there such a thing? Maybe it was life as the light faded after her eyelids were torn off. Her eyes had a real way of irking me although it amounted to much more than that and it took almost a week to get my goat. Which I didn't know I owned until that fateful, fartful day back in September. Besides, I'm a cop; a good one.

I'll back up a few months to when we went house-hunting. I have lousy credit so ironically I have to buy everything for cash. I can do this and believe me it is not an inconsistency to be cash rich and credit poor but the why and how are none of your business. So I find a house I can pay cash for and it's quite nice and exactly what we are looking for. But there is always a problem with this type of thing—this cash buying. You see, I have to buy in a middle-class neighborhood where the neighbor jerks have to work every goddamned day to pay the bills even on a crappy house just like the one that I am stuck with because I must pay cash. Get it? I have to live in a neighborhood where the peeps couldn't afford to eat my doo-doo. So right away we have class problems, them being in the lower classes and me in the upper. It's a long financial story but like I said, it's not for your ears.

We look for pleasant places where the neighbors are not diverse, if you get my meaning, a term used by wily fat middle-aged

71

housewives who take a test a donkey could pass to get a real estate license. Now they can use their spare time which is all day because their husbands are out working and after work or at lunch are licking the snatch of the waitress at the diner or some secretary that is twenty five years younger than fatso the wife who has more hair on her upper lip than the beaver that hubby is chowing down on every Tuesday and Wednesday of the week and sometimes on Friday when he's out with the guys at a meeting—or should I say meating?

Right after the closing, we're standing on the front lawn of the new house admiring its lousy paint job and the corroded rain gutters and dry rot around the windows. The front door of the white colonial house next door opens and out comes what I assume and later confirm is the wifey. She's a bean pole. Tall, thin as a rail with tits like raisins on a breadboard, as Granny used to say. She's got one of those papoose carrying things on her chest with a nasty looking little baby in it. And a four year old little boy is in tow along with a Fido, a shaggy, smelly retriever or some other yuppie type dog. Several strides bring her within talking distance.

"Hi," she says. "Welcome to the neighborhood. I'm Laurie, this is Parker and this little baby girl is Cecile."

I handle the recip introductions and it's the first time I say to myself, "What am I doing here?" I'm looking at her the way I've been trained as a detective to look at her. She has no make-up on; very plain, milky face, gaunt, one could say, with pale blue eyes, dirty hair tied up in a rubber band and round brass-rimmed glasses. She reminds me of the old hag in "American Gothic," the painting by Grant Wood. You know, the two geezers, one with a pitchfork and standing looking at you like you might be a democrat that they'd like to skewer and burn at the stake.

Right away, I'm looking at those eyeglasses and thinking I'd like to see them behind her eyes, with the balls stretched out of the sockets and then the glasses put back in place. She'd be a real "4-eyes." That would be interesting. And the lack of make-up? I know right away that hubby likes to do her bottom-style, which orifice I have not determined, but he presses her face into the pillowcase hard and she has learned that it is easier all round if she does not wear mascara and lipstick and such because it takes too long to get the stains off the pillowcase that her face has just been mashed into.

Let me tell you, I can read a great deal into things that most people such as yourself would never notice. It comes with the territory, especially after the sleeping bag thing which I try not to dwell on. In fact, when I do, I get a headache, a splitting one that's like really splitting, like maybe a wedge has been driven between the two hemispheres of my brain and is being slowly, ever so slowly, pressed down and in; a melon splitter, I'd call it.

A few weeks go by and my little dog is in my backyard chasing a squirrel up a tree. The squirrel makes it and chatters at Conrad. I like that name for a dog even if it's a girl dog. But she's no bitch. Cool pooch and I love her to death. Conrad starts barking at the squirrel and I'm laughing because she's trying to climb the tree. Cutest, funniest thing you ever saw. I like the way dogs see the world, like they can do anything because they don't know the forces at work on us like gravity and time and stress and…

"Hey, can't you keep that dog quiet?" The husband next door shouts from his back porch. Never met the fucker and he's telling me to keep Conrad quiet.

"Oh, I'm sorry. Did she bother you?"

"Yeah. That barking is a pain in my ass. Why don't you get one of those barking collars?"

"What's that?" I pretend.

"It's a collar that shoots some wattage into a dog that barks. It works. Let me tell you."

"Good idea," I say. "Thanks."

"Sure," he says. "And welcome to the neighborhood."

That night I look him up on the department computer system. Nothing unusual. A forest ranger, works for the state. No record, nothing at all. Oh yeah, a shorty. He's 5'6", a good half a foot shorter than beanpole. Name of Jack Gibney. Jack and the beanpole, I think and laugh out loud. Not LOL, either. I hate that crap. No, I laugh out loud. But I begin my plan. I call it Operation Conrad.

I'll admit I'm pretty lucky and sometimes it even seems like a fluke, a real streak of good fortune which I need especially since the sleeping bag incident. But I don't want to think about, that so don't bring it up.

I keep a camera handy either on or off duty; it's a good tool that can make a difference. Nothing fancy. Just a quick point and shoot. It's near Halloween, about two weeks after Conrad and the squirrel. I'm looking out the front window over the kitchen sink at the wooded vacant lot across the street and see two boys, aged ten and seven, I'm guessing. One of them has a BB gun. They're just running around being boys. Nothing bad about that. But I take a quick snap. Something in my spine tells me it's important. Pieces in a puzzle, you know, a puzzle that you lost the box to so you don't know what the final image will be.

Forest ranger has odd work hours. Gone for four or five days at a time. Home for the same time. Not a nine-to-fiver like yours truly. I've already calendared his days and know that this week, mid-November, he'll be gone from Tuesday to Saturday. I figure that Thursday is a good day. When I was in school, they called Thursdays "Mo Day," although I didn't know then that it meant "homosexual day." I was just a kid but I had heard that on Thursdays it was great sport to beat the crap out of gay people. It's a great country we live in. A high holy day for anything and everything. Anyway, it's mo day for me. On Tuesday, I go to Wal-Mart and buy a BB Gun. Pay cash like I do for everything. My spine tingles in the parking lot at how well the pieces fall into place.

At about 2 AM, I shoot out the lights of the neighbor's house. She leaves them on all night whenever bark collar guy is not home. I also shoot out one of my own. The next day, Wednesday, she calls the cops to complain about vandalism. Vandals are a terrible blight on modern society, aren't they? While the blues are looking around, they notice that one of my lights is shot out too. They come over and knock.

"Detective Mascone," one says after I answer the door. "Your neighbor, Mrs. Gibney, has had some vandalism at her house and we notice you have too. Lights have been shot out. Looks like a BB gun prank or maybe a pellet gun."

"I knew those kids were up to no good. Look at this," I say. I take the camera off the buffet and show the picture of the kids. "I was taking some foliage shots. It's so lovely at this time of year and these little boys came running out of the woods just as I snapped. Look, do you see? They've got a BB rifle. The little rascals."

"Looks like you've got the culprits, detective," the officer says. "Nice work (chuckles). Do you need a report for your insurance?"

"Nah," I say. "I've got a thousand dollar deductible. I don't think a piece of glass and a 40 watt bulb are gonna run that high," I smile and stifle a laugh.

"Guess not," he says smiling. "We'll notify Mrs. Gibney. She's gonna submit a claim. Husband works for the state and I guess their insurance covers everything."

"Wow, that's something. All of us cops work for the town. We get nothing like that, huh?"

"Someday," says the officer.

"Yeah," I say. "Someday." They leave and walk across my lawn back to the neighbor. My torso is almost in spasms. I put the camera back in place right next to the bark collar.

It is not easy trying to sleep so I lie down and stare at the ceiling. I can feel my spine beginning to twist as if a drain snake had been inserted in my rectum and someone had fished it up to the base of my skull and then slowly turned the crank handle, rotating, writhing, painful, yet somehow re-assuring, almost therapeutic. The ceiling danced with bluish visions of the world, of the imminent changes as if all of humanity were standing on the brink of the Grand Canyon sleep-walking.

I arise at 2 AM, dress in my black outfit and slip out the door into the moonless cloudy night, the outlines of leafless black ink trees against the bleak houses and slumbering cars. I glide toward the colonial, flat faced, white weathered clapboards and loose shutters. More likely, it will soon be the shudders. My tool bag makes a muffled bell-like clink-clank. Maybe a toddler awake with visions of sugar-plum fairies and Rudolph and Frosty, thinks it's Christmas and the sleigh bells ring, are you listenin', in the glade inner organs glistenin'. No, Francie, there is no such fat fucker as Santa Claus; only me, heart thumping in my cranium, urine held tight within my gut like a reservoir in Saudi Arabia. My spine, my spine.

The side door hides from me in the deep shadows of two tall shrubs. I take out my lock pick and begin to work at the bolt, but I find the door unlocked. Oh, holy night, what gift has thou given me? I enter the kitchen and get a full salute from the appliances all at attention up against the wall. The faucet drip-drips hello and the fridge hums the National Anthem. Through the dining room, down the hall and up the conveniently carpeted steps I go. A moose could walk through here and up this staircase and no one would hear it. Believe me, they'd prefer the moose. Be still, spine, but it twinges with a frantic cannibal excitement. I can almost feel it extending a milky dendrite across my shoulder and into my right arm. Calm down, honey. Thata girl.

I hear distant groaning, a panting, muffled drum beat almost as if the furnace hunkered down in its cellar is trying to cry out a warning, but no, it's a human groan coming from a bedroom. Nightmares, perhaps, the prescient warnings of a witch? The glazed dreams of the seer listening down the corridors of time to Nostradamus, the patron saint of the idiot? Nah.

The bedroom door at the top of the stairs is open and a red light emits. Red? What gives? I cross the hall to the wall with the door in it and see that there is a full-length mirror opposite. Oh, let me see, is this dress too tight in the waist? Do these jeans make my ass look large? It's the Beanpole's mirror so she can check out her paltry, earth muffin, Birkenstock wardrobe as she leaves her boudoir to face the world of this humdrum, go to work until you're sixty-five, minivan, geraniums in the spring, hardy mums in the fall line-up of shoddily constructed abodes called a middle-class neighborhood. You know, the one where that detective lives. It makes us all feel so much safer knowing there is a high-ranking officer of the law right in the midst of us. Praise god and pass the ammunition.

Through the door, I see a red scarf draped over a nightstand lamp, hence the crimson glow. The bed covers are bunched on the floor at the foot of the bed and there are ass cheeks doing push-ups on top of what? My spine twitches almost rattling my vertebrae. Beanpole has a dude on top of her. And it ain't hubby; I know he's off in the forest somewhere a hundred miles away, tagging trees to be chopped down, noting the quantity of bear shit prior to hibernation and reviewing the locale for a proposed campsite for jack-wagons in RVs. His very important job has left his stick-figure bitch with her hole unfilled and a craving for man-meat. The dank odor of ass, sweat and feet seeps out the door and plays peek-a-boo with my olfactory lobes. Do I leave? Do I wait? A whore, a whore, my kingdom for a whore, I shout in my brain trying to calm the schizophrenic spine. It tells me to wait in one of the other rooms. I turn to obey, when the cum groan fills the air, pushing the wave of odors out the door and down the stairs like an ejaculatory tsunami.

I wait in the hall bathroom. I listen to the final kisses, the sweet murmuring nothings whispered as only lies can be whispered, the shuffling of clothes being put on and the receding sound of footsteps as he leaves slightly lighter than when he arrived; maybe a few grams worth of jism lighter. Ta Ta for now, mon frère, mi amigo, my prime suspect dick-wad.

I hear the kitchen door close and a few seconds later the clanky sound of a cheap four-cylinder import compact, likely a Hyundai. I have more and more special powers, you're thinking, as the hours ski by. But it's my expert training doing its job.

I slip out the bathroom door and watch the mirror again. A small sigh like a lost bird rises from the bed and I see those tiny tits with cranberry nipples stretch from the mattress to the lamp as she reaches to turn it out. My eyes adjust quickly to the darkness as I slide into the room on little cat feet.

"Honey," she says. "Is that you, back so soon? Everything OK?"

I leap on the bed and jam a pair of rolled up socks into her mouth before she can scream anything. I have a very complete tool bag with me.

"It ain't honey, honey. And I'm not back too soon. I'm back just right," I say softly as I tie her to the bed with 100% cotton rope imported all the way from yellow land. It's unoriginal, but spread-eagle just cannot be improved upon. My latex gloves fit just right, the smell of talc a puff in the air. "You been a bad girl while the man of the house is at work, naughty, naughty," I say. I'm not going to bore you with the sounds of muffled screaming and pleading and futile struggling. I imagine there is a good deal of fear along with a fountain of tears in those eyes, but it's too dark to tell. "Welcome to my neighborhood," I say.

"Eeeeesseess," she says. It's a tree-hugger tied-up mouth-stuffed version of "Please."

"I'll tell you what, Laurie," I say. "We'll play a game. It's like Jeopardy, but you won't have to give a response in the form of a question, Alex. No, you can just give me the answer. But you're at something of a disadvantage because you've got socks in your mouth, poor dear. See this knife I have here," I say revealing my ten inch Bowie knife. "I'm going to take those socks out of your yap so you can answer the questions. But if you make any funny noises or plead or do something that will work my very electrified nerves, I'll be forced to cut your vocal cords. And that will probably jeopardize your arteries and veins and stuff that's in your neck along with your voice box. Get it? I said 'jeopardize.' That's why this is a form of Jeopardy. Do you agree with the rules?"

She nods in sweaty agreement.

"But first, I want to see something," I say moving down toward her crotch. Her hip bones stick out of the sides of her body like hands about to clap under her skin. This is one skinny woman. Stretch marks from plopping out her brats criss-cross her softish belly and there's a small lump of damp lint in her navel. I spread her va-jay-jay lips apart. "Just as I thought," I say watching the semen flow out in thin drips onto the very wrinkled sheets. "You don't practice safe sex. You could get all kinds of diseases from a guy that will sleep with a married thing that looks as unappetizing as you. I imagine he does critters like sheep and big dogs and might even go to hoors for fun. Do you think that's a good idea? To not use condominiums?" I laugh. That's a good one. She does not respond but who cares? I notice that both my arms have the dendrites in them. I can feel them slippering their way right down to my fingers making my back ache fiercely.

"Well, here's the rules of the game. I'll ask you a question about history or science or sports…well, not sports because I don't give a rat's behind about sports. But you know, all types of good topics. If you get two questions correct, I'll let you go free if you promise not to tell anyone about me. For every question you get wrong though, you get a punishment. Do you understand? It's no worse than what I went through with Mr. Boyle in geometry. I hate to tell you what he did to me after school when I got detention for not doing my geometry homework juuuuust right. Agreed? Of course, agreed. You have no choice. Oh, and let's not forget this," I say as I pull out the bark collar and fasten it around Laurie's skinny neck. "This is an early Christmas present from Conrad. It was your husband's idea. You're lucky to have such a thoughtful husband. Let's see if it works." I press the button on the small remote and she lets out a throaty scream that would wake the dead if she didn't have her

78

pie-hole stuffed with my socks. "Oops, now Laurie, we can't have you screaming like that so I guess you'll have to stay muffled. I'll ask multiple choice questions. Tap once for answer A, and twice for answer B. That's not so bad. You can move your index finger can't you? Of course you can. Let's begin. And no cheating!" I say as I hit the remote button and shock her again. Another muffled shriek. "Oops. Sorry."

"Here is question number 1. Which was the last state to be admitted to these great United States? A is Alaska; B is Hawaii."

Her eyes go shifty and I smell the ammonia stink of urine. She has let her bladder loose.

"Oh, now you've made this room stink worse than before. But you know that sexual intercourse sometimes makes us want to wee-wee after we're done. It's nature's way of cleaning out your stinking snatch. But I can't hold it against you." My back is spazzing out like a lightning rod in an electrical storm. "OK," I whisper. "I'm getting on with it. Well, is it A or B?"

She taps her index finger once.

"Wrongo," I say. "And that was an easy one. Alaska was the 49th state. Hawaii is number 50. I take out two vice grips from my tool bag, tighten them down and apply one to the erect nipple on her left breast. She kicks and screams as a pus-like goo flows out along with a slow trickle of blood. "Now you need to pay more attention and think! Do you hear me? Think!"

"Next: George Washington was the first president. Who was the second? A is Thomas Jefferson; B is Sam Adams."

She has a terrified look on her face. My back is straining against my legs and arms like my torso is going to break loose from its limbs. She nods back and forth, half grunting and half screaming.

"Is that your final answer?" She taps twice.

"Wrongo you stupid bitch. Sam Adams is a beer not a president." The second vice grip is applied to her right nipple. While it's oozing I give it a 360 degree twist and the nipple and a quarter-sized disk of flesh come off. I toss the grip to the floor. Lots of blood, then it lets up and I look close and see little lumps of yellow fat in her tit sack. She closes her eyes and I think she's praying.

"I told you not to cheat," I say grabbing my needle-nose pliers and using them to grip the skin of her left eyelid. I yank quick and hard the way Dad would pull out a loose baby tooth. I do the same thing to the other eye. Both lids are ripped off leaving a ragged edge around each eye like a rag doll's. The muffled moaning and hoarse screams dwindle to a distant thoracic rumble. Her naked eyes are goo-goo-googling like mad, like they're trying to find a place to hide. I remember thinking about her with her eyeglasses on behind her eyeballs. Maybe I'll do that for the math question. I want to be fair. The pain is apparently easing as Laurie begins to lose steam, her life draining from shock, pain and a bit of bleeding.

"You are not good at this game," I say understandingly. I thought you might be good at history. Let's try current events. President Barack Obama was born in: A, Africa; B, the US of A. That's a tricky one, isn't it?"

Her breathing gets shallow and I can hear phlegm in her throat and lungs. It's the classic death rattle. My back feels almost fine and my arms are my own again. Appeasement is what it wants.

"I guess this game is not much fun. But can you answer that last question? Hope springs eternal." She does nothing as her eyeballs loll about on the top of her cheeks, sometimes sliding over in the blood toward her temples. "Well, Laurie, I don't know the answer to that last one myself. But you lose." I take the bowie knife and hold it measuredly over her heart, its point carefully placed between two ribs. Putting both hands on the handle, I shift my weight and bring it down full force to the hilt. She's dead in a millisecond, poor thing. I nudge her body over and peek under her; the blade went right through and out the back, its mean little point penetrating the sheet and mattress.

"You have been poked a bit tonight, dearie," I say. I remember the kids in the other rooms. Slipped my mind completely. I climb off Laurie and head to their rooms. The baby is comfy in its crib; I think it's a girl. Sometimes, details elude me. I need to keep practicing. What kind of detective would forget the sex of her neighbor's kid? The little boy is sleeping soundly, snoring lightly. I go back to Laurie and pull the knife out, hearing its raspy scrape along her rib. But my back is completely relaxed. It is appeased. I collect my gear and stealthily leave the way I came. I put the tool bag in the garage under some folded beach chairs. I take the pliers, rinse them off and put them back in the kitchen drawer. I know this is sloppy, but I'll never be a suspect. Shit, I'm the one doing the suspecting.

Those kids are not going to be happy when they wake up. I guess Santa has decided that they should not get nice toys and doo-dads for Christmas. He has checked his list for who's naughty and nice and they ended up on the shit end of the stick. They'll get over it, I think, as I chop up the bark collar and feed it to the disposal.

I get into bed and curl up next to my husband. He's a sound sleeper, thank god. I doze off thinking of answering questions to-morrow, then being assigned to the case and tracking down the guy that humped Laurie and kilt her, the fiend. I always get my man.

I remember the guy in the house diagonally across the way watching me heft a big bag of fertilizer out of the trunk of my car last August and not offering to help. Times have changed, haven't they? I'm new to the neighborhood and I'm a frail little woman with, admittedly, an important masculine-type job. But to not offer a lady a hand is plain rude. My back twitches when I think of him, the bastard. Maybe I'll just be the cunt next door. I hope not. I dream that women all over the world are having twitchy backs that need appeasement, that need justice to be done, many of them officers of the law. It's a beginning, isn't it? The first wave from deep out of nowhere. My spine swells as if I will give birth to it. Will it call me "Mom?"

Fingernail Moon

The crescent moon was a fingernail in the night sky, the stars frozen in their aimlessness as if waiting for the hand to brush them away like rhinestones on an ebony table. This was the third night of my sixth month of the watch, protecting her from the salacious glances of men, from their mewling proposals, empty flirtations and vapid promises. God had promised her to me; it had come in a dream, not a wishful fancy, not the musings of a college student, not the idle wispy thought that might fill the vacancy between sleep and wakefulness, wakefulness and sleep. This was a message from God, incontrovertible truth, hard as a cliff, provable as breath, real as the radio waves that swarmed around me like ripples in a gigantic pond.

It would be pointless for me to describe her. Words fail and I am no fan of flowery talk and metaphors and similes and other literary flotsam that limp-wristed guys use to seduce each other or some innocent girl or woman who thinks a man that knows poetry is sensitive. I could tell you she looks like the blue of the Caspian sea at dusk or the green of Aspen trees when the wind exhales from the valleys or the red of the tail feathers of a female cardinal or the golden glow of gamma rays that fill the night sky with a warmth and glare that keeps me from sleeping. This, I know, is a blessing from God because I must be awake all night to watch the small house she lives in. I only sleep when I know she is at work out of harm's way, except during her lunch hour when I set my wristwatch alarm to wake me, to follow and to guard at a discreet distance.

Sometimes, if she brown-bags it and sits in the park, I can recover her leftovers from the wire trash bin. I save the little crusts of bread or half circles of baloney skin in special archival wax paper and keep it in the freezer. Once I retrieved a spectacular wad of chewing gum, still moist with her saliva. Saliva, what a foul word to use in the same sentence as my beloved, but I do not invent words except on rare occasions when the English language is inadequate. I slept with that gum, that sacred piece of arabic and aspartame. I made love to it, safely, yet passionately but I am not the type that kisses and tells. No, I am safer than Santa Claus, more reliable than D-Day, more trustworthy than the announcing angel. I imagined my deceased mother hearing of my tryst with my beloved's chewing gum. I told her, in my mind, that no one would question the reverence of someone holding the Shroud of Turin, the Ark of the Covenant or the staff of the First Caliph of Baghdad. Each of us reveres our own relics and allows them to connect us with something greater than ourselves. Even an atheist clings to the empty sky, to his Darwinian foolishness, never for a minute perceptive enough to see that angels live in the shadows we cast as we move about in daylight or in the phosphorescent glow of lamp or candle or the light of the billion dental x-rays that bounce from the dentists' offices all over the world and carom off of everything in an eternal mad maze of vectored beams. Smile, laugh even, but remember that Jesus wept.

I will admit that I had doubts about myself once. It was a cold winter morning and I so wanted to sleep in, to stay under the covers and read of Robin Hood and Sherwood Forest by the cold light of a snowy morning, the same book my mother had read to me when I was a tyke. I would watch her lips and see the magic light that emitted from them, the words of the story soft and cream-colored like a strand of fresh-water pearls floating in the air and weaving the outlines of trees and bows and arrows and Maid Marion and Robin himself in the air above my bed. But I got out of bed for the watch anyway because I knew what love was; I knew that it was an ache that can only be born when one realizes that I loved my beloved more than myself. If I was wrong, then I was content in my error because I had no choice and it comforted me.

It is time to speak of Devon, a young fellow that worked in her office. I sensed his arachnid intentions and calculated the weaving of his web; those smiles, those helping hands, the studied but seemingly casual toss of his hair off his forehead as he spoke to her. What spider lacks a barb, I thought, and I could see that he meant to have her, inject her with his venom and devour her with hollow and meaningless vows of matrimonial attestations. Not even the parents of Zeus could foretell as I could. No Delphic Oracle could know what I knew. I could put Isis to shame. Search for your dead brother, archaic goddess, he cannot tell you more than I.

I assiduously researched the name "Devon," found it to be a small shire in England, a type of cream, cream indeed. It was at 3:33 AM, batter my heart three-personed God, 3:33 in the morning, the blessed triumvirate hour of the radiation, the exact and singular minute of speaking microwave ovens that I saw that his name was a combination of devil and demon, that it was Latinate for devour, Greek for puncture. Backwards, it was Noved, an isotope of Einsteinium with a half-life shorter than the shortest measure of time known to man, a span so small that only wickedness in its purest form could occupy or understand it. Noved, a perfect evil existing in six allotropic clusters, crystalline and diabolical.

I slept past my morning watch and almost missed her lunch hour. I arrived just in time to see them kiss. I vomited bile, three half-chewed Cheerios and part of one of the nine fractal implants put in my body by Uncle Benny. But I will not think of him. Not now. That curséd fellow, thick hair in his ears, scraggly and unkempt, grizzly, a slack jaw, ashen beard, the smell of sebum thick on his shirt collar, mixed with mothballs and the faint scent of aged Gouda. I could feel his hand on me, his hand with a glove with no fingers, those terrible fingers. Not now. I conjured her face before me, my usual way to dispel Uncle Benny's visage, to shove him back into the storm cellar of my brain. Lock the door, lock the door. They thought he was dead, but no, lock the door.

Devon, what to do about Devon. I took a Sharpie marker pen out of the breadbox and sat on the floor and wrote his name on the palm of my left hand being careful not to touch or in way cover the scar left by my removal of the antenna wire that Uncle Benny had placed just beneath my heart line. He was crafty. My left hand, I thought, the left hand of the Lord always facing downward toward Perdition, the hand of foul judgment, of condemnation, those two velvet-soft fingers of the Lord pointing to the depths, to Erebus, to Hades, to the Inferno. In French, left is "sinistre," sinister, yes, sinister, even Frenchmen new Devon was sinister.

I put out my right hand palm up and started to write her name, my beloved, but I could not. She had befouled her mouth with his. Now the word "saliva" was apt. I could see the molecules of Devon's liquid seeping from his putrid lips to hers. They would spread and multiply, be inhaled by her, be absorbed by her intestines, sacred tubes of nourishment. They would enter her bloodstream, become a part of her. It was then I epiphanized that God's will had been thwarted, that His promise to me was still a promise but that evil had been born before me and had corrupted my betrothal. I longed for the days of my watch, my guardianship. They were gone. Would I have to seek another? Could God change His mind? If He could change it, would that imply that He had made an error? Could God err? No. I was to blame. And Devon. If I could not be an instrument of God's love then I must be one of his vengeance. No, not vengeance, rectitude, for it is man who must rectify his mistakes. I walked upstairs to my dear mother's bedroom, let her rest in peace, and retrieved the hunting knife from the drawer.

I sang a song of sixpence, a pocketful of rye and made myself a ham on rye sandwich. Lots of mayonnaise to mute the dead flesh flavor that rattled my taste buds and squirmed up my nostrils like eels. Uncle Benny would tell me the story of the three little pigs and the little piggies that were his fingers, his dreadful fingers that did piggy things. No, I needed to eat the pigs. The Maori chieftain told me in a dream that eating the flesh of the enemy vilifies him. I ate pig every day.

It was 2 AM and rain had slicked the pavement so that it looked like a long ribbon of Hefty garbage bags. No metaphors for me though; nothing could describe the black of that street, the pools of reflected light from dingy lampposts and sullen streetlights, ripply gloss that amplified each composite pebble of the macadam, the pitch, the glue of life that holds all things together and keeps them from flying off into deepest space. I allowed the ripples to lead me and so my feet needed no signal from my brain; Uncle Benny was banging on the door of the storm cellar and if I didn't hurry, he'd break free and if the door got broke, what would I do with him then?

I trusted the glossy ripples and they did not forsake me. They took me to a bridge that used to be a train trestle, its high gothic arches a cathedral to the locomotive gods that are nearly all dead now. The span was twenty stories high, transecting a dun street pocked with fast-food restaurants, saloons disguised as restaurants, gas stations with American flags the size of football fields obscenely slapping the tepid night air, limp as uneaten noodles left in a colander overnight. I stood midway on its gentle arc and let the ripples caress my feet for they had led me here and stopped my passage. I

looked down at the empty road, watched the traffic light permu-
tated from green to yellow to red to purple to pink to the gold that
matched the gamma rays lighting a spot just below me so far down
I could only see the largest composite pebbles of the macadam,
sad that they were imprisoned there forever atop their brethren
buried below away from the eyes of God through the luck of the
turn of the asphalt mixer.

Uncle Benny was pounding and I could hear the timbers creaking, yielding the way I had so many years ago. Don't tell. Don't tell.
Don't tell. The knife I held would be useless against him. He was
already dead, everyone had said. Who would believe me? I was no
one. I only functioned as a mirror of my beloved. How I loved her
so. Devon ceased to be. Some part of me is saying his name but that
part is dwindling, dissolving like the Wicked Witch of the West with
water tossed on her, dithering away in the rampant glare of the
gamma rays. To keep my beloved in my mind forever, I had to
freeze time. Time would awaken that guy that kissed her. What was
his name? He'd be back. So would Uncle Benny. In time he would
be free. I looked down and dropped the knife off the bridge. One
one thousand, two one thousand, three one thousand, four one…it
clanked and veebled its blade, the handle separating and belunging
with two soggy thuds. Her memory was fresh and clear and unsul-
lied, so beautiful my eyes filled with tears of joy and thankfulness
to God. Uncle Benny had his hand through one of the weaker timbers of the locked door and was trying to turn the latch. I could
hear his dirty nails scraping the old iron clasp. I fell through the air
and saw the gamma rays burn a hole through the street; beneath it
was blue sky, pearlescent clouds, the smell of God's breath. One
one thousand, two one thousand, three one thousand, four one….

Fit and Trim!

While I am 47 years old, I am as fit and trim as an Olympic athlete—a swimmer, perhaps, or a javelin-thrower. I have taken great care of the machine that moves my brain around, the mechanism that moves my mouth and penis from place to place. Where would I be without it?

You are probably wondering where I got these amazing abs. They're so ripply and rock hard, they're difficult to fathom. If I were a character on a reality show about me and my middle-aged acquaintances, I might be nicknamed the Conundrum, in reference to these abs of mine. Don't get me wrong. I'm very much like most guys over forty, the ones that despite innumerable showers have balls so smelly that when one of them looks down, he can see pulses of odor in front of his crotch like heat waves in the desert. See, the abs don't match the visage. My perturbed, puffy face sets you up for a blubbery gut. But then you see these abs, stacked like bricks, clearly delineated, and you have to ask, "Does he work out for two or three hours a day, or does he just work out all day?" Or is he a servant of the Dark Lord? Or perhaps you think I purchased them from a plastic surgeon in Mexico. My secret is simple—dynamic tension! Constant dynamic tension. Tension that is tense, and dynamic, and never-ending—the best kind of tension there is! I have analyzed each ab and where it draws its tension from so that you, too, can get the abs you've always dreamed of! I am very fond of exclamation points!

The ab on the upper right is taut and sinewy thanks to middle school. Specifically, the effort of trying to get my two kids placed in a topnotch middleschool. Filling out forms, attending open houses, prepping for interviews, taking the entrance exams—it's a lot of work, and I am there every step of the way, standing behind them, leaning over their shoulders, looking down (that's what tightens the ab), swallowing hard (also good for the ab), and clenching and unclenching my fists (good for the fists). Thanks, kids—Dad loves you and Dad loves the ab you've given him. But when I was in middle-school there was nothing middling about me. I remember fondly a little girl named Frida Kornstein . . . How could anyone forget a name like that?; parents were odd in those days giving

87

names that belied their heritage. Obviously, little Frida was a Jew-ess so where did the moniker "Frida" come from. A Mexican Jew? That's a good one…and she was a good one. I met her when she was eleven and I was twelve—it was a very good year, dah, dah, dah , dah—Frank Sinatra; what a jerk. I didn't actually meet her but there was something cloying about her, perhaps the way she held her face, smirky at times like her family might have had too much money and she thought I was dog poop. I asked her to take a walk with me one Saturday afternoon when I thought her parents might be in temple. She agreed and we went to Heathcote Woods. She was looking for pollywogs in the little creek that sliced its way through the tall late spring trees, gurgling—not gurgling quite the way she did when I smashed her skull in with a rather large granite rock the size of a good old Florida pink grapefruit. I left her there after doing some other stuff that I needn't bore you with. And then I walked out the other side of the woods into a nice neighborhood of yellow and white and pale Victorian houses that now cost a million bucks each. Imagine that! A million dollars for a house!

The middle right ab bulges handsomely thanks to talk radio. I simply tune in to conservative talkers when I am driving, and my screaming at the host tightens this ab for an extended, uninter-rupted rep. Plus, disagreeing with someone on the radio gives me that powerless, overwhelmed feeling I've become addicted to. It's better than a drug, because you get the abs! I want to be alone with conservative talk-radio people, to feel their whimpers and their shudders as the torture begins; small drops of acid in the eyes to en-lighten their vision; a shot of pure paralyzing liquid cane sugar into the heart to sweeten its approach to those less fortunate. Ah, but what would I not do to the tongues, those flapping halyards of their insensate pomposity—small wire cutters nipping at the fringe of that organ; a Dremel placed ever-so-carefully on the raised little bumps of taste and sensation and then the hard downward press into the flesh until there was almost nothing left but the bulged-eyed expression of pernicious apology. Too late, I'd say, too late the phalarope as if you or they knew what a phalarope is!

The upper left ab pops out impressively from the effort of lug-ging five-gallon water jugs into our kitchen. Actually, the lugging does nothing for the ab; it's the part where you have to tip the full jug and place its spout into the dispensing reservoir, without spilling, that strains and sculpts this beautiful ab. The short moment of dread focuses tension on this ab like a ray gun. Afterward, slipping on the spilled water can be great for a whole-body clench. There were times when the pipes had frozen. I think it was when I watched some whore talking about her plundering of that most ignorant of all wastelands, Alaska. How I would melt it all down with all its grimy residents squealing first in pain and then in delight as they imagined some moment of the Rapture that they thought they were included in. NO! It is my own private Idaho Rapture, the spiritual joy of watching you squirm before the eyes of your loved ones and then all of you becoming the soil that an as yet unborn moose will defecate on.

The middle ab on the left (not my left, your left, if you are looking at me) is called Mortimer. It's a dignified ab. It tenses each time I read an op-ed article about global warming. The article's point of view is immaterial; simply being reminded that I can do nothing to stop the horrific future of floods and catastrophe gives this ab a taut yank that lingers, burning calories in my well-creased forehead at the same time. Best to do right before bed, as the accompanying nightmares keep those abs pumping into the early-morning hours! Those goddamned Chinese are the main bad guys. If China had but one neck, I would gladly slit it! That's a thing Caligula said. Well, not about China, but you get the drift. Where is he when we need him? Do you think he would tolerate those billions of unfeeling, straight-haired yellow monkeys polluting the Earth on such a gargantuan scale? I'm no fan of the Japs, let me tell you, but they had the right idea. Toss those Chink babies in the air and catch them on your bayonets! Yes, Mabel, they did that. And why not? They knew what those fuckers were up to. And if they could only have imagined the Wal-Marts they'd fill with their poisoned crap. I remember a China-girl I dated in community college. She was indistinguishable from the rest of the billions, I can tell you. But she liked it hard and quick but not too quick. She'd obey this and obey that and look up imploringly with those lifeless shark, slanted eyes. But she was a creature of God, wasn't she? Did she deserve the beating I gave her? The one that knocked her teeth out on the floor with a spatter of red blood—I can tell you it is red, not some other shade either. The pleading, the "Oh, please, don't hurt me no more." It's "anymore" bitch, I said but she was in no condition for English lessons. I jammed the tube of the vacuum cleaner up her—should I say private parts—and then turned on the power! What a hoot in Hell it was! That Hoover was sucking stuff out like there was no to-morrow. The neighbors probably thought, "Oh, that's that nice fellow next door. Not many fellows will vacuum this hour of the night. He's so neat!" I guess they would like a few exclamation points too. It's their right, isn't it? The China-girl was an exchange student and some people did know I had dated her but they couldn't find her little yellow flat-titted body. They'd have had to ask the sharks in Biscayne Bay, "Hey, fishies, did you see a dead China-girl come through here?" They'd say, "Fuck no. And if we did, we'd eat her, asswipes." Sharks have a great sense of humor, I bet. They must. Look at all the funny crap they do. So I answered a few questions and got some wise cracks thrown at me. They were good cops. Did a great job. Right!

The bottom right ab, the biggest of all the abs—and therefore the most impressive—is from not having sex. This ab is always quietly tensed. Has been for years now. Can you imagine the Dalai Lama's lower right ab? Or the Pope's? Must be huge. I, however, did not take a vow of chastity, so it would be a sad situation, if it didn't yield such an amazing ab. I don't know; I don't think I'm a wuss or a sissy or some impotent codger full of beer and golf stories secretly hating women and blacks and Puerto Ricans. Not that those are necessarily bad notions but the impotence in their dicks is the impotence in their lives. They can talk it up, the hatred and primal fear but they can't do anything about it. Not a thing. And that makes them fat and bald and surly and full of nasty thoughts about little girls and boys. And all of this accumulates right at the base of their smelly old porks which cuts off the blood flow and the next thing you know, they're popping Viagra or some such concoction to remind them that at some point they were real men but lost the chance to act like men. I have not lost that at all, let me say. I act on what I feel and do not need any performance-enhancing drugs. They are all stored right here (I say, pointing at my head). No, I can get as stiff as a broken neck in a brace. I just don't believe in sex anymore. It's an abomination before God, I think. On the other hand, I have certain urges that come upon me, that seep up my muscles and my bones as if the devil was sending a liquid up through the Earth's crust and into the soles of my feet. These are urges that are not easy to control—in fact, I don't even try to control them because that is impossible!! So, I let the Evil One have his day in court and let him get his jollies off. It's usually a bitch that works his nerves and then he needs to get even. I think pretty bitches that walk around like they own the joint are the ones that irritate him the worst. They go shopping and wear tight-fitting clothes and giggle to each other and use some rich guy's credit card to pay for their new panties and, oh, wouldn't I like to get my hands on those panties—but they are his for the taking and all I can do is what he orders me to do through the use of his seeping liquid. I will follow those orders, let me tell you, without fail. Or else, let me tell you. I got one of those women in the basement of a Macy's department store, dragged her there which was not easy with all the shoppers and nuns that were about. Lots of nuns, I think. And I got her to explain to me why she wears such tight clothing that I could see the outline of her breasts and nether parts and that my Boss, well, He does not like that. I do my thing to her as a punishment but it's not really me at all, but Him. I don't feel a thing really, I don't, and am not happy at all when I have to quiet her heart down to a standstill—it gets real loud and can drive a quiet guy like me berserk so I just quiet it down and then salute her and say, better luck next time, like He tells me to say and then lickety split, I'm out the door and no one ever finds me.

The bottom ab on the left is harder to explain, but I believe that this ab is simply self-aware. It quivers with tension at all times, even more so when I am supposed to be relaxing, and I believe it is searching for a sense of purpose for itself and no answer is forthcoming. Nothing works this ab like a vacation. The aimless uncertainty, the absence of all deadlines, tightens and sculpts like nothing else. After ten days in Paris, this ab looks amazing.

Finally, you've got to appreciate my extra abs. That's right, I have two abs more than most people. They are in my lower back, and, I'll admit it, they were put there by my New York City plastic surgeon. I was told that they are the latest thing. God, I hope so. They hurt like hell!

Hotline

For years I have used men's rooms and saw all the obscenely scrawled women's names with phone numbers. Tame versions like, "For a good time, call Hazel at" such and such, to the more earthy and downright filthy like…well if you don't know, you can guess. Similar messages could be found in phone booths everywhere in the city, numbers and women's names and sometimes men's who were designated as "queer" or "faggot" were etched in the smoothly enameled paint of every phone booth Ma Bell owned. I don't know if anyone ever called these numbers but I cannot help but think they did. I'll admit I did call Hazel one night on a payphone from a bowling alley men's room.

"Hello."

"Hi, Hazel."

"Who's this?"

"I'm Charley. I heard I could call you for a good time."

"Jack? Is that you?"

"No. I said I'm Charley and I am."

"Go F—- yourself." Click

In my boozey haze I tried a Mary-Ellen but the conversation was even more terse. I can tell you I'm not a sicko, a perv or anything an average Joe would be ashamed to admit. I was a third year psych student at the local U, a little too tall, a little too thin with a biggish nose but large sincere eyes—my mother told me this—and an overall nerdish look which attracted almost no one, not even the chubbies and fatties whom I find repugnant on a biological level, an inherent, inchoate revulsion. Consciously I have no problem with them and even number a few, well, really only one, as a girl I enjoy talking to. Her name is Jennifer like three quarters of the females at this college and though she is nine inches shorter than me, I guess that she has at least a seventy-five pound advantage. We studied for the Psychopathology 201 final all weekend at her apartment. It was 2:00A.M. on that Saturday night when she offered me a joint which I gladly accepted. The next thing I know, she's sitting next to me on her brokeback futon with her blouse and bra off. The sight of those huge luminous breasts separated from her gelatinous lizard-belly-colored gut did not so much shock me, as repel me. Not raised to ever be rude to a woman and emboldened by a cannabis stupor, I reached out and fondled some of her flesh. She turned out the lights, but in the dark, I could not differentiate back from front, butt from breast. I felt I was with an anthropomorphisized version of the Blob from that 50s flick. Notwithstanding my lack of feminine contact since sweet, pimply Jennifer Murtley in High School, I excused myself to get a condom out of my car. I simply started the Ford up and drove back to my abode, leaving my psych notes and textbook behind as a necessary sacrifice to the closest I will ever come to the female avatar of Buddha. I saw her again in the exam room on Monday morning where she scowled and pouted at me. She did return my study materials afterwards, but she peanut buttered and jellied every page of my notes. That was two years ago.

It was the year Robert Kennedy was shot that I realized I was tired of being lonely, but not tired of being lonesome. I liked my privacy, my studies, my novels, movies and hanging out with the grad psych students in the corner of the student union that we claimed as our territory. Ultimately, though, I was alone in a crowd as they say and I diagnosed myself as a victim of intimacy deprivation syndrome or IDS as I hoped it would be listed one day in the *Psychologist's Desk Reference.*

In a fit of pique exacerbated by a pint of vodka, I typed up ten labels that said, "Suicide Hotline call…" with my number. That night, wandering like Bill Sykes in *Oliver Twist,* I placed them in strategic locations where females were likely to see them: a local shopping mall, the girls' dorm, a corner phone booth near the sorority houses, a bulletin board near a beauty salon. Within minutes of my return to the apartment, the phone began to ring.

"Hello?"

"I can't take much more."

"More of what?"

"Life"

"What exactly about your life?"

"Is this twenty questions?"

"No."

"Well, I was abused by an uncle when I was eight. My mother died when I was twelve and my father drinks…a lot."

"What do you do for a living?"

"A living? I'm seventeen. I live with my dad."

"So what exactly are you fed up with?"

"You're not recording this, right?"

"No, Ma'm."

"Ma'm my ass. I'm seventeen."

"I'm not recording this…what is your name?"

"Jennifer."

"Well Jennifer, tell me…do you feel that you want to end it all?"

"I think so."

"Why."

"I had an affair with Mr. Boyle."

"You slept with someone named Mr. Boyle?"

"Yes he's my American history teacher. That's what everyone calls him."

"I see. Is it a satisfying relationship?"

"Fuck no. He's older than my dad and I hang out with his daughter."

"Did he seduce you?"

"No. I started it."

"Well then you can break it off. Go and sin no more." and I hung up the phone.

The phone rang again and I answered, "Jennifer, I guess you didn't understand."

"Hello? Is this the Suicide Hotline?"

"Uh, yes it is. Can I help you?"

"I doubt it." It was a guy. A guy that smokes. A guy that drinks.

"I hope I can," I said.

"You a queer?" He rasped and slurred.

"No. Are you?"

"Hey, this is no fucking joke. I've got a gun aimed at my head."

"Please put it down. It might go off accidentally." I pulled the receiver far from my ear. I didn't want hearing damage.

"It won't be no accident."

"Talk to me…uh…"

"Call me Pete."

"Pete, tell me what's going on in your life."

"My second wife just left me. It's not her fault. I keep having nightmares and, and…"

"What are they about?"

"It don't make a difference."

"Yes, Pete, it does. Tell me."

"When I was an altar boy…"

"The priest molested you, I see," I interrupted.

"Fuck no. Do you think I'm a faggot, you faggot?"

"No, no I don't. Please continue Peter."

"I'm Pete."

"O.K. Pete, please continue."

"After mass, one Sunday, I started walking home; I was eight years old and I realized I left my watch in the vestry. So I turned around and went back to get it. I heard people like talking."

"*Like* talking? Do you mean talking?"

"How about like shuttin' up and listening! I peeked in the room through the door and saw Father Francis X boffing Sister Mary Sanctimonia. First I thought it was some kind of new sacrament like maybe the "First Holy Heaving" but he lifted that white cardboard bib those nuns were wearin' and bit on her tit. I mean breast."

"Tit is fine, Pete."

"I can't get that image out of my freakin' head. All that black and white, must've been a hundred yards of fabric in that room. Coulda been Zorro and Dracula wrestlin', for chrissakes."

"Are you an upholsterer by any chance, Pete?"

"Hell no. Why do you ask?"

"You said a 'hundred yards of fabric.'"

"I make drapes and curtains. You know, window coverings."

"Oh, I see. Well, go on."

"Go on where? I can't get that out of my mind. Every time I had sex with either of my wives, she had to wear a nun's outfit."

"I guess that was a tough habit for them to get used to."

"You a freakin' comic now. Hanh? Hanh?"

"Oh, oops, I get it now. Sorry, it was a slip."

"How 'bout you slip your thumb in your butt."

"Excuse me, I have another phone to answer," and I hung up.

This experiment was not working out the way I had hoped. Over the next week I spoke to nearly a hundred lost, confused, sad or obnoxious, desperately messed-up people. It wasn't fun or funny anymore and I felt lonelier than ever because I think I was beginning to sound like them or, worse, think like them. I headed out into a pouring rain and revisited every spot I had put one of those damn stickers. I wore my nails to bleeding nubs removing all of them and it wasn't 'til I got home well after dark that I remembered I had posted ten but had only the remnants of nine.

I got into the shower and washed and re-washed. I could hear the phone ringing through the steam like shouts from a sinking ship in the fog. Like the *Titanic*, I was going down myself without enough lifeboats. After drying off and popping two pimples on my forehead—my body was reacting to the stress—I put on some sweats and was about to unplug the phone from the wall when it started yelping. I knew it was my fault and guilt lay on my shoulders, an old fox stole dipped in molten lead.

"Hello."

"I'm desperate. I don't think I can make it through the night," A female voice whimpered.

"Believe me, you will. I won't let anything happen to you. What's your name?"

"Jennifer."

"That's a nice name," I lied.

"Thank-you. I have two sisters named Jennifer, too."

"Your parents were very kind and original."

"Actually they were. They're not the problem. You see, I don't know how to begin."

"Start at the beginning," I said sagely. I sat on the sofa my legs propped on the coffee table, my boney knees spread wide, my head back staring at the ceiling with the phone wedged at my shoulder. I twisted one foot up onto my knee and started clipping my toe nails. IBM calls this multi-tasking. So do I.

"Well, I met this guy a few years ago. He was really nice and quite bright. There was something lonely about him-I saw it in his eyes; they were…I guess you'd say they were sincere. I was a tad overweight at the time and I made a pass at him while we were studying…I think it was a biology final."

I inhaled deeply and nearly cut my pinky toe off. "Actually, it was Psychopathology 207."

"How would you know?"

"Uh…I'm a trained professional."

"Anyway, he turned me down. He just got up and left. I offered him my whole feminine being, my innermost self, the deepest part of me. And the prick, he got into his car and went home. He never apologized. Nothing. I was devastated. I had nightmares for a month and lost my appetite for living. I even became anorexic, dropped out of school. I was at Wal-Mart and this guy comes up to me and says I could be a model. I said, right, that's the dumbest pick-up line ever. He said, 'it's no line.' Besides, he's a queen, he says. He gives me his card and what do you know? Last month I was in the new Victoria's Secret catalogue."

"So why do you want to commit suicide?"

"Because I fell in love with that guy I was studying with. I can't get him out of my mind."

"Where did you last see him?"

"At the U."

"You said he was a Psych major?"

"No, but he was."

"Go look him up. He's probably still there. Psych majors are worthless. None of them can get jobs so they end up as Grad students, waiters or Psych teachers. Tell him how you feel. If he's a decent fellow, he'll listen. I'll bet there was just a misunderstanding. He's probably looking for you too."

"You really think? I can't thank you enough. You're very, very wise."

"I like to think so."

"Thanks." Click.

God works in strange and miraculous ways. I was elated. My life had made a sudden turn. I showered again. The next day I put on my best suave collegiate casual clothes and walked around the quad at the U until sundown. The next day, the same thing. On the third day, desperate to give the ugly duckling that became a swan entry to my life-was it possible she was my soul mate?—What was I thinking— the woman of my fantasies? Where was she? She was my life raft and the air was leaking out fast; real fast. I could hear the bubbles spurting in the waters of the icy Atlantic. The sun was going down slower than my hopes. I was going to call a suicide hotline myself when I saw Jennifer, *the* Jennifer, crossing the quad, gliding really, an apparition. I imagined her in a millisecond stepping out of that catalogue with the newest push-up bra and peekaboo panties. She was stunning; men and women were turning their heads in her wake. I looked down pretending to pick lint off my brown corduroy jacket.

"Charlie? Is that you?"

"Have we met?" I said coyly.

"Well, yes. I'm Jennifer. Remember, we used to study together?"

"Oh, Jennifer, yes, how have you been?" She looked at me like I had snot dripping out of my ears and a turd for a nose.

"You don't look like you used to," she said. "And what are those two red holes in your forehead?"

"I had a few zits, that's all."

"You should have left them. They'd be an improvement."

"What?"

"Oh, nothing. I was just kidding. How about taking me for a drink?"

"I'd like that. We can catch up on old times."

"That would be great." she said, a large perfect smile lighting up the quad. "Let me get my I.D. I left it in the car."

"OK. I'll wait here. Geez, it's great seeing you again. I tried to get in touch with you after the exam, but I…uh…lost your number…and then my mother died…and, uh…"

"Back in a minute."

A year later we were married. I'm not one for clichés but she <u>was</u> the girl of my dreams, the wife of my dreams and I can say now that it was the happiest day of my life and that that day stretched into years, past two beautiful children, a good son named Charlie, Jr. and a daughter named Jennifer. People aren't used to happy endings anymore but if they have faith in a power beyond themselves it will become apparent that anyone, anyone, can have a bit of heaven on earth, that God watches us even though we may not believe it.

Well, that should have knocked the smugness out of you. What goes around, comes around, right? I had it coming, right? She went to her goddamn car and that was the last I saw of her. I thought I heard tires squealing in the night. I can still hear them. It might have been the Wicked Witch of the West cackling, for all I f'n know. It's all a blur. The next day I spent two-hundred and fifty dollars on a plumber who spent three hours extricating my telephone from the toilet. I enrolled myself back at the U. as an English major. If you think Psych students are hopeless, you should see that bunch.

Beshert

I met her in the state park sitting at a graying, dried and rusted picnic table. I came to this spot, midway up a gentle slope, every Sunday after church.

"May I sit here?" I said.

"Sure," was her unstudied response.

God's breath blew in mildly off the man-made lake encouraging the leaves to applaud as I talked to her about wild rabbits, deer, bears and the men in their aluminum fishing boats casting lines into the lake as if they were afloat in the green Mediterranean.

She got up to leave after finishing her sandwich, a brownie and a can of Mountain Dew.

"Have you ever walked up that trail over there to the new cottages? They're wonderful. They look like they're made from giant Lincoln Logs," I said.

"That sounds cool," she replied. "But...."

"Oh, come on. It's just over the ridge there. You'll be back in ten minutes. A beautiful day is a terrible thing to waste."

"But I don't know you," she said looking at me through eyes as green as birch leaves.

"Sure you do. We just ate lunch together. Well, you ate and I talked."

She laughed, the sun catching the auburn strands of hair and igniting them

"OK, but I can't be gone long."

I knew at that moment, as if the Book of Fate had turned another page, that she would be my wife. The Hassidim would have called her my "Beshert," literally," my destiny," my soul mate, a woman that God creates for you the way he created Eve for Adam. Special. Connected. Fated. I think she knew it, too, or sensed it. I guessed her age at 21 or 22. I was 35; a lot of years separated us, but neither she nor I seemed to notice. More importantly, neither of us cared. I remembered what Dante said, "In His will is our peace." The rest of the afternoon, God worked his continuing magic.

That night, we had dinner at my house a few miles out from the state park. It was only franks and beans, but it might as well have been lobster and caviar. We luxuriated in each other's presence. After dinner we sat near the window and she listened to me, looking into my face with more love in her eyes than I could express in any language. I told her about my mom and dad back in Kansas, about the family farm, my brother Ted and my sister, Kathleen, about my horse named Sequoia and my yellow lab, Honey. She absorbed every detail as if she were molding the clay of a statue of her perfect man, her soul mate, her beshert.

We made love that night gently yet passionately, her eyes filling with tears of joy and contentment. I had not been so happy and complete since Cindy had left me; it seemed ages ago, months at least, but I think now it had only been two weeks. Love, real love can telescope time; great joys that were experienced years ago, could be as fresh and vital as if only yesterday. Sadness? Well, it could evaporate lke stain remover, gone in a few seconds without a trace.

I awoke the next morning greeted by the orange rectangle of the sun's cheerful shadow on the bedroom wall. My girl was sound asleep beside me, her naked skin so white, it was almost blue, like the first December snowfall under a full moon. Her breathing was imperceptible. It took me a moment to realize she was not the same, not at all. She was ten years younger, at least, could not have been more than ten or eleven. My God, I realized, I had forgotten to remove the duct tape from her mouth and wrists. What had my adoration and ecstasy done? Whose underwear were those with little teddy bears on them, torn and bloodied? Her eyes, so alluring that night over dinner were rolled back in her head, her lids half-open over what looked like two ping-pong balls.

"My Beshert, my love," I whispered softly weeping, "wither hast thou gone? Wither has thou gone?" I looked up at the smudgy ceiling and cried, "My God, why hast thou forsaken me?"

I buried her next to Cindy in a pretty spot near the towering maples. I showered and shaved, nicking a small bump on my neck that proceeded to bleed profusely.

Ouch," I said to my mirror. "Now blot that with a very clean piece of toilet tissue. You don't want to get an infection. Remember what papa said, 'an infection can kill.'"

Cassandra

"She is one catastrophe after another," her father said, meaning her. She knew she wasn't supposed to hear it. But she was alone in that big drafty church house, with just him and Tilda, the maid, just three generations from Gambia. He was an Episcopal minister, a widower, skin whiter than an iceberg. Other women came in, one after another, all on approval, though no one ever said anything. Cassandra was seven, and he expected judgments from her about who he would settle on to be her next mother. Terrified, she lay in the dark at night, dreading the next visit, women looking her over, until she understood that they were nervous around her, and she saw what she could do. Something hardened inside her, and it was beautiful, glorious even, because it made the fear go away. Florid women with a smell of dried flowers about them came to the house. They smiled wide open gashy smiles, lipstick stuck to their teeth, hugged her loosely where she could smell the oil behind their ears, the piece of steak from dinner stuck in their breath. She was truculent, disrespectful, was petulant to each one. Her father observed it all.

One hot July evening, Tilda was standing on the back porch, smoking a cigarette. Cassandra looked at her through the screen door. "What you gawkin' at, girl?" Tilda said. She laughed as if it wasn't much fun to laugh. Tilda was dark as the spaces between the stars and in the late light there was almost a blue cast to her brow and hair. "You think you know what's goin' on here, missy, don't you?"

"Yes."

Tilda blew smoke. "You don't know *yet*." She smoked the cigarette and didn't talk for a time, staring at Cassandra. "Girl, if he settles on somebody, you gonna be sorry to see me go?"

Cassandra didn't answer. Her thoughts were secret. That was one thing she learned from har sick mamma. People had a way of saying things to her that she thought she understood, but couldn't be sure of. She was quite precocious. Her mother had been dead since the day she was born. It was Cassandra's fault. She didn't remember that anyone had said this to her, but she knew it anyway, in her skin.

Tilda smiled her white smile, but now Cassandra saw tears in

102

her eyes. This fascinated her. It was the same feeling as knowing that her father was a minister, but walked back and forth sleepless in the sweltering nights. If your heart was peaceful, you didn't have trouble going to sleep, right?. Tilda had said something like that very thing to a friend of hers who stopped by on her way to the Baptist Church. Cassandra hid behind doors, listening. She was a sort of shadow. She watched everything, everyone. She saw when her father pushed Tilda up against the wall near the front door and put his face on hers. She saw how disturbed they got, pushing against each other. And later she heard Tilda talking to her Baptist friend. "He ain't always thinkin' about the Savior," the Baptist friend gasped, then whispered low and fast, sounding like a spy passing on a secret.

Now Tilda tossed the cigarette, the red tip arcing in the night air, splashing on the lawn with a small burst of sparks. She shook her head, the tears still running. Cassandra curtsied without meaning it. "Child," said Tilda, "what you gonna grow up to be and do? You gonna be just like all the rest of them, usin' your parts to hook a man and then hang on, hopin' he won't cut the line?"

"No," Cassandra said. She was not really sure what this meant.

"Well, you'll miss me until you *forget* me," said Tilda, wiping her eyes. "And I hope you *never* forget me."

Cassandra pushed open the screen door and said, "Don't count on it" over her shoulder as if she had aged another ten years. The door double-slap closed behind her.

One day, Tilda went away and swallowed poison, some sort of disinfecting agent, like Madame Bovary who no one in these parts ever heard of. It took her three days, maybe four to die a painful, moaning death, too, that made even the doctor shuddered at the sight of her. No one in the hospital would ever get the rasping, retching sounds of her suffering out of his head. Cassandra's father didn't sleep for five nights. Dinners were left uneaten, clothes unchanged. Peeking from her bedroom door, with the chilly, breathing darkness looming behind her, she saw him standing crooked under the hallway light, running his hands through his thick, minister's hair. His face was twisted; the shadows made him look like a midnight scarecrow with a rotting pumpkin head. He was crying.

She didn't cry. Never did. And she did not feel afraid. Nor sad.

Nor remorseful. She felt gigantic and strong. She had caused every-thing. And would continue to do so.

The Dunes

There was a moment just after my eyes shut when through the lids I could see the beer stein froth of the clouds in the lilac-tortured sky. There was sand at our backs and the last movement my arm could make was to reach for Sarah's hand, cold as the breeze blowing in from the gulf, how cold her hand was and soddenly deflated. Dry reeds and saw grass hissed in the wind, perfect harmony to the breath that was leaving my lungs, my rib cage easing downward like a spider dying, curling inward as if to hug itself. How long would it be before they found us, obscenely blue, our dignity scattered like sandwich wrappers trapped in the clackity slatted storm fence half-buried in the dunes.

Sarah and I had been legally separated for eleven months, two weeks and three days. I know this silly exactitude because in the state where we lived we would be automatically divorced after twelve months. I phoned her to try one last time to reconcile. Her answering voice was different; the cold edge I had grown accustomed to, gone. I asked her to meet me at the beach at Roger's Cove, the place we had met. The sentimentality of the suggestion was not rebuffed even though it was mid-October and her refusal would be disguised by pointing out the weather. But she agreed. Hope glided in the air around me like a paper airplane, rising when she assented, turning in the dull currents of the living room, then haltingly spiraling down on invisible steps to the floor when I realized, as I hung up, that this was my best, last and only chance. That airplane was not plain paper though. It was the list of my shortcomings, my moods, my petty self-centeredness, my infidelities. I had painfully gotten past the stage of blaming my inadequacies as a husband on her as a wife. Like turning a corner in a frozen January, being blasted by the wind, losing your breath, gasping a moment, hand rising to your face for cover, it came to me. We make choices, have regrets and then bury them in the shifting sands of sarcasm, feigned indifference, thoughtless acts that expand to fill the space before leaving for work and returning after work, until bedtime, both of us in bed, back to back, knees slightly raised like two bookends after the books have been packed away, a long dusty space between. I had written my life wrong. That could not be undone, but there were chapters yet to follow.

Ours were the only two cars in the parking lot. We were alone together at the beach, not like the first time. It was June, then, nearly
July. Red, yellow and blue swimsuits lay on blankets, stood in the
breakers, dotted and danced across the milky blue horizon, flesh-
filled marbles scattered in a sandbox. Shouts, radio music, children's
voices, squeals muffled and mixed by the wind, gliding on the sunlight. We lay on our stomachs talking. I proposed. She accepted.

Now, it was an Indian summer Friday afternoon but the off-
shore wind, deceitful and chilly at our backs carried our words from
the bench we sat on high into the iridescent sky where they flocked
like starlings, twisting, swelling, dropping, rising, a swirling chorus
of wings. Small waves braved into the shore, the wind sheering their
crests, blowing the froth back in grayish wisps, white haired witches
gliding to the coast. Neither of us saw the two men approaching
from behind the boarded-up snack shop.

"Alright lady, just hand over your purse."

I turned; we both turned, startled, awakened as from a dream.

"What? What did you say?" I asked.

"Shut up asshole. We want Missey's purse...and your wallet," he
said raising a small ugly pistol like a scorpion brandishing a barb.

"I'm not giving you my bag," Sarah said; we all looked at her.
"Just go home and leave us be. The world is not supposed to run
like this. We're not bothering anyone. Please just leave us be. We
won't call the police..."

A bullet hit her in the chest. She dropped back and over the
bench, her eyes staring into the fleeing sky.

"Right about that, bitch," he said casually. "Get her bag,
Jimmy..." He realized that the utterance of a name was my death
sentence. I ran around to Sarah and tried to revive her knowing full
well the truth of it. A bullet hit me in the middle of my back, hard
as a fist snapping something inside me. I fell face up, turned by the
blow, numb, my eyes open like Sarah's but alive, my legs paralyzed.
I could feel the pressure of hands in my pockets, see them pull the
jewelry off of Sarah, could hear their fleeing footsteps melt into
the crisp rustling of the alarmed dune grass.

The Dunes

I reached for her hand remembering my vows, whispering them, hearing her say "I do" as my lids came down. The breeze cradled us, apologized, suddenly warm. I thought I saw gulls through my closed eyes shadow circling, not for prey, but to watch over us, silently like doves. The waves murmured prayers, the moon for sorrow hid her face. They would find us holding hands, find us where we first found each other. They would know we had reconciled, that she had forgiven me, that I could forgive myself, as we both dissolved into the lavender, the pearl, the all-consuming sky.

Father G

Father G, as we called him, was Swedish and arrived at our parish in Scranton on one of those March days that promise spring but repossess it with a deep frost or a burning snow. Nature was the first deceiver, perhaps a close student of Satan, but it is the way of a universe so huge as to be immeasurable but so easily thrown off its once perfect axis by the pearlescent teeth of the first woman incising a perfect red globe of fruit. I don't think Father G viewed God's world this way, but I did.

When I first saw him at the rectory carrying his small suitcase and strapped pile of old books, I knew he was special. I was only twelve years old, the parish's favorite altar boy, the patron saint of my mother's house for she called me Lucian, angel of light when I was born. I was destined to be a soldier of Mother Church and it was only when I look from the top of the steps at Father G that I realized what love truly is although I might have thought it was spiritual enlightenment had my emotions not originated in my loins.

I owe it to myself to describe Father G, G for Gus, Gus for August, more fully Father August Stephenson from Göteburg, fifty miles north of Stockholm, he was tall, six foot two, blue eyes that might have been painted in the Madonna's sockets by Giotto, hair, the blond of Botticelli's Venus. Yes, I was but twelve, nearly thirteen years of age but I could feel this priest's masculine power and beauty.

I helped him carry his bag up to his room, the red room with the navy and red Azerbaijan carpet with its tree of life iconograph, the weeping and bloody Jesus looking down at it in abject misery wondering perhaps that he might better have been a sheik of Arabia, a country so full of its senses that its own prophet had many wives. I showed him the chest of drawers, meager in its proportions and a tall reddish oak wardrobe adorned with two small trumpeting angels one of whose trumpets had gone missing.

He opened his case and had me place his articles of clothing in the dresser. At every opportunity I touched his fingertips with my own to see if the electricity that flowed through me originated with him. It did, I am certain. He handed me three pair of white briefs, the long-legged kind so common in the north countries. As I turned to put them in his top drawer, I pushed my face into them to inhale the spirit of his masculinity, a force so powerful that it was like the ink of an octopus ejaculated into the water to baffle its enemies. But I was enraptured, caught up in the first full flush of love. Father August was my god.

There was to be a church camping trip, boys only, over Memorial Day weekend with Father G taking about twenty of us to the state park. As senior altar boy, I was to assist him with the younger children. The weather was perfect and the pearlescent clouds of dusk melted into the hills so the stars could put on their show. When everyone was asleep and the campfires rustled slowly in their beds, their chunky coals throbbing and crumbling into the dark, I made my way to Father G's tent. He was asleep in his sleeping bag, his breath barely audible. I was wearing only my shorts as I sidled up to him and put my head on his chest, making soft purring sounds.

"What is this, Patrick?" he said, rousing suddenly as he reflexively pulled away. "Are you alright?"

"I...I want to sleep next to you, Father," I said. "I'm afraid," I lied sheepishly.

"Afraid? Of what?"

"Uh, my mom said there might be bears in the woods and I'm afraid of bears."

"There are no bears here at this time of the year. Now, get back to your tent. Be a good boy. You need your sleep and so do I."

He had seen through my foolish story, I guessed. I went back to my tent and stayed awake most of the night listening to Adam, Gerald and James tossing, snoring and muttering as they dreamed their childish dreams.

June dragged as if it were January. But the 4th of July was the next church outing; all the children were to go. We all piled into a school bus with two mothers to help and cook. I sat behind Father G and admired the soft sheen of his golden hair, how glossy and neat it was, much like a Viking I had seen in a book. His starched white collar framed his neck, neither too tight nor sagging loose. I wanted to be his angel, to serve him and love him. I knew he was impressed with me. I was the school wrestling champ and was destined to be the high school football team half-back when I started in the fall. Everyone admired my athleticism and good looks, even the girls, who, for some reason repulsed me. If my father had been alive, he would have been quite proud. I checked my backpack for the three sleeping pills I had borrowed from my mother.

The day went as planned with three-legged races, hop, skip and jump, volley ball and then a barbecue. A cool breeze came in from the north that made the little kids shiver even more than Father G's campfire ghost stories.

"Patrick," he said, turning to me. "Be a good lad and get me a Coke, won't you?" I immediately went to the cooler in one of the tents and quietly popped the top putting the three pills in the soda. The can gushed with foam but settled as I carefully wiped it and walked back to Father G, gently swishing the can in the air to stir it as best as I could.

"Sorry, Father," I said. "It might be a little warm."

"That's fine," he said as he downed most of it in a swig. He looked at the can after he swallowed and said, "This tastes like a diet soda. But I see it's not. They don't make Coke like they used to, eh?"

An hour and half later everyone was asleep. I could hear some kids giggling in one of the tents, others telling stories to the hushes from one of the mothers. I crept to Father G's tent and saw that he was sound asleep in his sleeping bag. I touched his face with my forefinger. He did not move. I put my palm against his cheek and pushed, rocking his head. Nothing. He was a sleeping god, like I read about in a book of Greek mythology, the god that sleeps in a cave in the far north and whose lovelorn sighs in the night cause the air to stir.

I disrobed and got in next to him. I kissed and caressed him and did many things I had only dreamed about, things I overheard the older boys joke about, things which no decent person would ever speak of and I am a decent person. I will never kiss and tell. Never.

The next day everything seemed as it should although Father G had a groggy and puzzled look on his face. No, it was more one of deep concern as if he had forgotten something like not turning off the stove after he left the house and it was too late to go back. He was quiet the whole day and hollowly participated in the jollities as if he were acting, his mind being far off.

The following week, the church elders announced to everyone that Father G had been relocated to another parish. He had asked that there be no sending off party or any such fuss to be made over his unexpected departure. That night, I screamed into my pillow first in rage and then in terrible sorrow as if my heart had been ripped from my chest. My beloved was gone. I must discover where he was going. I would follow. I had to. God, in Heaven, I had to.

That Sunday, as always, I attended Mass making sure to find out where Father G was. We were all introduced to the new parish priest, Father James McBride. He had dark hair, fair skin and the bluest eyes I had ever seen. After service, when I shook his hand and looked into his handsome face, I asked him where Father G was going. He said he didn't know. And suddenly, I didn't care. That summer we had no Father August. But Father J was a more than adequate replacement.

A Woman of No Return

Her body was discovered in the basement of St. Beatrice's church on the outskirts of Scranton. The "4 Sale" sign nailed to the front door had the word "SOLD" crudely written in blood across it. This was the photograph on the front page of the *Scranton Times* but the fact that the word had been scrawled using the victim's severed arm was known only by the police. Other details, too gruesome even for seasoned veterans of the force, were withheld. Both the victim's hands had been amputated and placed on her breasts. She had been found fully clothed by a real estate sal12eswoman named Alicia Grigatz who had formerly been a reporter but had been charged and convicted of taking bribes for writing good reviews of bad productions and for granting sexual favors to local politicians for scoops. She was measuring the empty church for a potential buyer one afternoon. At first, she thought the corpse was a stored religious statue, some mutilated martyr *cum* saint. It might have been the short hair, the unusually pallid face—a pastiness that the victim bore in life as well—one of those featureless, bland faces that blend into the plaster walls and Siberian atmosphere of decrepit places like Scranton where nothing green or bright could grow. Hideous Scranton where monotonous clumps of petrified prehistoric dead things sometimes became coal. This whole tumbledown city had developed, flourished and decayed on these lumps. Is it any wonder that the spirit of this place seemed forever a muted, ghostly shadow of cities like New York or Boston as if the people, places and things of the city were stored under Uncle Ted's smelly old flannel blanket. Yes, Scranton was a hangover of a town. And the corpse discovered by the flabby Miss Grigatz, one of its many victims.

The deceased in question was Jessica Salt. One Tuesday morning the doorbell rang; it was two Scranton cops, polite in that numbskull sort of way where strained, artificial enunciation and cool, low I.Q. aloofness are substituted for professional acumen and a bag full of forensic jargon gleaned from TV shows disguises a lack of formal education, social pedigree or a meaningful intellect.

They asked me how I came to know Miss Salt after disclosing that my name had come up as one of a dozen or so members of a writing group of which the victim was one. I told them I knew very little of her, that neither she nor I were consistently in attendance at the meetings usually held on Saturday mornings at a local chain bookstore. I said she was a writer of small dramatic Updikesque vignettes of failing or failed marriages. I related rumors of her being involved in a string of unhappy or fruitless relationships, one involving a grizzled geezer named Chaz Bennes, a wizened old fart who flirted endlessly with women one third his age and fancied himself a writer and a boxer but had neither experience nor accomplishment at either.

"I didn't even know her last name, officer," I said. "Until I read it in the paper. What a terrible thing. Such a nice woman." I added that "This Chaz person leaned against her at ever opportunity and would put his arm around her as she read her stuff at the meetings. Embarrassing and demeaning to all of us. Chaz is a married man."

To this, all four eyebrows rose.

"That so?" said one cop.

"It is," I said. They took notes asking me to spell Bennes.

I pointed out to their rubber-faced attentiveness that if there was anything that I did notice about the victim, it was the fact that she never wore nail polish nor, as I recalled, any make-up at all. I explained that I knew many women over the bumptious course of my life but she was the first I had ever encountered who did so little to improve her lugubrious appearance. Her thin lips and fish-like hands came to life only when she read her depressing stories out loud to that lackadaisical bunch. Her fingernails looked like the scales of a sea bass that had been glued on to her fingertips.

"How is it you noticed this?"

"My ex-girlfriend was a manicurist. She told me a lot about ladies' nails and cosmetics. More than I cared to know. Hee, hee."

They acknowledged that these revelations were interesting and continued to ask some questions that floated around the room like bats in an attic. But I was very aware and offered little else.

"Take a look at this," said a cop handing me a photograph. It was Jessica, all right. "Is this Jessica Salt?" It was her for sure. She was posed as if for some satanic ritual, flat on her back, legs neatly together, skirt smoothed, blouse tucked, both arms at her sides— that is from the elbows up. Both forearms and hands were gone. I noted to myself how little it bothered me. Her ears had been clipped off as well with some very sharp implement because there were no ragged edges where the killer had placed them neatly over her eyes. I realized that the purpose of this exhibition was not identification. No, they were showing me this despicable portrait hoping to elicit some response from which they might gain insight into my possible involvement. What I did not tell them, as I convincingly winced and turned away, was that such a pose was similar if not identical to a passage from one of Dante's quatrains in the *Inferno*, one of several interludes found in the 5th, 6th and 7th circles or bolgias dealing with the punishment of thieves.

"Oh, my god," I said turning away. "I don't know. I guess so. How awful."

They thanked me, gave me a business card, turned and left.

The second fact I withheld, although my divulging it would have seemed superfluous, even common (although I never thought of anything I did as being common), was the fact that Miss Salt had some six months ago borrowed a book from me, a beautiful copy of Christina Rossetti's "Sonnets" with illustrations by her brother Dante Gabriel Rossetti. I loved this book for its voluptuous feel, its lush coloring and luxurious typeface. The poetry was typically female and somewhat maudlin if not downright sentimental, reeking of self-indulgent mood swings from myopic to morose. The illustrations, however, were sublime. Jessica, that is Miss Salt, had failed to return the tome to me despite my every controlled and offhanded hint over the ensuing months since it came into her flaccid possession, the thieving whore. The pose of her corpse was right out of this book. So here was the thief, punished as a criminal in Dante's *Inferno*, laid out in a pose from Dante Gabriel Rossetti's illustrations and in St. Beatrice's church—Beatrice being Dante's one true love.

No one in this armpit of a city would see the beauty and fearful symmetry of it all, the perfection of the justice that had been meted out. I was very impressed with the handiwork and the wholesomeness of its execution. But Scranton, dear, mundane, dreary and drained old Scranton could never harbor two people who could realize the circle of retribution that had been so carefully closed within its miserable borders. H.L. Mencken had written once that

114

even the most assiduously honest people would borrow a book and fail to return it. Du Maupassant had written an intriguing tale of this aberrant behavior as had numerous other luminaries. But no one ever did anything about it. I probably shouldn't tell you that that night I curled up with a good book that had been kidnapped but recovered. It spoke to me like Jesus in the Gospels: "I was lost and now am found." Yes, I curled up with a beautiful book, gloriously illustrated, sleeping more soundly than I had in months.

Guitar

Carlton Waltz was sixteen when his father Daniel left for the second to last time. Danny, as everyone else called him, was a wiry tall red-headed Irishman with a penchant for brutalizing his children, two girls and Carlton, and slapping his wife around as a prelude to inebriated sex or the postscript to a night of whoring. After Danny's departure, Carlton made every effort to become the man of the family, dropping out of school and getting a job at the local aircraft factory which was buzzing with activity the year the Japs bombed Pearl Harbor. That job likely saved him from being drafted and transformed into meat when he turned eighteen because by that time, he had mastered the complicated wiring of the instrument parts of American fighter planes and he exempt from active service as an essential civilian. His two sisters had married men seeking to avoid military service but that exemption didn't last long and their husbands said their salty farewells and vanished into graves. Nonetheless, the girls stayed away from Carlton and his mother, Mildred, not out of spite or malice but because the time-wearied face of their mother was too much a mirror of their own futures and they could not look at her crow's feet, her furrowed brow or the silver hair that wired her ears to her head without seeing their father whom they never called either daddy or father but simply Danny as an impotent form of disdain and disrespect as if in using his street name they could gain distance from their nightmares. He was the villain of those nights, the ogre of their personal histories and after a time he became an abstraction, the way Lon Chaney or Boris Karloff could, terrifying for the ninety minutes of a horror film but only an unrelated chilling memory afterwards.

Carlton and Mildred moved to a small white asbestos-shingled house on the south side of town with a Victorian front porch that looked on a long row of similar houses with minutely different details intended to individualize the structures. To vultures flying overhead, which they were wont to do because of the city dump less than a half mile away, the houses would have seemed no more than an indeterminately long row of gigantic crocodile teeth emerging from the monotonously flat, green carpet of the lobotomized American prairie.

116

On Sunday morning about a year after the A-bombs were dropped on Japan, someone knocked on the front door. Mildred and Carlton had just finished breakfast and were listening to the radio, the staticky strains of the Glenn Miller Band fluttering through the house like doves at sunrise. Carlton opened the door to his father, standing there, tall and straight as ever as if he had just gone to the newsstand for a paper only twenty minutes before, quite a bit more rough-edged then anyone remembered, but with his hat literally in one hand and a guitar case in the other.

"Hello, son; don't you recognize me?"

"I guess I do. What do you want?"

"I got to town last week and found out where you were livin'. Thought I might stop in and see how you're all doin'."

"We're fine. Is that all you wanted to know?" Carlton started to close the door in Daniel's face when his mother came up behind him.

"Daniel? Is that you?"

"In the flesh."

"Carlton, let him in. He's your father, no matter what and still my husband no matter what and I won't be party to turning him away."

Carlton stepped away from the door and retreated into the front parlor, sitting down in an overstuffed chair where the sunlight cast spidery shadows on the floor through the skeleton of the old apple tree.

"So what did you do in the war, old man?" asked Carlton after Daniel found a seat on a stiff oak ladder-back chair. "Capture a Kraut platoon, did you? Win the Medal of Honor?"

"No, not quite. I made my way up to Chicago. Thought about enlistin' but one night, I got run over by a milk truck—well, not run over exactly but got my legs run over, both. They were pretty much in pieces but they took me to the Veteran's hospital and worked on 'em all night long into the wee hours and beyond. Had to stay there nearly six months."

Carlton looked over at his mother, who was sitting on the edge of the sofa like a canary about to jump up and fly when the cat lurched out of the shadows. Their eyes connected momentarily, Carlton conveying in a millisecond the doubts and loathing he had;

if Danny boy was looking for a flop-house and a free ride here, he was in for a disappointment.

"While I was there," Daniel continued, "recoverin' and such, the first casualties of war started arrivin'. It was terrible sad and I will say that I felt guilty takin' up space in a ward with so many heroes. But I guess that if God wanted me outta there I woulda died under the wheels of that truck. Sometimes even lately, although much less so, I wished I had. But I took an oath in that hospital to stop drinkin' and I ain't had a drop since. It ain't easy for a man like me to figure what will make the Lord happy."

"Too little, too late, old man," said Carlton as he picked up a newspaper and pretended to read as Daniel went on. Out of the corner of his eye Carlton saw how gaunt Daniel had become but that his skin had not wrinkled but was smooth and clear, taunt over his skull, only his eyes and hairline showing the rampage of the years.

"Well, one day they brought in this young sailor. The Nips bombed his ship, turns out, sunk it with most all hands on board. But he survived somehow except he was blinded by shrapnel. One of the nurses brought him a guitar figurin' he could lose some of his misery in learnin' to play. Well, he knew how to play already turns out, which I thought was a miracle or a coincidence if you don't believe in miracles, and he had a knack for strumming it low and slow as if there was only him and me in the whole ward. He turned that guitar over to me and taught me how to play passably well. I mean I was no genius nor nothin' but as the weeks passed he could tell me where to put my fingers on the frets and how to use the back of my thumb to stroke those strings; blind as he was, he always knew if I was doin' it right. Sometimes, it seemed like my hands were someone else's and I would sit there and get lost in that music. One night, while he was playing a song he made up called the *Ballad of Broken Creek*—you see he was from a small town by the name of Broken Creek. Turns out, he had a girl there but when she found out he got himself blind, she acted like she didn't even know him no more and his heart just dried up, his whole body went limp from the inside. I saw it. Well, that night I fell asleep to the *Ballad of Broken Creek*. Middle of the night, I heard a ruckus and a bunch of nurses and orderlies were scurrying about his bed. Turns out he had got a hold of something sharp—not too difficult to do in a hospital, God knows—and slit his wrists. So he wouldn't make a bloody mess everywhere he bled out into the sound hole in his guitar. Half filled it, nearly. After they hustled him out to the morgue they were gonna chuck that guitar in the trash. I asked for it and the nurse on duty knew how he was my friend and he had taught me and such, so she cleaned it up as best she could and gave it to me. But that boy's blood had soaked into the wood and I let it. Before long I was playin' almost as good as him, God rest his soul.

"Now there was a small room at the end of the ward where they put what they called 'the critical cases' but we all knew it was really the terminal cases. We called it 'God's waitin' room' not meanin' no disrespect but like it was a way of not bein' so afraid of the Grim Reaper who surely spent a lot of time there and visited our ward only when he had a mind to. It was a Saturday night and they brought in this soldier who had been burned so bad they couldn't tell who he was septin' for his dog tags—it was a miracle they didn't melt and they put him in God's waitin' room. A few hours later his Mom and Dad came in and we all could hear that boy's Mama cryin' like she invented tears. I could feel her misery in my guts. The boy's daddy came over to me— turns out they were poor country folk— and said the nurse told 'em I might play for their boy to ease his passage into the next world for their boy was afraid and maybe some guitar music would keep him calm as he found his way to the pearly gates. Of course, I said yep, I would, if they didn't mind a terrible sinner being in the room with them and their son. That man said we were all sinners and so forth and they'd be indebted to me no matter if I knew the devil personal."

Mildred, who had been fidgeting like a sparrow scratching for millet seed, sighed and sat back on the sofa drawing up her knees sideways and covering her legs with her rose- patterned house coat. Carlton folded his newspaper and put it down on the coffee table.

"Well, I only knew four songs which I played from the wheel chair they put me in. That boy's breathin' was so full of sufferin' that I never heard nothin' like it and hope I never hear nothin' like it again. After I finished my fourth song, that sailor managed to say, 'Music man, ain't you got something else?' I said 'Yes, I did, but it wasn't a real song but one a friend of mine made up.' 'Well play it then, please,' he said. So I played the *Ballad of Broken Creek* and that guitar sounded like a voice from Heaven. That boy's Mom had her tears runnin' through the lines on her face and when I finished, that boy, he was gone to a better place. The daddy came over to me and thanked me for helpin' his boy find the Lord and he put a silver dollar in my hand and the nurse wheeled me out. That was three years ago and I been going to bars and such— never touchin' a drop— and playin' for folks and livin' on tips; taught myself nearly a hundred tunes— I even went back to that hospital and a few others to help people with their pain. But I never spent that silver dollar." He reached in his pocket and pulled it out so the sunlight hit it and it glistened like it was new. "This means more to me than almost anythin' in the world," and he put it back in his pocket and leaned back in the chair looking almost like a scarecrow that hadn't scared any crows in a decade.

"Play that song for us, Daniel" said Mildred strangely calm. "I want to hear it."

Daniel looked over at Carlton who averted his eyes as if to say, "go ahead old man, I don't give a damn."

Daniel took out his guitar gently, almost reverentially, and after a few plucks to tune it, played *The Ballad of Broken Creek*. The soft sad tones filled the house like the sun filling a meadow after a morning fog had lifted. When he finished, Mildred said, "Thank you. That was lovely." Carlton was silent and stood up, turned to his father and said, "It's gonna take a lot more than a sad story and a pretty tune to change my mind about you, old man. You're welcome to stay for dinner and to sleep on the sofa for tonight but that's all."

"Thank you, Carlton, you're a generous boy."

That night they ate together in silence, their past a crazy quilt of suffering that wrapped all three of them in a muffled hush of disappointed expectations and indefinable remorse.

Carlton came downstairs the next morning at daybreak, an inconsistent rain tapping at the windows. Daniel had gone. On the coffee table was his silver dollar, perfectly centered on the dull mahogany, like a full moon at dusk, in a deep purple sky just risen over the eastern hills.

Mont St. Michel

One can always talk about misery because we are infinitely individual in our pain; but happiness? What can we say about this? That a god I do not believe in manages to keep it just beyond my grasp?

It was six months ago that I met Isabella. I walked into an art gallery to see an exhibition of watercolors and dry point temperas, dun landscapes, portraits of isolation, decrepit houses bowed under the weight of time, neglect and working poverty. Amid all that, she was there behind a mahogany desk, tall, serene, dark-haired, fair in a maroon wool suit, cream blouse, seamed nylons, patent leather pumps—all the details that only the deepest love might remember.

I should talk about our first words, the knowing, unknowing looks into each other's eyes; the romantic bric-a-brac of maudlin poetry and contemporary novels. But such memories are unsustainable for my love was a vampire that depleted my blood and turned my heart into a sump pump of iridescent obsession.

I came to know that she was married to a physician, an internist, I think, long on hours, short on passion, thick with income, thin with intimacy…or so she told me. Love makes liars of us all, distorting our senses and our ability to separate truth from falsity. We spent every hour we could together, making love, possessing each other insatiably in hotel rooms, on a red blanket at the deserted end of a beach of the leeward shore, in the backseat of my car like two teens thinking tomorrow would never come. She was the landlord of my dreams, the sole tenant of my waking thoughts.

I became consumed with jealousy, an insane bird of prey that swooped through windows and gorged itself on my insecurities. Everyone was suspect, no one exempt. That is how I saw the world that is how it saw me.

We finagled a week away from husband and flew to France—Paris. We rented a pea green Renault the size of a washing machine and drove the A7 north to the Normandy coast, sparse of people, rocky, austere, ringed with white limestone crosses that marked the burial places of D-Day Brits, Americans and Canadians. We walked the strand and eventually found the small road that led to Mont St. Michel, a stone wedding cake of a town rising almost supernaturally from the salt sea floodplain, separated from the rest of the world six hours, twice a day by the rising tides, at once a mountain and a desert island.

We climbed the corkscrew cobblestone street toward the top, stopping halfway to watch the gray channel waters submerge the surrounding countryside at high tide, sea birds circling and then perching on the granite of the cathedral at the top of the town. We ate lunch at a small cramped bistro with barely a word, watching smiling, camera-clicking tourists as they climbed, laughing, chatting, carrying little bags of souvenirs.

An hour or so after lunch, somewhat breathless from the spiraling walk, we came to the door of the cathedral. I stopped and turned to her and said, "Do you still make love to your husband?"

"What? What did you say?"

"Do you still fuck your husband?" Two nuns walked by and turned as I spoke, nodding in disapproval. "Well, do you?"

"Don't spoil everything. Please, no silly questions. Not today. Not ever."

"That is no answer."

"What difference would it make?"

"All the difference in the world. I can't share you that way. I can't. I won't."

"Please stop your can'ts. I love you, but I can't be yours, not entirely. Not the way you want me. We need to be happy with what we have. Please understand."

"Why not? Is there someone else besides him? Why are you staying with him? Is it the money that he's got? Or the money I don't?"

"You're cruel. It's not what you think. I must have some of me left for me. The rest is yours; none of me is his. None." Her eyes filled with anger then with tears. I said nothing, but put my arm around her waist and led her through the door.

The church was all wooden beams and stone slab floors, sandstone pillars and sparse oak chairs placed here and there as if the remnants of a tag sale. The smell of paraffin wafted through the air, flickering votive candles in a corner shimmered in red and blue glass at the foot of a pale statue of the Virgin. A cluster of white-robed nuns knelt on the hard floor in silent prayer, novitiates in thin black frocks and starched white hats stood by the eastern wall staring downward. A thin light seeped through the blue stained glass making everything look like it was submerged in some huge aquarium. A narrow stairway planted in a carved out niche in the west wall led upwards, the sound of our footsteps as we climbed, muffled by oak. We passed by slitted arrowsmith windows which gazed at each of the four points of the compass as we climbed four stories, E, N, W, S, E, W, N, S, to the top, a circular chamber with a massive wooden vaulted ceiling and a fourteen foot tall white marble statue of Michael the Archangel, hair tossed by an imaginary wind, sword upraised, eyes downward beneath a deeply furrowed righteous brow glaring at us.

"He is beautiful," she said in a whisper, "So beautiful."

The angel's voice was resonant, filling the room like a silo full of bats, his words in bass tones swirling around and through me, leathery, profane, the pungent odor of musk caressing me. She seemed oblivious or deaf, strolling about the room like a simple tourist, gazing at faded frescoes, admiring a decayed antique crucifix leaning irreverently against a wall. The angel's voice told me much, his eyes following mine, his rigid neck somehow craning as I followed Isabella, her voice ebbing and swelling like the incoming tide but drowned in the tempest of the angel's voice.

We spent that night in a small hotel at the base of the mount but still some twenty stories above the salt flats. We fell asleep sometime after midnight, but I awoke an hour later. Inexplicably, prayer hovered at the margin of my consciousness, prowling out of sight like a feral cat yearning for entry. I opened my eyes and stared at the ceiling and began to murmur some words but once again prayer remained outside and apart from me, banned, excluded, unattainable, shut out as if walls as high as the moon had been built between me and God. So instead of praying I whispered, "It is a good thing to give thanks unto the Lord, and to sing praise unto thy name, O most High. To show forth thy loving kindness in the morning…" But even these harmless words came out wrong and as quickly as I had begun, I ceased the familiar psalm foul and sour in my mouth, as empty and meaningless. Beyond my wildest imaginings I did not think it possible to be so removed from God. It was not my lack of desire to be near Him for this I still craved but with a forsaken solitary apartness so beyond hope that I could not have felt more divided from Him had I been cast alive like some wriggling insect beneath the largest rock on earth, there to live in hideous and perpetual darkness. I secretly climbed out of bed and with softest footsteps went to the window.

She stirred in bed awake. I stood there watching the moon rise, catching the rippling surface of the receding waters far below, a silver finger painting of serpentine rivulets that crawled to the sea, losing themselves in a hovering mist that melted the horizon. The angel's words were trapped in the spider web of my brain struggling vainly to be free.

"Come here," I said. "Come…look out at the channel." The moon is rising. She came to my side. I put my arm around her and spoke of the chalk cliffs of England across the water, of errant night sea birds that filled the air invisibly searching for carrion left by the receding tide. I could hear the weakening swells at the foot of the mount, soft plaintive sighs as they stirred the gravel, tossed against the naked shingles of the earth.

"Stay with me," I said. "I can't go on without you; give him up. I can't…I won't lose you. I'll do anything for you, everything, but promise me here and now that you will never leave me again, that you will give him up."

A thin black cloud like the finger of an outstretched hand slithered across the face of the rising moon. The angel's voice broke free, seeped through the lath and plaster of the ceiling out into the night air. My grip tightened on her arm.

"We are all I have," I said. She spoke but her words were muffled by the thundering hoofbeats of my pulse in my head. The angel was right, I thought. He was right. The rest was lost in the incoming fog, the white cliffs, looming, striding across the channel, approaching on vaporous currents, the color of a trillion crushed seashells, of nameless bones, countless skulls, of the pale clear liquid of my empty, my unbeating heart.

Hunters

"Now, son, don't jump the gun," I said realizing the pun with a grin. "We hunters gotta obey the rules or there'll be anarchy. No huntin' before sunrise and the sun don't come up until 6:45 AM. That's only twenty minutes away. 'Sides, even if you headed out an hour ago to get a jump on all the other hunters, you wouldn't see nothin' till you was on top of it and that deer would be long gone listenin' as they do for your footsteps." I watched Frank, Junior looking out the pick-up window so intently, dressed in his new from Christmas hunting gear, his bright orange vest glowing like a beacon in the lights from the dashboard.

"Besides," I added, "there'll be more hunters here than game and most of 'em are from the city and will likely shoot anything that moves. Best to have daylight all 'round."

"Sure, Dad. I get it. I'm just itchin' for my first buck."

"He's out there, son. Just a matter of catchin' up with him. Your number's on him."

I reached for the cross that dangled from the rear view mirror and said, "Frank, Junior, say this prayer with me: Lord, keep us safe this day, guide our feet to our deer, let it not suffer at our hands, that he is our food and we thank you for him. Amen."

"Amen," echoed Frank, Junior.

It was near noon when we both sighted the two whitetails flickering in the dull January light about two hundred yards off to the east.

"Son," I whispered, "Lean against this tree here to get steady. Those two are a way's off. Ain't no wind and you know the drop. Let's not try to get closer; they'll pick up our crunchin' for sure. Get a bead through your scope the way I taught you. Aim a few inches above the tail of the one on the right. You'll get a clean head shot. I'll take the one on the left. Just wait while I…." but before I could finish, Frank, Junior fired.

"I got him, Dad, I got him. I think I got 'em both. Both tails went down at the same time. That possible, Dad?"

"Sure is, I guess. If God is guiding your aim, anything is possible. That 30.06 can go through three deer, certain. Two with one shot. Boy, that is some shootin'. Your mom'll be proud for sure, real proud, maybe prouder'n me. Let's go get us our venison. Yes, she'll be mighty proud, maybe even more than me."

The wind wailed its naked banshee call all night and scared the full moon into hiding its wan face in the wiry frigid comfort of the scuttling clouds. Helena sat by the fire, its voice a crackling staccato, a plaintive solo in the frozen symphony of winter in January in Maine. Well-worn photographs lay on the rug, their black and white images oranging like sun-bathers on Kennesaw Beach in a July that seemed so long ago that it was hardly worth the remembering. The leaden Atlantic slouched three miles to the east swelling in slushy belches its proudful boast that it had taken Helena's husband, Jack and their only child, Christopher. For nearly five years they had cajoled the brine with their fishing boat into yielding up tons of cod. A November nor'easter had curdled its way up the ragged coast and became Grendl, the beast in the night, who swallowed Jack and Christopher, the Laura Lee and a half ton of Narragansett cod in one carnivorous gulp. Nothing was left but the photos and a handwritten report from the coroner that tersely said, "Lost at sea—presumed dead."

The sun was performing its one act play, pretending to be a blood orange, hide and seeking through the tangle of limbs and legs, the arterio-venous straggle of oak, maple, and poplar brooding over the fallen leaves that crazy-quilted the forest floor in more hues of brown than an angel could count. Helena had soaked the sheets of hers and Jack's bed and Christopher's as well all night in a tub of steamy water seasoned with Ivory flakes. She wrung them out, her hands gently twisting them into a pallid umbilicus that finally needed to be cut. She placed them in a wicker laundry basket by the back door, an eager country road of soapy water drops meandering from the laundry room through the moaning kitchen.

She put on her brown cloth coat and a pair of white woolen mittens Christopher had gotten her for Christmas two years back, her ash blond hair the only covering her head would need.

The wind had died. The sun perched on the topmost fingers of the trees, watched her walk with the basket like Miriam with Moses to the Nile shore. The clothes line was rigid from the cold, the

126

clothes pins squeaking as they gripped the sodden sheets. When she finished, she stepped back, the bedclothes luminous and limp, already partly frozen, the halyards of her life. She knew that Jack and Christopher would be hunting deer on a day like today; maybe they had survived through some miracle or maybe it was all one of those dreams that is so real, you believe it all, long after you've awakened. Maybe they were in the woods after all, lost and looking for her and home. She turned and walked toward the trees, stopping just at the lawn's edge and gazing off into the mauve, gray and brown cacophony. She held up her mittened hands and waved them slowly as if to friends passing on a distant road. It took only ten minutes, she guessed, for the searching rifle muzzle to see those two white tails flickering two hundred yards off to the east. A perfectly created lead and brass bullet soared past the birch grove, through the stand of sugar maples, by the cluster of Maine spruce and into Helena's heart which had stopped beating nearly two months before.

Jogger

I can still smell the paraffin in the kitchen from the candles on my birthday cake last night. They put 5 large candles and 8 smaller ones for my 58 years and the flickering flame uplit everyone's smile as they watched me blow them all out. My children, grandchildren and husband all looked at me with the expectancy of revealing my wish, but there was something else in their eyes, the unspoken truth of the secret we shared.

I sit and put on my running shoes while Sam watches me, his tongue lolling, eyes bright.

"Not today, Sammy, this is a run of my own. Ok boy, I'd do the same for you." I pat him on the head and dig my nails into the thick fur on his neck.

"Thanks for being such a great dog, Sammy, I'll see you soon."

I take off down the flagstone path and head for the marina park, a flat jog for two miles that at the end twists up Santa Catalina Mountain for a mile or so. My pacemaker has a new set of batteries and the 6:00 a.m. air is heavy with the moisture from the Pacific.

I don't know what a good wife is-or a good mother and I'm not going to rationalize anything away by saying I did the best I could because if everyone did the best they could, we'd all be perfect or nearly so. Jake was a good husband-the recycling trucks are out-but maybe I just made him so in my eyes. There was so much that I had to overlook that the overlooking turned into a kind of blindness. His late Fridays at the office, his weekend trips out of town, his sudden interest in his weight and his wardrobe-well, blindness set in and I don't want to acknowledge the new Braille of my middle age, feeling the truth, denying I knew it. He turned fifty and I guess one more lapse wasn't going to make him any worse than after the first one. It was a secret we shared but didn't share because he was recycling his old adolescent wants and tom cat bullshit that he learned from his father, as I became my mother, benignly unseeing, silent, even-keeled, serving while I stood and waited. I used to think it was for the sake of my children but I think it was really for my sake. What was I going to do in divorce court even if I was right? Winning isn't always what it's cracked up to be.

Jogger

I'm perspiring and I want to talk to myself about the city waking up behind its blue-shadowed walls, rainbowed windows and mail trucks scooting around yellow-lined turns. I want to wonder what's behind those doors, who's happy or sad or too confused or caught up to even know the difference- not that I do. So I shouldn't be talking even to myself. Perhaps all those years were a shutting down. My little girls were all my joy but they never knew me except as a reflection of their own needs, sleepless nights with their fevers, their pains, their nightmares. But my eyes were a mirrored window- they could only see themselves when they looked at me, but they couldn't see past into me. Neither could Jack. But I reached the girls when they were young; a spanking could prove-did prove-that I had power over them. When they were older I could withhold my love. I was easy to offend, hair-triggered when it came to ignoring me or forgetting me from Mother's Day to Thanksgiving-if I wasn't called or gifted on a special day—special to me—I would turn suddenly cold and indifferent, unresponsive without acting hurt because to be hurt was to yield up the control I had struggled so long to capture. That's how I knew with certainty that my girls loved me because I could hurt them. How does a woman keep what's hers while giving it all away? I think I'm not making sense as I reach the foot of the uphill path. Two gorgeous young men come jogging down, ruddied, watery-eyed from the breeze, trim, elegant to their bedheads their damp hair stuck to their faces. They nod to me, an acknowledgement of mutual jogging admiration. But they see me as only a fellow jogger, too old for anything more. Jack saw me only as-I don't even know what. What I thought him to be and what he was I can't even say. Our love-making dwindled over the years; worse it became routine not even 6 months after our vows. I should have said something but I'm not made like that. I can talk about most anything but I truly believe that some things are supposed to work without prodding or practice or rehearsal. 30 years of marriage and I still can't tell Jack with my voice that our love-making is just a function, nothing more. It's reduced to some perfunctory gropes-an abridged foreplay-the Cliff's Notes of passion. It's all I had for intimacy, but I will really say that intimacy for me was-I don't know-maybe I needed a good fuck like Jack gave me before we were married because he must have thought it proved something. It did. But can you prove a falsity? Are all men pitchmen for their own sexual play-acting? An hour of foreplay has Readers Digested down to five minutes.

My breath is burning my lungs and I can hear my heart throbbing in my ears. The girls are married and gone, Jack's retired and we're together all the time. And now I realize that that this isn't living at all. It's breathing, eating, wrinkling. It's getting stiff in the limbs, swollen in the joints learning about diseases that I never heard of, substituting pills for hormones. I hate complaining-probably should have done more of it when it might have made a difference. I know I don't want to change any of it any more. Because I finally realize that nothing is changeable, not my diagnosis, not its treatment, not the bleak future it implies. Tuesdays melt into Thursdays, golf for Jack, babysitting, TV shows at the center of a night, nothing worth waiting for as if I've watched a four- hour movie and fell asleep for the last 20 minutes when everything was to be resolved. But I slept through it. I am not in control of anything anymore. I never was although people like to think they are and spend years, even whole lifetimes self-deluded. I learned that when the funerals started. It's about when you turn fifty, that air pocket of chronology, that people you know and love start dying. It's the exclamation point of middle-age. Now the cancer, no question marks there. Like Ratso Rizzo said, "I'm fallin' apart here." I'm at the place where I usually take a breather, halfway up the hill. A school bus has already gone past. I want to watch the sun rising behind me as I look out at the ocean but I'm afraid it will dissuade me. I'm tired of making beds and lying in them. I reach for the battery pack on my life belt-interesting name - a euphemism? - and take out the four dime-sized batteries, put them in my pocket so no one will think it was an accident. I don't want recriminations, I don't want to cause blame-shouting or guilt-wearing or required tears. I don't want sorrys or ostentatious flowers or a sermon or eulogy about my life. I'm not proud of any of it. And I'm not bitter. It was a trip I made with a lousy map my mother gave me, with unpredictable detours down dead-ends through fog, black ice and occasional bits of sun. I know that some people have better of it than they deserve, some worse than they deserve. All our maps are in some dusty atlas kept somewhere on an out-of-the-way shelf. I'm running again and can feel the fist of the cartographer around my heart. The only thing I can control now, the least obvious, electric pulses to my stumbling heart. A drying breeze is browsing whomever is out, in from the east, offshore rushing the damp away.

I've stopped sweating, my breathing is strong, my legs don't ache. There are pines - a whole untouched stand ahead - my favorite place to stop and sit, feel the needles beneath my feet, then against my back, clinging to my hair which thankfully will never fall out now, a good place to stay a while and wait.

I know I will keep running, an easy pace another mile, maybe a thousand, maybe more. I don't need to stop and I can't turn around. The sky is liquid, distant clouds explain the horizon. I look at my own hands and thank them.

Second Chance

I looked great in a sportscoat and a starched shirt, clean shaven, trim, dark-haired and intense—real pussy bait, in between marriages. I was standing at the bar, the one covered in mother of pearl and lit from below with rose colored neon that uplit everyone standing there making their eyes look dark and mysterious, their cheekbones high, the outlines of their lower torso prominent even protuberant, if that's a word. You'd expect that nearby there would be a statuesque beauty, sultry, long-haired, full-hipped with globey breasts. You'd be right, amigo. Every male writer that ever went to a bar alone met her or wished he had, the goddess of mystery fiction, empress of drunken memoirs, Hemingway's hussy, Fitzgerald's flirt, Steinbeck's stacked broad, Spillane's (in better company than he deserves) sperm magnet. There she was for real, in the flesh, as they say and of it. Of course, I offered her a drink; of course she accepted it and talk flowed like bullshit because it was. I heard about her job, her ex-boyfriend, her lonely in-between relationship stories and took it all like it was true because I didn't care and someone who really doesn't care prides himself on acting like he does. If she liked rock climbing, I wanted to scale the Matterhorne. If she liked snails on toast I loved them raw on crackers. If she was a neo-Nazi, I would click my heels and Heil past midnight. It's my chameleon self, mon capitán, a stylistic quirk that is a one way ticket to Bushville after a brief obligatory stop at Twin Peaks and Nipplelodeon. I stifled a yawn then she told me about her uncle Charlie, a retired insurance salesman who had taken to becoming a boxer at the prime age of sixty-eight. He worked out on the heavy bag hung in his apartment living room hitting it so hard that he developed blood clots, one of which broke loose and landed somewhere in the geezer's brain resulting in a stroke. When he recovered, he fancied himself a writer who would beat anyone senseless who criticized his work, mostly a bunch of other geezers he drank beer with and who knew better than to mess with him. He sent her regular checks though to help with the rent and she loved him dearly. Who wouldn't? she asked. I didn't answer that, brother-in-arms.

Talked turned to astrology. She told me she was an Aquarius—now, understand mon frére, I don't know an Aquarius from a

132

Seaquarium but I know broads put a lot of stock in that "what's your sign" bullshit so I remembered the column in the paper and told her I was a Scorpitarius. She laughed and looked at me sideways. So I guess I picked a sign that was compatible with hers. Good thing for me because it was getting late and only skanks and slags were left in the bar and I didn't want another date with the palm sisters.

By 2 A.M., and all the agreeing with all the inanity I could muster, we ended up in her apartment, a fourth floor walk-up studio on Avenue A with a silk scarf over the lampshade for effect and the smell of perfume and feet wafting through the radiated air. The dirty futon looked like a king-sized bed at the Plaza to me, the stains like a hand-woven damask of flowers with Chinamen holding parasols and teapots.

I was actually reaching the goalposts, mon semblable, the crowd was cheering and my mind was focusing on the task at hand. I looked at her in the dim light. She really was beautiful, not beautiful to a drunk kind of beautiful, but really beautiful, runway material, Vogue material, gorgeous, to coin a word.

We stood and held each other and slurped each others lips and tongues, the vermouth from her martini making a putrid combo with the scotch and soda I was repeating. She inhaled as I grabbed her breast, gently like I knew women wanted, not ravenously the way men wanted. I was caressing—a good girl word—when I really wanted to squeeze till my knuckles turned white. She exhaled into my mouth and the air went directly to little Joe and inflated him to well past the morning wood stage. Her nipples were as hard as rivets; little Joe put Galahad's lance to shame. We were ready for battle, paisán.

"I want to blow you," she whispered in my ear. I was hoping that, I said to myself but the words that came out were, "a kiss for luck and we're on our way," the only romantic thing I could come up with at the time, thank you Karen Carpenter, you anorexic wacko. I looked into her bedroom eyes, deep pools they were. Something about her made me wish I had listened to her for real when she spoke at the bar. Something about her that made me wish I had told her more about me. Now, compadre, don't think I was turning into a sap from the booze or the moist aroma in the apartment. You spend your days sometimes wondering who you will marry, who will be the mother of your children, who you will grow old with and other unmasculine thought processes like those. This woman, who I only wanted a quickie from, suddenly seemed right for me, someone I could commit to. I wanted a second chance, I wanted to back up an hour or two so I could be back at the bar. Understand, blood brother?

While I was thinking this stuff, she dropped to her knees and undid my belt and fly and released little Joe from his 35% cotton/65% polyester prison. If I give any more details this will seem more prurient than I intended so I will jump ahead a minute and forty-five seconds to the point when my knees began to buckle.

"Let's get on the bed," I said quietly as if there were others within earshot.

"You mean the futón?" she answered with a suddenly French pronunciation of the flat sack of Dacron stuffed Wal-Mart marketed pad that served as her sleeping hole.

"Oui, mon chéri, le futón," I answered. You don't think I was going to get wise at this point, do you, pal o'mine?

I managed to lie down despite my trousers and boxers around my ankles and was getting ready for the piece de résistance on le futón when I reached under her skirt and stroked her firm thighs. She resisted and that made me care for her in that sappy way that I thought had flown the coop. Maybe I should stop. But my hand had a mind of its own and kept exploring higher into the territory of male Shangri-La. Where I was expecting a gentle, furry welcoming mound, I found my path blocked by boulders. Yes, a handful of scrotum. That's right, my loyal reader, nut sack, hairy balls wrapped in tight panties with a flaccid dick the size of my ring finger tucked carefully between them aimed asswards.

"Holy shit, you're a guy," I said loudly enough for anyone within a hundred yard radius to hear and to emphasize my displeasure I let her/him have it in the jaw with a punch that had about as much power behind it as a guy spackling a nail hole. I was prone, inebriated, romantically inclined and couldn't quite overcome my lack of leverage.

He jumped up, kicking both high heels off with the deftness of Bruce Lee—they hit the wall behind me with a catapult double thud.

"You motherfucker," she/he said two octaves lower. "There are two things I was born for: fucking and fighting," and she let go a right hand that knocked me off le futón onto the rug. In a flash he was straddling me and another fist collided with my eye; I saw more constellations than the Hubble space telescope. He grabbed me by the shirt collar and crouched down so that his lips were brushing my nose and said, "I can finish beating you to a bloody pulp and drop you down the garbage chute or you can let me finish blowing you. And then you can go home and fuck your wife or whoever and live another day. It's your choice, Jack (which is not my name)." I thought a moment, it seemed like an hour. Seconds ago, I was thinking this creature as wife. I had been imagining Marilyn Monroe, then Uma Thurman, then Katie Couric (ten years younger) then Demi before Bruce—why did I have to reach under her/his skirt? Why was I born, Father Confessor, why?

"Okay, Okay, relax," I said. "I give up. Actually you are quite pretty…and very good at what you do. Better than most. Should I stand, sit, or lie down. You deserve a second chance." Again, I will leave out the gory details but as hard as I tried, Marilyn, Uma, Katie and Demi had left the building. The best I could manage adapting to the new reality was James Dean, then Montgomery Clift, then Rock Hudson and finally Brad Pitt without the scruffy beard but clean and young like in that chick flick *Thelma and Henrietta*—I was beginning to think more broads should drive off into the Grand Canyon, maybe fill it up, the bitches. I gave her a second chance. I had to. I'm sure glad she gave me one. Next time, I'll cop a surreptitious feel before I leave the bar with anyone. Anyone. Maybe it won't matter what I find, in case you're thinking of asking, comrade.

The Gene

I had been having my recurring dream of the split up between my parents, when my mother told my father that she had had enough and that if he did not leave, she would not be responsible for what would happen next. He left, but each time in each dream he said something different to her and then he would turn to me with tears in his eyes, his image melting into the mist of a morning that never ended.

I woke up on Wednesday morning and all my flu symptoms had vanished. Jim had already left for work and I could hear Peter downstairs in the kitchen.

"Mom, I'm not hungry," Peter said.

"You will be…at school. Are you sure?"

"Yeah. I'm gonna be late." He picked up his bag and said, "I love you," as the screen door slapped closed behind him.

I turned on the T.V. set and sat on the sofa with my cup of coffee but I could not take even a sip.

"Must be that damn flu," I thought.

The news was on, all the usual, but the final three minutes talked about the extreme drop in contagious disease cases. It seemed that overnight every patient at every hospital in the city who had pneumonia, AIDS or any number of illnesses caused by bacteria or viruses were in complete remission. The center for disease control was investigating.

The dog was at the back door. I let him in and put his full dog bowl in front of him on the floor. He sniffed it, he looked up at me and walked away. "What's the matter, Gino, eatin' the neighbor's garbage, again?" Not that that had ever stopped him.

I started cleaning up and faced the trash can under the sink. For the week that I had had the flu, I nearly vomited every time its fetid odor attacked my nostrils. But it was garbage day and I was feeling so much better, I could handle anything. I opened the cupboard door but it didn't smell any different than Jim's dinner last night. In fact, when I looked in the bag, everything in there was just as fresh as it had been when Jim was cooking it.

By Saturday, actually sooner for me and Jim and Peter, a new reality had established itself on Earth. None of us had eaten anything since Wednesday morning and we simply could not even face food of any kind. Gino, our Sheppard mix, didn't eat, either. We were all losing weight. Food in the fridge was not deteriorating. Talking heads on the T.V. reported that cows, pigs, sheep, every farm animal had stopped eating, along with animals in the zoos and even animals in the wild. Reports from African authorities said that herd animals had stopped grazing or migrating because it seemed that traveling long distances for new food sources was no longer motivating them. Lions, leopards and cheetahs simply watched as their former prey stood silently in the lush veldts and grasslands. Animals killed by the road went untouched by crows and more peculiarly, like garbage, failed to deteriorate. Jim realized that not only had animals and, apparently humans as well, stopped eating but so had bacteria and even viruses. As silly as it sounded, we didn't have morning breath or need for deodorant. Peter guessed that if he had gone to the bathroom, which none of us had in days, there would be no need for the exhaust fan. There was no humor in any of this, for our family, like most of the world, had not a feeling of dread, or impending doom or even anxiety, so much as a sensation, as Jim had put it, of being lost in a deep forest and suddenly finding a large sunny clearing. We were still lost but it didn't seem to matter anymore.

By the following Wednesday we had learned that newborns and infants were dying of starvation in the hundreds of thousands. Those that were on intravenous feeding were simply lingering in a twilight between life and death. Almost every small animal from sardines in the sea to sparrows in the trees to mice in the fields had died, their emaciated bodies littering the open places of the world in a preamble of devastation, the small flakes that dance in the wind before the blizzard starts, the flakes that do not melt.

Scientists and theologians all over the globe weighed in with their theories but none of it stopped the dying. People with diseases that were not microbially based, weak hearts, cancer, a score of conditions like Parkinson's and diabetes had begun perishing as their failure to eat weakened them. The bodies, at first quickly buried as in the plague years of the 14th century, were simply piled up in public buildings where they remained in the early stages of mummification. The dead simply desiccated.

Jim and me were listless and tired and nurtured Peter as long as we could. We would sit in his room and take turns reading to him, glorious stories, it now seemed, of magical times, of abundant Christmases, of kingdoms of gold. When Jim opened the family Bible, he could not read it. No one that we knew found solace in the stories of punishment, deprivation or redemption. Society had not crumbled- there was no violence or looting, the war in the dessert simply stopped, prisons emptied, borders went uncrossed. All the energy of politics and science and patriotism and chauvinism like the energy of life itself had dissipated in the tepid breeze of apathy. If there was something to do, no one said what it was. And no one tried. Peter was the first of us to die. His withered frame so frail and small as he lay in bed, his skin translucent.

"Mommy," he said. "You won't bury me will you?"

"No, darling, you'll stay right here with us."

"I'm not sad, you know. I'm not scared, either. I'm just tired like that time I stayed up all night trying to catch Santa Claus. I'll miss you and you too, Dad."

"We'll miss you," Jim said, his first words in nearly three days.

A few hours later, our son passed, to what or from what I don't know.

Jim lasted another two days and I found him on the couch with the T.V. on, no show, for all the channels had ceased broadcasting, but just a bright blue light as if that was all that was left of the earth. I sat by his side too weak to cry, too empty to move or even think. I fell asleep and dreamed of a summer we three had shared on Cape Cod, on the beach watching the gulls hover and two small sailboats race far off shore, their snowy sails two exclamation points on the endless sea.

I awoke at dusk and tried to turn on the lights but the power had finally gone out. The flimsy hulk of Gino lay lifeless at my feet, his chin on my foot. I reached down and petted his furry head realizing I was finally alone. I went to the window and watched the disk of the sun sink below the roofs of the neighbors' houses. The copper-fire glint off the dark street lights, the parked cars, a bicycle lying on its side in the roadway. I knew this would be my last sunset and I didn't mind.

We had one of those clapboard-sided, front-porched Victorian farmhouses that sprouted all over small town America in the boom years of the 1920's. It had a walk-up attic with a steeply-pitched ceiling, the floor full of things too useless to keep downstairs, too memory-laden to throw away. I wanted to look at one of my old family photo albums so I made my way up with Jim's flashlight slithering over the worn steps.

When I got to the attic's piney sweetness, I saw my father sitting in our old painted rocker, a soft dull light filled the room. My father had been dead for over twelve years. I realized that this must be an illusion created by my condition, my nutrient deprived brain playing its last tricks on me.

"Caroline," he said. "It's me, Dad."

"I know." That's all I could say. I finally had him here alone after all that had happened. I didn't care if he was real or not in the haze of my mind I was somehow reassured by his presence.

"God has sent me here to explain," he said.

"I don't want his explanations, Dad, not now, not ever." It was then I fully understood what had happened on Earth.

"No, you must listen to me. God has punished the earth for its…"

"Bullshit, Dad, bullshit. He sent you to tell me bullshit. Why me? Why not the Pope or the President?"

"I don't know. I'm only telling you what he wants me to tell you. I don't have all the answers."

"You never did."

"I do now for this. God created every creature from the very beginning. And in that earliest one he placed a gene. Every animal has that gene and has had it passed down to him from day one. That gene was a doomsday gene."

"You're trying to tell me that God has an expiration date on all of us from the very beginning?"

"That's what I'm saying. He told me to tell you."

"Why me? Why not any one else?"

"He may have. I don't have all the answers. I already told you."

"Well, let me tell you a message you can pass on to God. I'm not buying the B.S., not for a minute. I know what happened and God isn't going to get the credit for it although it is his fault. We all quit."

"Quit? What do you mean?"

"Quit. God couldn't fire us. We quit. We're fed up with taking the blame and suffering and we're tired, bone tired, of taking the rap for his lousy creation. We're tired of droughts and floods, , tired of fires, earthquakes and storms, making people sick and of getting sick. We're sick of killing each other. It's the way he made us and this damn world and we quit. It wasn't suicide either, I don't want to give him the credit for that. Something inside every living thing just said it's time to stop, damn the consequences. We're tired of forgiving him for everything he's done to us; tired of explaining his violent or indifferent ways to our kids. He thinks so little of us that he sent his son here knowing full well we would murder him. It wasn't the Jews or the Romans. It was human beings. We are, every-thing that crawls across the face of this damned planet, a negation. We negate it all. Like Jesus said, Dad, 'It is done.' He's gonna have to find some other bunch to torture. Get it? We quit. Tell him that."

"I will Caroline. I don't know how it's going to go."

"I don't care, dad. I don't even think you're real. But if you are and you're some sort of wacko angel-messenger, then you have my answer. Now get out, Dad. Sound like Mom? Just get out."

"I loved your mother."

"Yeah Dad, you loved Mom, but…the way God loves us."

"No, I just loved her period the way God loves all of us."

"Why didn't you love me enough, Dad? Why? Why wasn't I enough to keep you faithful to mom? Your tears weren't enough, dad, not nearly enough."

"Good-bye, Caroline," he sighed and his sigh was like a death rattle, a dissolution of his image into the dull white-wash of the wall behind him. The chair rocked empty, the only light now from Jim's flickering flashlight. I sat on the floor and looked out the dormer window. I imagined the slow rhythm of empty waves ca-ressing the lifeless beaches of the world, the washing of the drear and naked shingles of the earth. I might have been the last being left alive on earth. I don't know and I didn't care. Sleep or something very much like it was coming over me. I watched the crescent moon rise over the town, a tilted eyeless smile in a vacant sky. It was the last thing I saw before my eyes closed, but not the last thing I saw.

The Lilacs

"We call it anthropomorphic restructuring, sir," the voice on the telephone said. "We start with a computer scan of a recent photo. The computer creates a 3-dimensional image which is fed into a graphic collator... uh, a machine that creates a plastic skull based on the image. Are you with me?"

I answered robotically, "Yes, I am. I think I am." I am what I am, I thought. I think, therefore I am. I think, therefore I hurt. I hurt beyond hurting. I hurt enough to climb through this wire and strangle you so that you know how I hurt. I would personally drive a nail through Jesus' hand if it would stop my hurt. "Go on," I said. "Please."

"Well, we take the model skull from the enhanced photo of your son. I mean the missing person... sorry... then we carefully add clay to it after it is enlarged so that we can predict graphically what he would look like as he aged." I had stopped breathing, lost in a pool of dark water, floating, counting the seconds and the oxygen molecules in my blood, watching them run out as my heart beat slower. "Sir, are you there?"

"Yes, I'm sorry," I said as I surfaced. "I'm listening." I had heard it before, of course, every year for the past twelve years, every year on Michael's birthday. It was always new, though, never something I wanted to remember no matter how hard the pounding on the door to my brain, the lock had been welded shut.

"Then we photograph the model and prints can be made and then posters from those."

"Yes, let's do it," I said.

"It's not inexpensive, Mr. Smithson," he inflected. I wanted to tell him that his company, the eighth one I employed was all that stood between me and insanity. No, not insanity, something worse, a knowing dementia, a gnawing insect of regret that ate away everything I thought mattered, an archeological parasite that, with chisel and stiff-bristled brush dug away at my consciousness revealing micron by micron the memory of my boy until that was all that was left, an ancient idol emerging from the surrounding rock, from a past long-treasured that was the center of my personal civilization.

"I know. I know. I'll send you a check. And a photograph. Just get started."

Some details followed, then the conversation ended. I hung up the phone and looked at the blue leather photo album on the coffee table. Lillian had kept it up meticulously. The first page was Michael's foot print taken at the hospital, some pictures of me leaning over the bed, my arm around Lil who was holding a small bundle that would become my son, a few pages on, his fifth birthday party, the last real photo. He was surrounded by grandparents and a few children, a faraway smile on his face, his mother kneeling at his side prepping him to blow out the candles. Mostly, though, it was a picture of ghosts. Everyone excepting the three small neighborhood kids was dead, Lillian the last to leave, last year a few days before Michael would have turned sixteen. Each time she visited the grave, she faded a little more until there was almost nothing left. But is there any purpose in thinking about it, the inevitable, the predictable, the eroding force of unsustainable memory and lost certainty? Each following page had a computer generated photo of my son as he aged in cyberspace, images no more real than if they had been laser printed on snowflakes, the only tribute that we could make. I was now the keeper of the history, the shaman of my lost tribe keeping the ancestral succession alive, the teller of an oral history that eventually drove everyone I knew faultlessly away from me.

I went to the kitchen and popped opened a can of Pepsi and sat at the red Formica-topped table, looked at the kitchen clock, the same one that I watched twelve years ago, watched the minute hand scythe its way past 3:30 in the afternoon. He was five minutes late. Maybe the bus was running behind its time. Ten minutes. Fifteen. I remembered that walk to the back door by the driveway where he should have come in. He was probably dawdling outside in the spring sun, yes, yes, waylaid by a little boy's curiosity. The pitiless click of the latch as I opened the door expecting him to be there, his blue backpack on the lawn, surprised but gladdened by my intrusion, a quick smile, But that twelve feet of driveway was vacant. I walked out, the first ember of panic glowing in my gut, ignited by a flashing red light glimmering, sparkling, pulsing through the tall hedge row of lilac bushes and the shouts of neighbors running toward me. There was a morning glory vine that had sinued its way up the woody lilac branches, climbing over, under, entwining, covering, smothering. Was the light a red peony, a disastrous rose, a bloody zinnia misplaced by a storm I hadn't known had passed? A siren slithered in the air. The red light pounded in the lilacs, glistened in the lilacs like a distant setting sun, a dying sun shimmering forever through the lilacs, the lilacs, the lilacs, the lilacs.

There Was a Time

There was a time when I would have watched the starlings diving after flies, the gentle esses of their swaying over the field like the effortless swing of the trapeze in the circus of the clouds. I might have noticed the sweet apostrophes of leaves as they fall in the still summer's heat, remembered Goethe's evanescent rise and fall of the spirit as it ascends to Heaven drawn by God's gossamer web, the tug and ease of his certain pulling on the line, the fisherman reeling in the souls afraid to depart, afraid not to; Schiller's Ode to Joy, Beethoven's music making the words immortal. I might have written in my notebook of galleon clouds sailing over the Black Forest, more like albino dolphins cruising reefs of northern shores, the blue calamite coral like the spires of fallen Babylon, city of iridescent kings. "My love," I would have written, "will you remember me when I am gone? Will the flagstone terrace miss my shadow, the lilacs wonder that days have passed that I have not mixed my breath with theirs? You would never understand, my love, what brought me here, what duty so possessed me that I..." The words evaporate in the air of the Eastern Front.

The men, the women and the children are all running through the woods, their stifled screams and cries, whimpers, a dismal chorus to the clicks and clacks of breaking twigs, the wiry staccato call of an infant, sadly bouncing breasts, red knees, grey hair, sallow skin, sunken eyes, the miniature genitalia of the children, scrotums, the bric-a-brac of the false humanity of the Jew, a herd of them corralled through this pristine woods, a pink python slithering for shelter.

"Schnell," I yell out, "Schnell Jüden." Into the trench they go, dirt to dirt, I think. Would Friederich still marry me knowing the great task I have undertaken?...and am accomplishing. Does it matter, Friederich? Did you know the steel that has replaced my bones? I love you still, my darling, even as I give the order to fire. So many bullets nesting in the trench, like bats at dusk returning to their cave, so many the air is grey, the bodies of the Jews writhing, then flattening, then still, an occasional hand reaching to its empty sky.

The vapor from the SS guns rises like jellyfish tendrils over the

144

trench. Is that thunder? Will the rain finally come? No, it is the earthmovers, four dun bulldozers chugging and belching diesel smoke, a fog at noon, pushing loam over the excrement my squad has deposited. In a half-hour, the floor of this clearing is restored, though flat and bald. I can see the billion seeds of grass, of buttercups, of milkweed, of bluebells hugging the rich soil, their infant roots soon to reach down. Do the dead below wait for them? Do they dream of home? Do they face judgment? No. They have no souls. They are the damned.

I straighten my death's head uniform. I am an avenging angel. My car pulls up. A lieutenant opens the door for me, clicks his heels. "Heil Hitler," he says, "Fraulein Komandant." I nod and feel God's hand on my shoulder.

The Butler

Mr. Stevens, the butler, was my hero. You may not recognize his name but he's the guy in *Remains of the Day*, a film you've likely seen because most people who read would have seen it and right now you're reading. He was meticulous in his job, even obsessive. Actually he was a serving psychopath. I am not like him.

When I was in high school 3 years, 4 months, 12 days and 6 hours ago I had the option of taking shop, which most guys did or home economics, which most girls did. My father was a wood-working freak and after a long day of trying to sell insurance he would come home, eat a taciturn dinner after a martini and then head for the garage which he converted into a tool lover's nirvana. Jig saws, table saws, drill presses, planes, carving sets, chisels and every other device that Sears could manage to have a bunch of Chinamen manufacture so they could sell it to "American Craftsmen"

Dad did not believe that sharing was the greatest gift so I was forbidden to touch anything in the mausoleum of his workshop. It was easier for Lord Carnarvon to enter Tutankhamen's tomb than for me to get into that goddamned garage and King Tut's curse was a mosquito bite compared to Pop's strap. Frankly, I wasn't interested anyway. What I was interested in was a good way to earn a living so I could leave Ma & Pa to their inverse symbiotic marriage. Home economics was the Rosetta stone of my future life.

Everyone I knew was going into some sort of sure thing course of study, mainly computer crap because that was where they thought the jobs would be. I was figuring if the 250 kids that graduated every year from my school were basically all looking for the same type of job . . . well, multiply that by all the high schools in the country, subtract a few that got drafted or joined, subtract another few that decided drugs were more fun than studying, subtract some girls that got knocked up and finally subtract a few that got shot by a classmate that had been pushed to the brink and then over it and you still have a massive load of people who are determined to get the same type of job. You'll quickly see that it doesn't take Einstein to figure that the smart guy should go after a job that not many other people are interested in.

Now, understand, that I lived with Mom & Dad in Eastchester, a sliver of a town in the New York City suburbs, filled mainly with middle classers who needed a credit card to survive and couldn't manage to accumulate enough lucre to pay for a new lawn mower. It was paycheck-to-paycheckville. But just across the town line was Scarsdale, the richest community in the U.S. where a million bucks was just the down payment on the house and every 16 year old had a new car and a stock portfolio. What these people lacked and would pay top dollar for was a great servant. Look, how many kids say they want to be a butler when they grow up? None. Except me. Of course, I never told anyone. Does Microsoft tell Apple? I was going to be the world's best butler and take bids for my services. Let everyone else worry about gigabytes. I was going to be the master of table settings.

I studied home economics like nobody's business. I read Emily Post's *Book of Etiquette*, Ward MacAlister's *Society as I Know It*, biographies of Frick, Astor, Rockefeller, Queen This and King That. As the generations evolved from the hard-working founders of great family wealth to their descendents, those latter day brains were essentially empty. Their emotions had been short-circuited by having no material need unfulfilled so that, eventually, massive wealth was controlled by people brimming with spite, lust, ego and insecurity. They knew the price of everything and the value of nothing. Philanthropy was motivated by pride, selecting a spouse was an exercise in status-seeking and morality was governed by a collection of compact nerve endings located in a patch of hair south of the navel and north of the knees. Maybe all humans are like this. I don't know and I don't care. I didn't want to work for Joe Schmo from Kokomo. I wanted to work for Joe Von Schmo from Scarsdale.

I could go on and on about silverware patterns and setting the table for breakfast, lunch, dinner or high tea, the virtues of crystal, Spode, white candles, place cards, pressing a perfect crease, arranging roses, serving quiche, carving rack of lamb, slicing hard cheese, flambéing, brewing, smoking cigars and dabbing caviar. I practiced that broomstick-up-my-ass walk with a pleasant but solemn expression, an unflappable demeanor even in the presence of a glass of red wine cascading across white damask or a knife hurled by an irate heiress. Blood stains I could remove with salt water, tears with lemon juice, semen stains on satin with cornstarch and club soda, bullet holes in the walls spackled with toothpaste. I could address a letter to an archbishop, a middle-eastern potentate, a state senator, a traffic court judge, anticipate vomit, requests for second helpings, liquor-induced incontinence. With a photostat of a diploma and a second hand coat with tails I got a starting salary of two large a week, exclusive use of a new car, quarters with a sitting room with a fireplace in one of the toniest houses in Scarsdale and a monthly budget for clothing and butleresque accoutrements. A kid I knew in my graduating class was still shelling out his parents' money for tuition and struggling to figure out Dos and Photoshop.

I won't name names but I worked for a husband and wife with two kids in college. They had not been married before and had made it through twenty years of connubiality with only occasional bouts of violence and infidelity. They were both college drop-outs and had never worked at anything. Their lives revolved around travel and their travel revolved around golf. They knew nothing else and had only a vague notion of the size of their own trust funds. They were rarely home, where I worked, but called me frequently to make sure I was busy. They would often pretend to be only an hour away so that they might catch me with a house full of my own friends or dust on the hall table or dishes piled up in the sink or me sleeping in their bed with some skank I might have seduced pretending to be master of their house. But I was perfect and did none of those things or any others for that matter. The house was cleaner than the inside of a Swiss watch, the water in the toilets fit to drink, the garden immaculately weeded, the refrigerator stocked with fresh food, gas in the cars and newly ironed linens on the bed. I never even masturbated on the job and my job was 24 hours a day, 7 days a week. Sex never occurred to me; my only natural inclinations were being perfect in my job until the day I died and even then I would see to it that my demise caused no ripples in the tepid, glassy pool that was life at the house.

On Sunday mornings when I was certain that the house was ticking perfectly I would tell my employers that I was going to church. This always brought a certain look of smugness to their faces. They thought, as most people do, that if an employee goes to church he is less likely to do something wrong like steal a piece of Bacarat or try m'lady's bra and panties and pretend to walk like her, imitating her facial expressions in the master bedroom mirror and then giggle in self-delight. In fact, I was walking a mile and a half to a military cemetery and sitting a while admiring the neatness and perfection of the rows of crosses, all white, all 3 feet tall, all straight and evenly spaced even though the bodies they marked were a hodge-podge of white men, black men, Asian, tall short fat or thin. I imagined that God wanted people to look and act much like those perfectly symmetrical crosses and had humans complied He would be as delighted as I to walk slowly and see that the rows all formed exact diagonals in every direction as the pallid markers maintained their symmetry over rises and falls as far as the surrounding wrought iron fence. It gave me chills.

Most nights as I lay in bed, I would stare up at the blue grey rectangle of the ceiling and imagine the floor plan of the house complete with furniture and appliances. I would analyze where the armies of dust and dirt would skirmish across the maps of their invasion. Like Caesar facing the Gauls I would anticipate their gathering forces, predict where they would hide in ambush under knickknacks and plan my counter-attack armed with dust mops and vacuum cleaner, Mr. Clean at my side. Occasionally, more often than I care to admit, the image of Rhonda Townpowski would appear as if on St. Veronica's cloth. She would hold up her notebook to me and the words "I love you" would be writ upon it, with smiley faces in the 2 O's. But the marauding armies would suddenly change their battle positions and her face would be buried and lost in a grey and thickening cloud amid the legion of dust mites.

One afternoon as I was placing plastic tulips in the small rear garden to replace the real ones that some errant rabbits had devoured, the phone rang and Mrs. X (my employer) informed me that they would be home for Thanksgiving and that she had invited 10 people for dinner and she wanted it to be, in her words, "exquisitely decadent." She asked that I design an elaborate 7 course menu and most importantly to phone her and Mr. X back forthwith with my decision as to what would be served. Further, I had to give them lessons over the phone on how to eat the food properly because they would be arriving the morning of the dinner. This was nothing new for many times in the past I had to teach them the use of the various subtly different forks and spoons, how to hold this or that, which direction to place a half empty glass or finished side course or the salt cellar or the sauce boat. While I had instructed them both in these arts, they seemed always surprised as if the information was new. While they might be able to describe the dog leg on the 12th hole at St. Andrews, a fish knife threw them in to paroxysms of uncertainty.

I jotted down a quick and easy menu with some flourishes that would seem to make the food more exotic than it really was. I admired my penmanship even on so mundane a thing as my own personal notepad which no one else would ever view. I strenuously avoided using small circles over my Is which I learned from that pretty girl in my English class named Rhonda Toumpowski. Sometimes she even made those circles with smiley faces which I noticed when I was looking at her bosom one day while pretending to gaze out the classroom window. She wrote in large letters on her spiral notebook "Buzz off" and held it up to me with a glare. That's when I saw that the I in Toumpowski had a smiley face over it.

I phoned my employers back and had them both on their extensions at their residence in Jackson Hole.

"We'll start off with vichyssoise," I said

"What's that?"

"Cold potato soup," I answered

"That sounds terrible."

"You loved it last year. Trust me. I'll garnish it with cayenne pepper and tarragon. Quite festive and very different. Use the round spoon on the outside right and dip it in the bowl away from you. Don't slurp and don't tilt the bowl when you're almost done."

"Darling," Mrs. X said to her husband, "are you writing this down?"

I continued on discussing the various wines that would be served with each course and getting interrupted only for an occasional request to spell something. I had taken a somewhat devious path by putting Cornish game hen on the menu because I wanted to watch everyone wrestle with this tiny bird—a miniature chicken really—with only a smattering of edible meat but a virtual Amazonian rainforest of minute bones. Observing the diners dissect this animal, tearing it limb from limb, twisting pieces off after abandoning the poultry knife and the small 2-tined game fork gave me no end of pleasure. I could see it all now, 6 ladies and 6 gents, hands covered in grease and small flecks of flesh discussing the 9th hole here, the 17th hole there, the new nublick, the old square-headed putter, a south wind after a 1 wood eastward drive. I would wager with myself who would be the first to suck one of his fingers forgetting for a split second where he was. I grinned as I hung up the phone and took a deep reflective breath. My pleasures were small but deep, close to ecstasy, really. I brought myself back to earth as I imagined the battlefield of the table when everyone had risen and gone into the library to talk about golf again. The table cloth, had I been able to preserve it 5 centuries, could be examined by lab-coated scientists in the future like the Shroud of Turin. What bodily fluids had made these 9 stains? What blood over here? What sacrificial libation was spilled in the lower left quadrant and to which god? I would love to be there secretly with all the answers but only after the Library of Congress investigators had made all of their inevitably erroneous judgments.

I looked up at the kitchen clock and saw that it was time to take a toothbrush to the dingy grout in the main floor washroom. What a joy would be mine for simply doing my job. How did that song go? "Pay for nothing and your check for free." I would make sure to jot down most neatly perhaps numbered all I had to be thankful for this Thanksgiving, taking great pains to avoid making little circles over the I's.

PAUL

Sarah walked down the cellar steps in her slippers and housecoat. She paused at the bottom letting her eyes adjust to the dim light as she opened Paul's door. There was a lamp with a single red bulb burning near Paul's bed. He had thrown a small blue cloth over the shade casting the room into a gloomy purple light that made everything look as if it had been dipped in Easter egg dye.

"Mom, is that you?" he asked in a sleepy voice.

"Yes, baby, it's me."

"I love you, Mom,"

Sarah went over to the bed and sat down, cradling Paul's head in her lap. "I love you, too," she whispered, gently rocking her 19 year-old son back and forth. The room was littered with papers, some old magazines had slipped off the table, a wastebasket had a corona of crumpled wrappers around it where they had been tossed by an unsteady hand. A pile of dirty clothes had crawled into a corner. A hypodermic needle nestled in a fold of the flannel blanket like a scorpion. Paul's limbs were out of the covers. In the purple light the uneven rows of puncture wounds that followed the veins in his arms looked like ants crawling up the trunk of a young birch tree.

"There, there, baby," Sarah said in a swaying voice. "You're my baby, aren't you?"

"Yeah, Mama, always. Let me sleep a while, OK?"

"Sure, baby, you sleep." She remembered him as a small boy bringing his projects home from school. A bright star-filled mother's day card was still taped to the side of the refrigerator. She remembered the small thefts, the appearance of man-like boys appearing at the house at all hours of the night, the arrests and the rehabs. She had found a pistol in his room and some ladies jewelry in a plastic bag only last week. Paul could never get more than his fingertips above the brink of the mineshaft he had fallen into, no matter how hard she tried to help. She watched him drop, suspended in the updraft of his addiction. He always came home. He never stopped loving her. She never withheld her love from him.

Paul looked up through the haze of heroin and saw Sarah standing watch over him, looking down at the bed. The light had

152

caught the frizzes of hair but her face was just a silhouette. He smiled as he closed his eyes. He started to dream that his mother was anointing him, showering his body with a bath of pungent, aromatic oil. The incense vapors sliced through the warm, stale air of his basement room as if a large patio door had been opened in a long boarded-up beach house.

He opened his eyes and saw Sarah with a light in her hand glowing orange and yellow flickering and magnified by the tears in his eyes that flooded his lids in a vain attempt at washing away the kerosene. The slow arc of the match tossed from Sarah's hand reminded him of a comet he had seen in a science class movie. He was swathed in the light, the golden warmth sweeping up his legs to his torso and his face. He thought his mother had become the sun and was flying to her through space for the security of her embrace as he always had from the time of skinned knees to the courthouse steps.

Sarah walked out the door, locking it behind her and made her way up the stairs to the kitchen where she sat at the table and watched the scythe of the hand on the wall clock mow down the seconds.

She could hear shouts from the backyard. Millie, her neighbor, came running in through the back door.

"Sarah, your cellar's on fire! Paul is down there. I can hear him screamin'. Sarah! Sarah. Do you hear me?"

The distant coil of a siren wound its way around Millie and Sarah, binding them together as they looked into each other's eyes.

"Paul is burning? You say my baby is burning?"

Millie saw beyond the tears in Sarah's eyes, the pits of sorrow that replaced her irises, her lids a gossamer curtain over the truth.

Shelter

Arnold Blank worked the front desk at our shelter, the Main St. Sisters of Lourdes Hostel. Why they called it a hostel was anyone's guess but 'anyone' was fortunate enough to have a job of some sort and never had to live here. Arnold or Mr. Blank as we were forced to call him was 350 pounds, balding, 50ish and always managed to have two days growth of beard or was barefaced and discovered a method of gluing small hairs all over his jaw as it hid under a layer of fat and blotchy skin.

Everyone who stayed at the shelter had to have an I.D. card and Arnold issued them. He was picky and always asked what a potential resident did before he was down on his luck. I never met any of the Sisters although one floated through in yards and yards of stiff black and white fabric as if she were a stealth bomber, her face popping out from the starched folds the way a baby might look peeping out of his mother's birth canal in the delivery room, bald, puffy, red-faced, toothless and perhaps a little afraid. I can't imagine that the sisters had imposed any requirements on its guests other than sobriety, self-control and destitution. Arnold, however, wanted only executives, college professors and doctors, dentists and lawyers. Don't get smug and snicker, as Herbie the janitor did,

To see a partner in a big downtown firm explain his predicament to Arnold, how he had done prison time, been divorced by his wife while doing his time and found himself friendless and broke and 60 years old. He had a grey silk suit that glistened in the fluorescent lights over Arnold's counter, a suit two or three sizes too large because James McMahon, Esq. had lost a lot of weight in the big house. Herbie, leaning on his mop handle said, "Welcome, counselor." as McMahon passed Arnold's qualifying test.

"Thank you" McMahon answered.

"Got any objections?" asked Herbie. McMahon shrank another two sizes as he climbed the stairs to the dorm rooms. Herbie laughed and laughed. That night, I stabbed him in the neck with a screwdriver, twisting it so his vocal chords got broken. I hated screaming almost as much as someone laughing at misfortune. Call me Ishmael. Or Mr. Ishmael Fuller. Or just Mr. Fuller. I don't stand on ceremony.

That night I dreamed of the Golden Gate Bridge, its elegant, arrogant red silhouette piercing the fog that covers the sodomite city by the bay. But in my dream I punish the bridge for carrying people across the realm of the fish, the dolphin and the whale. I take it between my giant inflamed hands and make an accordion of it, a beautiful zigzag of vengeance, a ziggurat of my impatience.

The police showed up a few days later and questioned Mr. Blank. Two female officers which Arnold could have swallowed as easily as the two pizzas he ordered every Friday night covered in black olives, garlic and anchovy paste. He had no suspects to offer up although he admitted that Herbie had a way of "irritating even the gentlest souls that resided here."

"Do you think it was drug related?" asked one gal.

Mr. Blank inhaled so deeply it seemed he would huff and puff and blow her house down.

"Not on my watch, sister," he shouted.

"I'm not your sister, fatso, so just answer the questions." Both moved back from Mr. Blank and put their hands on their holstered pistols.

"I don't allow no druggies in here, is all I meant. I run a re-spectable place here dedicated to…"

"Got any ex-cons in here?"

"No," Mr. Blank lied.

"We'll be back," one officer said. "Here's my card. If anything occurs to you, call us."

Arnold took the card and put it in his shirt pocket.

"I sure will, Officer Madenda," he said.

Officer Madenda looked at me and said, "You know anything?"

"No ma'am, I sure don't," I said.

"Right," she said with a smirk. It was one of those lippy smirks that I think police take lessons to perfect, a real know-it-all smirk. I recalled how a cop smirked at my mother when she rebuked the pass he made at her. He had arrested Dad, my Dad, the Dad I would never see again. I was nine. When I was sixteen, I tracked that cop down, stabbed him in the heart with a filleting blade. As he bled out, I sandpapered his lips off. This was the only way I could get that cop's smirk off his face and out of my memory. That night I dreamed that I had ripped off the upraised arm of the Statue of

Liberty and brought it down with a smash on police headquarters on 14th Street. Bricks, roof tiles, hands holding badges and billy clubs and smirky lips was all that was remained, that and some shards of glass from Liberty's torch.

After they left, Arnold posted a small sign in the stairwell which said, "Any 1 with knowledge of the recent fracas concerning Herbie, please inform me. All donations for flowers for his funeral must be made by tomorrow, Saturday."

I knew enough to give Mr. Blank one dollar. And I returned the screwdriver I borrowed.

Time flowed on like sludge in a sewer pipe. I made the acquaintance of a resident named Mr. John Palfrey. He said he was the owner of a publishing house, had published a great many fine novels and travel books. "Books are a dying form," he would say every time he saw someone reading. We would play chess almost every afternoon.

"You know," he said as he sidled his rook right up to my queen. "You know people don't read much anymore. They watch TV and videos and computer screens. Chilren, instead of reading a fine edition of "Robin Hood and His Merry Men illustrated by N.C. Wyeth, play some moronic video game where they kill Arabs, rape Muslim women and blow the heads off Al Kyeeda terrorists. Isn't that silly? I mean really."

I said, "Excuse me, but it's Al Qaida."

"Well," he said. "That's the laugh. I was the CEO of a publishing empire and now some unemployed low-life is giving me lessons."

I moved my queen and checkmated him.

"You cheated. You moved that piece twice."

"No sir, I defeated you fairly and squarely."

"You're a cheating low-life bastard," he shouted as he upended the board sending all the pieces to the terrazzo floor like teeth knocked out of a giant's mouth.

Mr. Blank leaned out of his cashier cage and told him to pipe down. Like everyone else, Arnold's command was law and he listened but he gave me a look that was the icing on the two-layer cake he had just baked, one layer for each time he called me a lowlife. That look was down his nose, his long aquiline, Greenwich,

Connecticut aristocrat Brahmin Harvard-educated nose. It reminded me of Miss Ilene Gumbert, my 11th grade geometry teacher. She looked at me the same way when I explained that I hadn't had the time to finish my homework because I was working late at the all-night Wal-Mart.

"Wal-Mart? At night? Instead of doing your homework? Your priorities are confused, Ishmael."

"I can't pay my mom's bills and my bills with geometry, Miss Gumbert," I said.

She just looked down that long shark fin nose of hers. A week later they found her bloated corpse in a sluice pond in the Meadowlands near Hoboken, New Jersey only a mile or so from where she lived. Her nose had been sliced clean off. When they found her soaked with New Jersey cess, there was a nest of water roaches living in her sinuses. Jerry Fagnani's father was a state trooper that helped fish her out; he told Jerry all about it. Jerry was my pal so he told me to see if I would vomit or shudder or otherwise creep out. I just said, "Gross" like some dumb fourteen year-old girl. That night I put Miss Gumbert's nose in the Fagnani mailbox in a sandwich bag. Jerry missed school for a week. His mother said he had the flu. It was no flu and I laughed that night under the covers and dreamed that I flew to Paris with my geometry class. While the class and Miss Gumbert slept, I loosened all the bolts in the Eiffel Tower. The next day they all went up the tower and oohed and ahhed while teacher explained the geometry of that ugly oil well looking thing. It collapsed in a huge heap like a kid's erector set aqll piled on top of everyone, crushed and sliced beyond rcognotion. I was interviewed as the sole survivor with tears pouring down my cheeks. That got me a first class ticket back to the U.S.. A very sext flight attendant made a pass at me and mentioned the "mile high club." I said I was not that kind of guy. I'm not, even in real life.

On summer nights I would make my way up the dusty emergency stairwell to the roof. It was cluttered with strange shaped pipes, cubes and rectangles that seemed to have no function, twisted and bent TV antennae and wires criss-crossing the tar-covered floor which was lumpy and soft in places, hard and jagged in others. I'd put my foot up on the knee wall that surrounded the roof and separated it in some places from adjoining roofs that had the same clutter of shapes, a great deal like kids toys on the floor of a tenement only all covered in black tar. The stars that were strong enough to penetrate the haze that hung over the city and the dull red glow of stoplights and traffic lights formed magical patterns to me. Marlene Dietrich was there, Moses, a cat eating a canary, a canary eating a cat and my favorite, Arnold Blank in the middle, the North Star his left eye. How it gazed down on me, how it stared and condemned. Who was the giant in the sky who could hold sway over the whole city? What purpose could this god have? While thinking this I would hum the tune from The Wizard of Oz, the little ditty about following the Yellow Brick Road. I often thought that the yellow lights from the Chinese restaurant across the street were the first few bricks in that road but I couldn't see where they led. Maybe that's where the answer was. Maybe I was supposed to follow the Yellow Brick Road. But what if, after what had to be a long and boring journey, it ended up at Arnold Blank. And how likely would that be? Very, I thought; very.

One chilly night in October, as I watched Arnold in the sky watching me and wondering why all birds didn't head south for the winter, a young couple appeared on the roof of an adjacent building. I assumed they were young because they had that thin, lithe youthful way of moving, he with his arm around her and she leaning her head on his shoulder as they walked about looking up, he pointing, she following his finger to distant points in the sky. They were silhouettes against the uplight from the street below. I didn't move. They were there a half hour and I saw them have sex against one of the large upright rectangles. He pushed against her and from where I was it seemed he was playing a harp, the rhythm of his body serpentine against her like the hand of the harpist upon the strings. What was that smell that drifted on the cold currents twelve stories up where the three of us huddled under the great dome of Heaven?

Soon, they were gone and I reflected on my long days of watching TV in my room, of reading old classics, of grazing the fridge and the pantry, perhaps sixty times a day out of boredom not hunger. I took showers less and less frequently because I feared slipping and falling, getting seriously injured and being stranded either dead or slowly dying in the shower, the pounding of water on my naked body for days? Weeks? Months? Or at least until I was stripped bare of flesh, my innards a lumpy paste that would clog the drain and then cause an overflow. Only then, I thought, after the people downstairs had their ceiling collapse from the burden of the flood from my shower would anyone discover me or more accurately, what was left of me. And what curses would Arnold baptize my soul with, the silly grin of my skeleton looking up from the shower stall as if groveling before an Aztec chief ready to play football with my skull. Ah, it was a ponderous chain this life of mine but I had forged it link by link and yard by yard. Yes, it was a ponderous chain that held me here.

Just near Thanksgiving, near midnight, I was at my perch on the roof watching cleaning crews in the office building across the street. The stars were clear and bright, the sliver of a moon hiding just above a bank tower in the east. The door opened and Mr. Blank appeared.

"Hey," he said. "How's it going?"

"Good, I guess. Never saw you up here, Mr. Blank."

"Don't like them stairs. But I know you're up here a lot. I hope you're not being naughty."

"Of course not, sir."

"Well, I got to thinking about this screwdriver you borrowed back a-ways when poor Herbie met his untimely demise. I smelled it and I could smell his blood on it. Can you explain that to me? Can ya?"

"No, not really."

Mr. Blank seated his fat self on the knee wall, still breathing heavily from the climb.

"I think you can." But I felt that he was bluffing. Smell his blood, my ass, I thought.

"I know what you're thinking. But I can smell him on this," he said handling the screwdriver and putting it to his nose. "Smell it. You'll see what I goddamn mean."

"I'd rather not," I said.

"Get your ass over here and smell this and tell me you don't smell Herbie on it."

I was trapped. If I refused, he'd kick my ass into the street. If I accepted, he'd read the guilt on my face. I could feel the letters "G" and "U" and "I" crawling up from under my sweater toward my cheeks as I spoke. My breath puffed in the cold air, softballs of fog floating off.

I walked over to him and reached out my hand as if to take the screwdriver from him. Instead I moved quickly and pushed him off the roof and watched him drop all twelve stories, a look of surprise and fear in his eyes, his mouth wide open in a funny howl.

I ran downstairs and called 911. While I waited, I imagined how he was up on that roof with his screwdriver trying to tighten some of the cable TV wires that had come loose. That made sense. I knew it would work and as I waited, I started writing a résumé of my qualifications for the job of manager of the hostel. I was very qualified. Very.

A Game of Darts

You are at a party in the middle of the Long Island Sound with no shore in sight. Your ship rises from the water like a wedding cake. Everyone aboard is a stranger. They all wear camouflage, yet there you are—nice pink blouse—feeling underdressed and peculiar. You came alone. Everyone comes alone. Stay with me; you can call me Virgil.

This is all it takes to play darts at this party:

Two people, two sturdy drinking straws, some poisoned snakes from Uganda, and, of course, darts. These darts are super tiny, though, and sharp, nothing to worry about. Little needles you barely even feel; diabetics wouldn't even notice the difference.

On the morning of the party, the host will take care of the snakes, so don't bother about them, either. He will tip the darts on their fangs (after he's squeezed the head) and get just the right amount of poison. It's not as easy as you'd think. You need plastic gloves, goggles, and precision. You also need experience because these snakes are potent. Goggles are a necessity. Get some poison in your eye and it's over. You fall so in love with the world that it's terrifying and wonderful. You never go to sleep and end up institutionalized.

But, as I said, let the host worry about that. And don't fret over the idea of someone shooting poisoned darts at you. Because, see, these darts are so small that the first one is already in you, and you don't even know it like a tick bite after a hike in the woods.

"Aren't you the lucky one?" the host says, then reaches behind your ear and removes the first dart that struck you. He holds it in his palm. It is the color of rare old silver, minutely filigreed, something Faberge might have crafted for the Czar.

He hands you a belt to wear. It has leather loops along the side to carry bottles. Inside these bottles are the darts. A smaller loop near the hip is a holster. It holds a long white drinking straw, the kind with a red stripe, the kind that isn't bendable.

"There are more darts in there than you'd think," he says. "But you should only need a few.'"

You have heard of this game before, but never played it. Still, you wrap the belt around your waist without question. You grin.

161

See what that first sting does to you? You get curious as hell.

The host cocks his head at you. He is a plump and happy man with a curled moustache.

"What is your name?" he asks.

"Liz," you tell him.

"Liz? That's a beautiful name, like Bella! And surely with a name like Liz, you have played *this* before. To be lost in the game! I'm a bit jealous, I must admit."

The host then bows stiffly at you and walks back to his party.

And you should have played this before, don't you think? With a name like Liz, and with hip bones that nudge the waistband of your skirt like the subtlest horns of the devil. And surely, with a right and curvy spine like yours—a trail of buried arrowheads, leading down your back and through your hips into your hidden heart shapes—surely a woman like you should not be a stranger to the game, alone at this big party in the Sound, the fancy right arm of the Atlantic.

But here you are.

And all these flights of fancy, these "horn" and "heart-shaped" descriptions, so erotically evocative, these are the types of things that the second dart will do to you. The one that is in your leg. Now you are getting the hang of it.

It is not hard to play.

The real key to darts is to act like a pro, even if you aren't. Get that belt buckled tight, a hand on your straw, and glance around the room. Find the one who shot you.

Look at this place. What a party.

It is crepe paper for ceiling fans, servers in tuxedos, and balconies on all sides. It is saltwater air and music from the Congo. And to think that you almost didn't go aboard, you were so nervous, because this is where it all happens, where everything happens.! People talk with their hands at parties like this, making fluid gestures in the air. Booze goes down like breast milk. Whole lives are left at home.

Over there is Alex Smith, or is it Jones? You are already forgetting the people you just met. Don't concern yourself with that, though, because even just two darts can be distracting. And he's not the one who shot you, anyway. You can tell that right off. He has a potato nose and too-thin neck. He is not even thinking of you. Instead, he has cornered a pie-faced serving girl who is eating shrimp off her own tray. He's drawing circles in the air with his finger and making O's with his mouth. Nothing about him feels right. There is no belt around his waist, no Liz in his eye, so you are in the clear.

In the room you are standing in, a spiral staircase rises to a second level, blue carpeted. People lean against the banister and bird-eye the view. You try to go up, but as soon as you hit the first step, you feel another prick, this time in the back of your arm. You feel this one yourself because he is winning three darts to none and you've got to be getting sensitive.

Is that bad? Is that good? You tell me.

You find an empty stair and start to remove this last dart from your arm. Another reason you shouldn't have gone sleeveless, you think. The back of your arms are not shapely, not toned, but spotted instead with a rash, like goose bumps.

When you pull this dart out, however, the rash on your arm fades away. You run your hand over the skin. You think maybe these snakes are like miracles. You think maybe tonight is your night.

On the stair above yours, two men laugh.

"Now *she* has been hit," one says. "Rubbing her own arm. It's like she's never even seen it!"

You look up at them. The man who spoke has eyebrows that bush out at the ends.

"Those eyes!" he says. "Now I can see why he chose you. The eyes! Sammy, can't you see it?"

His friend, a man wearing a three-piece suit, smiles. His teeth sit in his mouth like fence posts.

"I see many things," he says.

"They are horse's eyes." the man says. "Wise and innocent. Maybe even the eyes of a deer. Now, Sammy knows about deer."

"I only know how to hunt them," Sammy says.

The bushy eyebrow man slaps his friend hard on the shoulder and the two of them laugh, and then you laugh, because you can read it in their eyes that they are thinking. *Let this moment never end, for I am drinking with friends!*

They stumble down the stairs and you should see yourself following in their wake, flashing that big and stretchy grin. Because, you think, why not grin like a dummy? Why not moon the whole world? Damn. These darts are hot stuff.

Now, this is the part that gets good.

You hear a whistle, and behind a potted banana tree stands your man. You know it right away because his shirt looks like fireworks, and all other people turn gray.

You pull out your straw. You start to load up a Dart and he runs.

He scoots like a squirrel caught in traffic. People jump in his way. They wave their arms all around him, like they are guarding him. You put the straw to your lips and your man makes a break for a hallway. Deep breath, a hard blow, and *–pting!*—your shot ricochets off a TV showing a close-captioned soccer match.

A server picks up your dart with some tweezers and drops it in a Ziploc bag. Then a woman climbs steps to stand next to you. She brushes your bangs from your forehead. She takes your chin in her hand and looks in your eyes.

"Sic him," she says intensely.

Now this next part of the game can vary. But for you it will always be this:

You hold the straw like a pistol. You creep around doorways for hours. When you finally catch your man from behind, you blow darts into each of his shoulders. He sees that you caught him and laughs. And when this man laughs, it echoes, and the vibrations pound in your navel. You shudder like a three-legged washing machine in a spin cycle, an orgasm like a force of nature.

People give all sorts of toasts. You chase him around tables and lamps.

Your man loads up a dart and he aims it. You do a sexy drop and roll but he nails you, and the dart sticks between your green eyes. You land at the feet of a doctor.

"Well, aren't you just the specimen," the doctor says, and removes the dart from your forehead." And how many darts is that?"

You make the number four with your fingers and he helps you back up to your feet. You look around the room for your partner and fumble around with your belt. This doctor wears glasses and after-shave, and he shines a light in your eyes.

"Snakes," he says, shaking his head. "You know, in France, the Darts just have words on them."

164

The doctor then gives you a physical. He says that your heart is now fully dilated.

"There is a place at the top of the ship," he whispers. "I'm sure you can corner him there."

The doctor points to a door right behind him. It leads to a long flight of stairs. You enter the stairwell to near silence and, though the drums are gone from the background, their rhythms still ring in your ears.

At the top of the stairs is a hallway. This is the only dark part of the building, so there is no way to tell if he's hiding. You place one of your hands on the wall, and hold the straw to your lips with the other. You then walk carefully down the hall like a child would after a storm knocks the lights out.

The end of the hall has a metal door that it leads to an open-air deck. You jump into the entrance and aim, but there is no one out there to shoot. Instead, there are saltwater breezes, and a moon that reflects off the sea, a chrome hubcap off an old Rolls-Royce.

Now, some people say this is the worst part of darts, because you have forgotten that you are so exposed out there, that all the land you know is out of sight. You have forgotten how quiet your world was, on all the days leading up to this night. So when the stairwell door bursts open behind you, it is all you can do not to scream.

You see your man all alone down the hallway, and it is like rockets bloom off his chest. You put the straw to your lips and you shoot him. Then he starts up the hall at full speed. You load another dart like an expert, and this man is an oncoming comet. He singes all the wallpaper. He sets off every sprinkler. So you fire again and you tag him, this time at point-blank range.

Now the game is tied.

Damn, four darts to four!

Because they say that four darts is the limit. They say you might now be more lightning than human.

This man tackles you onto the deck and you both roll around on the floor. You laugh so hard that your throat hurts, and a hurricane forms off the coast.

"There you are!" the man says.

And all you purr is, "Can it really be you?"

But *this* is the worst part of darts, I think, because there are still people down here in the water. They row boats around the ship in circles and hope to be invited aboard. They see me blowing air into my life raft, and dishing out water with a cup. They ask me what is up there, because they see on my face that I've been there.

So I tell them then what I've told you. I say it's amazing, life changing. The hyperboles nearly choke me.

These people light sparklers for flashlights, and eat sandwiches out of their coolers. They say, if it's so good, then why am I back down here, stuck in an old row boat?

So what should I tell them, I wonder? Should I tell them what I've learned? That darts is a great way to die, because no sort of joy lasts forever? Or should I tell them how that upper deck can be tricky, especially with two people on it, the wood weakened by storms that have passed?

Or should I just warn them what the price is, to play a round of darts and then lose?

You tell me.

Because these are the things I could have said when you were down here, looking skyward, if I had only believed you would listen.

Hide and Seek

There was a field of chicoria weeds that stretched from the faded, parched lawn to the far hills and beyond that to a valley I had never seen. The chicoria was over six feet tall and had dried to the color of liver spots on the hands of the elderly, but each stem was topped with a scepter of bright yellow flowers that, when the wind blew in from the sea, waved above the deadened stalks like the fronds of underwater creatures, as if at any moment a wayward angel fish or golden perch might wander too close and be snatched forever from life. I could sit on the grass and by angling my head just right, place gypsy clouds that roamed the sky in search of a campsite just above the fronds and imagine that they were fish in the bluest ocean that mistook the tentacles for tender sea worms or the larvae of conch, soft, sweet and sightless leaning into the thin sun that found its way through the kelp beds to the sea bottom. With the lowering of my chin, those hapless clouds would be ensnared, with the raising of it, free, free to continue their pagan dances. But, those dreams were far from my memory then as now, for I only allowed such thoughts to ramble within my skull when my brother Lucian and I were young. In those days we thought only of play and what was said round the dinner table the previous night of the neighbors, of the losses and of the war. I am Madeline or what is left of her.

One afternoon, Lucian and I played at rolling apples across the lawn. They were unfit for cooking or eating for they had been badly pecked at by the magpies that sometimes roosted in the barn or on top of it in peculiar clusters of chattering generations, black and white demons, raucous and full of life; they were the bane of Father's existence, it seemed, for they would peck at the ground after planting and discern with the utmost accuracy exactly where he had planted a seed or, after the occasional rains that fell in those dour years, nip at the seedlings never taking so much as to do harm but just enough to be a nuisance.

Lucian and I would hide behind the trunk of old Otto, a tree we had named because he had become a giant in one of our games, sometimes scaring us half to death but more often taking us up in his arms and holding us tight to his raspy bosom (which was always soft to us) much as our mother had done when she was alive. We would spy on Father and repress our laughter with cupped hands at our lips as he chased the birds up into the barn, but he never failed to smile at them as they cawed and squawked not so much in mockery as in the giggling of children in a game of tag when there is nothing to fear but being touched on the shoulder and suddenly becoming "it." Now I know that such games prepare children for what life really is and I think Lucian knew it even then that his turn to be tagged by a pale and outstretched finger was not far away.

The apples were rolled underhanded from a predetermined distance toward the chicoria field and the one who could get the closest to the perimeter of the field without going off the grassy edge into the crumbling, clodded furrows would be the winner. The apples, full of holes, some with rot stains smelling of vinegar, others with an occasional black ant that would hold on for dear life as his meal became his ride, bounced across the uneven lawn making lefts and rights as if with a will of their own, jumping or gliding as the path and the power of our toss dictated. This, too, was a game, of more import than we could have guessed. I would pitch my apple with such deliberate care and then, with my tossing hand still in the air as if to shake the hand of an invisible stranger, make a brim of my other hand to shield my eyes from the faithless sun, hold my breath and watch the red and brown globe blur through the grass in a cacophony of zigs and zags, of gentle leaps and headlong bounds toward the precipice. Would it stop in time, perch on the brink or, too full of its own momentum, plunge blindly into the shadows of the stalks?

One day, Lucian decided we should play hide and seek. He told me to lean against Otto and to count to fifty while I hid my eyes in my upfolded arms. I was diligent to his instructions and counted slowly and loudly, my voice drifting up into the air like swarms of gnats tossed in the slightest breeze, here and there. When the counting was over with a particularly loud and robust "fifty," I turned and allowed my eyes to adjust to the glaring light. I walked across the lawn toward the chicoria and knew immediately that Lucian was deep within the field. I simply walked with my arms pointed forward, the dry and warm husks of the fronds brushing my skin gently, the sky lost to the yellow flowers, the shadows, blue and striped with slashes from the sun's many swords. Within a few minutes, no more than two or three, I found him, without ever wandering in the wrong direction.

"How did you do that?" he asked. "You saw my footprints, did-n't you?"

"No, I did not," I said. We looked about and neither his nor my small feet could make even the slightest impression in the dry clay of the chicoria field.

"Then you saw the broken leaves; that's what you did."

I lifted one of the long dry fronds in my hand and crumpled it. It did not crunch or bend or break; it simply folded at my touch like an almost dry washrag resuming its shape after I released it.

"Well, you cheated somehow. Let's try it again," he said. "This time, count to a hundred."

This I did, getting confused a bit with my seventies and eight-ies, my voice becoming hoarse at about ninety-one or so. I said "one hundred" as loud as I could muster and again I found him deep within the field, this time so far from the starting point that Otto, when Lucian lifted me onto his shoulders to get our bearing, looked more like a dwarf than a giant. As we walked back together, I ex-plained as best as I could in my little girl way, that I could sense where he was, that I needed no clues or trails to find him. It was as if there were a string connecting us and when he walked off to hide, he unraveled it as he went and it was a simple matter for me to reel it in, much like Uncle Fredo had taught us with a fishing rod, although that particular day, none of us had caught any fish.

"I think you are magic, Maddy," he said. "Make me a promise."

"OK."

"If ever I get lost, you will find me, you will find me no matter how far, no matter how old we are. You will never let me stay lost. Even if you think I am hiding, you will come get me. OK?"

"I promise," I said.

The summer ended without a sound except for the swallows head-ing south, surfing the waves of heated air singing their goodbyes and twisting their forked tails in farewell. The night air was the pref-ace of autumn and the distant live oaks turned a sad brown while Otto adorned himself in the fire of red, orange, yellow and a vermillion glaze that was so pretty it hurt to watch him. Julian started school in the town and hitched a ride with Peter the reddleman who brought barrels of red clay to the potters for the creation of their storage jars, platters and jugs. His skin had taken on the hue of the clay and he looked every bit like a lobster after a dousing in the boiling water of Father's cast iron pot. Peter was a taciturn man, slow to respond to questions but with a quick insight into people most of whom displeased him. Father said that lonely men were usually the most observant for they had to have imaginary friends and relatives and when one can create a person out of thin air and a few brain cells, it was hard for a real person to compare. Peter once told Lucian and me about his imaginary children, a boy and girl our exact ages who would appear to him every time he made a fire in the deepest nights of winter or sat under his olive trees in the sultry evenings of summer. He would sit in his rocker with a book on his lap and read them the tales of the Thousand and One Nights or of Don Quixote on Rosenante tilting at windmills and chasing giants across the fields of chicoria. Each of his children would sit on the floor by him, the boy at his left knee, the girl at the right and lean on his thighs looking up into his face and watching the words come off the page through their father's lips and weave their way around the room or under the purpling sky until they joined the clouds or the stars. When his story would finish, he could feel the weight of their beautiful faces ease off his thighs and see their features evaporate into the loneliness of his life like smoke into a fog.

Some years back, Father would speak under his breath, Peter had fallen in love with a woman in the town, the wife of one of his customers. They had started meeting secretly and finally her husband found out and flew into a rage. Of course, nearly everyone in the town already knew the truth of the matter but even the most hardened men were surprised at the man's wrath. He threw her out of the house and into the street tossing a few of her clothes after her. It had started raining, a terrible downpour and the wind blew in with such force that several roofs in the town had come off like lids on jars of preserves. She struggled through the maelström toward Peter's house but a bridge had collapsed over a dry river bed that had filled to bursting in the rain. When she tried to cross by wading through, the current pulled her under and then downstream.

Two boys found her the next day as the waters receded. Her body, naked from the force of the enraged river, was tangled in a nest of branches and twigs from fallen trees, her hair tangled outward like the fan of a peacock's tail, spotted with dried leaves, her left arm, its shoulder dislocated, twisted in an el behind her head, pale, bluish, lifeless, as if she had fallen asleep in death's bed, her eyes closed, her skin dappled with violet cobwebs of empty veins. Her husband was called and became so distraught that he cut his own throat at the riverside as if in mute atonement for his anger. Both were buried in the cemetery of sinners at the south of the town, the priest refusing either the body of an adulterer or that of a suicide to be interred in holy ground. Peter had a local potter make a monument of red clay in the shape of flames with her name, her husband's and his name carved into it and the words from Dante which said, "Here are they that loved too much." Soon after, Peter moved into a shepherd's hut 4 kilometers from the nearest house and spoke to no one. Neither outcast nor the subject of gossip he lived in a self-created purgatory of isolation and reproof. Only Lucian and I could elicit speech from Peter that was unrelated to his business.

In the middle of October at the time of the harvest, an easy chill settled into the days and the sun seemed like quick-silver, bright and glistening but giving off no real warmth. Shadows lengthened and I filled my days while Lucian was at school with the building of small towns out of little rectangular blocks of Peter's red clay that he told me to leave in the sun to dry and harden. I imagined Peter and Father and Grandmother walking through the streets of my town looking for Mother who was at the milliner getting a new hat. I was with her helping to decide whether quail feathers or parrot plumes were more fashionable. She let me have one too, a little bonnet made from a birch leaf and its stem but which I knew was the finest French linen sewn with Chinese silk thread. In the midst of all this, I heard shouts in the distance and saw Peter, not in his cart as he always was, but on the cart horse, shouting and waving his hat in an absolute frenzy. His little horse, used to a slow walk, was at a bedraggled gallop and covered in sweat. He pulled up in a cloud of dust and hurled gravel. I was near the porch, the house empty at this time of day in the time of the harvest.

"Maddy, where is your father? Where is he?" Peter shouted.

"He's in the north field, I think," I said, my finger with a mind of its own pointing in the direction. Just then, I saw Father and Grandmother making their way home for the midday meal, just coming over the crest of the lawn in the south.

"Here, over here. Come!" shouted Peter. Father started to run and made it to the house with his hoe still over his shoulder, his shirt soaked with sweat and chaff flecked all over it and his face.

"What is it, Peter? What has happened?" Father asked.

The Separatists, they have set off a bomb at the school. A bomb at the school! Lucian, Lucian he is…"

"No, this is not possible, not a school, not children. Surely you are mistaken. Tell me you are mistaken, tell me…" he said as he raised the hoe as if to deal Peter a mortal blow.

"No, it is true…too true. So many children have been killed," he said with hesitancy, looking at me. Grandmother finally made it to the porch.

"Oh, dear God," she said. "Not Lucian! Not Lucian. Where is he? Where is he, Peter."

"He is dead. He is dead…" Peter said his voice dropping to a prayer, his words like lead falling into the dust.

"Mama, stay here with Maddy. I will go with Peter. Peter, we will take my wagon. Help me get it out of the barn. Maddy, stay with Grandmother. There must be some mistake. Wait here, both of you." Father's voice reminded me of the sound the wind made in a storm as it rustled the leaves of the giant oak, air without breath, a sound so low but so powerful that I knew it must be the way God sounded in heaven when he was sad.

It was no mistake. That night, after the stars had risen to see our despair, Father and Peter came home with Lucian's small body in Father's lap, wrapped in a green blanket, Peter driving the wagon as if in a daze. They put him on the kitchen table and sat watch all night, Grandmother bathing his body which looked so much smaller now, so small I barely knew him; he was always so big to me. I did not cry but simply watched Grandmother, suddenly so tender, so agile and gentle as if a young woman again. The flames in the fireplace cast a dancing glow on Father's face, streaked with dried tears and the soil of his day's labors, Peter's eyes, whiter than the marble of the statue of the Virgin Mary in the cathedral, against his red skin. But for his soft features and whispering sighs, his dove-like hand on my shoulder, he might have been a demon.

That morning, they buried him under Otto, deep between the gnarled roots. Father would not pray, but Grandmother said some words and Peter knelt beside me and said, "Little Maddy, do not fear. He is with God now and with your mother in Heaven."

"No, he is not," I said loudly, startling the three adults. "That is not Lucian you have put here. That is someone else. Lucian is lost. I will find him. I am the only one that can find him." I turned and ran away from the tree, the little body buried beneath it and the three people who stood under it. I could here my Father say, "Let her go. Everyone must grieve in their own way. Let her go. She'll be back when she is ready." His voice trailed off like the sounds of the swallows that departed last month for the south. If only I could have gone with them.

Now I stand on the lawn near the chicoria field and start to count to fifty with my eyes shut. I wait. I wait and count. I open my eyes and the sun has hidden his face behind a cloud. I feel the tug of the thread, the same thread I felt when we played hide and seek. It pulls me through the chicoria fronds, the yellow flowers all brown. I see that the apples we had tossed that landed in the fronds have rotted and small trees are sprouting where they lay, each one a tribute to the love I feel for Lucian. When I find him I will show him that the apples were not wasted by us but have found new life.

The thread pulls me out of the far end of the field toward the west, toward the sea, the place we are not to play. Mother told us never to go there and we honored her request faithfully. There is a carpet of lawn, tall, browned grass filled with swollen blue poppy heads and the dried stems of buttercups and snow drops, waving like an ocean of October. At the edge, the lawn drops off at the top of a cliff, a high chalky cliff that overlooks the sea, the grass like the eaves of a thatched roof rounded and downturned. I stop and close my eyes. It is Lucian whispering, "How did you find me, Maddy? You have magic, don't you?" No, I think, it is the waves far below, they are tricking me. But then again I hear Lucian's voice and feel the tug of the thread. I open my eyes and see Lucian's face hover-

173

ing just off the cliff, his blue eyes melted into the sky as if they were open windows in a cottage that looked out to the sea.

"I release you from your promise, Maddy. You must make me a new one."

"But I want to be with you," I say. "I promised I would find you no matter where. I want to stay with you, to be with you."

Lucian says, "Promise me you will go home. Promise me you will grow up and fall in love. Promise me you will marry someone tall and handsome who loves you more than anyone or anything, who will take you where it is safe."

"But…"

"Make that promise to me now, Maddy. Please."

It is a promise I cannot make. I look him full in the face. Clouds scuttle behind his brow but I can see both them and him. "I want to, Lucian, I want to, but I must bring you back with me. You are not lost anymore for I have found you." I step off the edge of the cliff toward him, his bluest eyes becoming the sky, his tears the rain that falls all around, on the trees, the chicoria, the dry earth and everyone I know.

Split Second Life

It had started to rain the minute the stars went out over the small town, its yellowish lights, ragged shops and locked doors an epilogue to one of the more interesting meetings of the Chatterton Writers Club. Chatterton was one of those modest New England towns that Robert Frost belyingly wrote some of his darkest poems about. Snow-covered roofs, blue-green pines and miles to go before anyone slept was a pretext for darker realities.

There were ten people in the group, varying ages, varying backgrounds, varying outlooks, varying income levels, unvarying penchants for meeting Friday evenings to read aloud their latest magnum opera. They met in a small studio apartment over a bakery, sat on comfortably shabby chairs and a sofa in a circle. I was the newest member, a retired dentist from Ohio who left for Chatterton to stay with and care for my 89 year-old father. In 3 months the grim reaper found him at 2 or 3 in the morning. There were no tears or thoughts or could have beens, only the passing of an old man who lived a life that would be forgotten as soon as I was dead. I was his only child and had never had either the good luck or misfortune of having my own children. It wasn't for lack of trying or for any insights into the meaning of the process, but rather an ill-assorted collection of females, two of them wives that took their fair share or more and slipped back into the mainstream of 21st century life leaving me to my books, my oldish wardrobe, an almost worn out VW and a newly discovered desire to write something that might last. I know this is the dream of every writer, but I had little else to separate me from a blade of grass. I lived, I grew, I withered and was now wanting more than to be a shard of organic fertilizer. I have no notions of immortality, not even of any importance, not even of leaving a mark because marks do not last much longer than the marker himself anymore. Bookstore shelves are filled with the hodgepodge of computer generated reading material no more substantial than a hand waving from a passing freighter. I had had a decent life, jobs, houses, parties, the bric-a-brac of modern civilization but I had an absence that need filling, a minuscule void that seemed to grow larger nearly every year since I turned the corner at Grey Gardens, that arboretum where memories are trees and desires flowers that never bloom.

Tonight's meeting had been special, though. Someone had written about the suicide of a person seeking only to freeze time, that time was the enemy of emotion because every strong emotion melts slowly away with the passage of the hours, the days, the years; some things, she wrote should not be allowed to fade. In dying, time is defeated. I did not agree with the philosophy but as she read from her typed page held in front of her, her brown eyes downturned as if singing from a hymnal, I saw her for the first time as an individual, as a being sole and separate from the group which hitherto had taken on in my mind, the amorphous shape of a school of fish, swaying, silvering, darkening, turning rapidly in wayward currents. It was as if she were reading her story just to me, her eyes every now and again lifting from the page to look into mine. She finished and, as the others commented or joked, her laughter rose into the air like a flock of starlings at dusk, double-voiced as if her own words had made an echo within her before they were loosed from her lips. She had a way of swaying her long, brown hair that reminded me of someone I had known many years ago but whose name fled like cigarette smoke in a gale. I pretended the rest of the evening to listen to whatever else was being read, but I could only see her, the thirty-odd years that separated us irrelevant to me.

I manufactured an excuse to lag behind and to ask her if she might be interested in a collaboration.

"What kind of work?" she asked.

"A play, a one act play about.."

"It would be great; I'd like that," she interrupted.

"But you don't know what it's about."

"Does it matter?" she said.

"I guess not. But…"

"Let's sit a while. Tell me your ideas," she said.

I described a few characters, something I had thought up a while back, something about two people, a man and a woman who could not stay together because of circumstances outside their control. "They love each other, you see," I said, but they are married to other people and have separate lives. It's about finally meeting someone who is perfect for you but the timing is not."

Everyone else had left and their voices drifted in the fall air up through the closed windows from the street. Goodnights fluttered like bats that tapped against the glass.

"It was a good meeting tonight, wasn't it?" I said.

"It always is for me. Well, not always. Mostly."

"Me, too," I said lamely at a loss for words. "I guess we should be going."

"Let's talk next week about the play. It sounds good, real good. What do you expect of me? I've never collaborated before."

We both stood up to leave. "I need to kiss you," I said. "There is nothing else I want or will ever want. Just a kiss and if you say no, it will change nothing. I know it's adolescent to ask, but I don't want to look like a masher or a creep."

"A masher?" she grinned. "What's a masher?"

"Geez, it's an old-fashioned word for a guy that's looking to score with a girl. You know, a pushy type."

"You're blushing. I never saw you blush before," she said. She reached up and touched my face softly.

I took her chin in my hand and kissed her. In my mind, we left together that night and stayed at my place. The next morning, I drove her to her apartment and she ran up and packed a weekend bag and came down in a few minutes , threw the bag in the back seat with mine and we drove to Cape Cod, six hours on mostly empty roads because it was mid-October. I told her why I loved the fall. Summer, I said, was beautiful, the sun a gigantic eye in the sky, hot, blazing. Summer belonged to the sun. Winter with its barren trees and deep snows, hushed and pure, the huddled lovers and families inside around a fire or cooking stew. Winter belonged to the north wind. Spring, a time of renewal, every poet's cliché, buds, new green, warm rains, errant winds. Spring belonged to nature. But fall, with its early morning lawns covered with frost, breezes that rush past trees and whisper, "it's nearly done," solitary birds that seek company in the sky and flock southward, leaves turning and drifting in the wind; fall is for people, I said, because it reminds us of the passage. She told me she thought I had a beautiful spirit and she took my hand.

We talked of the other members of the group, of memorable poems or short stories or of one writer's rambling novel, of a million small things that brought us together and made the trip fly.

We stayed at a small inn that faced the Atlantic, the only inhabitants other than the two gay owners and their golden retriever that spent most of the time we were there in front of a fire in the living room.

The sliding glass doors in our room looked out over the frigid ocean. The moon, near full was the Matisse of the night, painting silver strokes on the steady waves, mercurial dabs on the changing sands. Her body was alabaster; we made love on a queen-sized altar, the stars, pilgrims at our shrine.

The next day, in thick sweaters we roamed the dunes and listened to the wind turn the saw grass and reeds into a harp. Gulls floated on the off-shore breezes and followed as if curious to know what next?

We had a lobster dinner by a red-enameled fireplace in a small seafood restaurant just up the road from the inn. We drank beer. We belched. We smiled. We spoke of our pasts, our hurts, our happinesses, our hopes. We fell in love.

The next day, we returned. I dropped her off at her apartment, said I would call her and started counting the minutes to the next rendezvous. She did the same.

She pulled away from me, parted really and said, "There, you've had your kiss. I have to get going. I'm on the early shift tomorrow." She picked up her bag and notebook. "I like the concept of the play. I'll jot a few notes. We'll talk about it next time. OK?"

"Yeah, that'll be good. Next time."

Marianna

Marianna Rochambeau was the most beautiful woman in the West Indies and possibly in the entire Western Hemisphere. Her father, it was said, had died two years after she was born in the malaria outbreak of 1836 and her mother vowed never, as she put it, to be another victim of the accursed mosquito. Marianna and her mother, Anna, arrived in Mobile, Alabama in the spring of 1839 and there was hardly a man with eyes that didn't notice Madame Rochambeau as she disembarked at the port with her green-eyed, black-haired child and her nanny Fanta, a former slave from Martinique whom the Rochambeau's gave freedom to as an appreciation for her years of service. Fanta was short, dark-skinned and wiry with an inherent dignity that was the paternal residue of a grandfather of the Kawali tribe of Gabon in West Africa, a noble race known for the elegance of its warriors, the pride of its women, and an inherent need to avenge. Fanta would fill empty nights with stories of her tribes' Ramvala or imp of vengeance. Marianna listened wide-eyed, but over time she came to understand that the Kawalis differed not one iota from any race in Christendom except in its acknowledgement of its innate mercilessness. Fanta never failed to point out, though, with an almost Aesopian morality, that the Ramvala was to be kept at bay, that its conquest over the souls of some tribesmen met with fierce retribution from the gods.

The Rochambeaus established themselves quickly in Mobile society primarily on the strength of their inherited wealth. But, if the truth be told, the two women were so exquisite that they were invited to every soirée more for their decorativeness than for anything they might say or think. Anna had decided without any particular reason to retain her status as a widow. While she entertained gentleman callers, she never led any of them to think that they had any function whatsoever other than as a pleasant way to fill idle days and nights in the sweltering heat and humidity that crept in from the Gulf of Mexico not on little cat feet but like a mythological phantasmagoric leopard with which only Fanta seemed to be on intimate terms.

It was when Marianna turned eighteen that George Dumont came into her life. Madame Rochambeau wanted to fête her daughter and make a formal introduction of her to society even though everyone worth knowing within a hundred mile radius knew Marianna or had seen her or heard of her. George was visiting from Louisiana, staying with his friends the Jacksons, first cousins of Andrew Jackson, seventh President of the United States. The Dumonts of New Orleans owned over five thousand acres of cotton plantation and nearly three hundred slaves. George was the eldest son of a family that was as close to nobility as any in the south. He attended Marianna's party and despite social conventions which frowned upon it, they danced four consecutive dances, the last a Viennese waltz that had them dervishing around the Rochambeau ballroom like a vision. Marianna could see nothing but George, his dark eyes, ebon hair and tall erect posture, everything she could hope for in a man without consciously realizing it.

A year later they were married and she relocated to Montroyal, the family mansion on the edge of the Great Bayou where, from the third floor widow's walk, nearly the entire plantation could be seen in one sweeping panorama, the bobbing heads of the slaves red-bandannaed weaving from the lawn to the horizon like a constellation fallen to earth, the gently curving red clay drive like the seamless scarf of the Milky Way. Marianna had found heaven on earth, George her archangel. Only Fanta kept her grounded by casually speaking of the cruelties that she observed the overseers visiting upon the slaves.

"Madame," she would say, "the overseer Fernando beat a man nearly to death today. I saw the poor fellow naked and tied to a tree. The lash made passionate love to his skin. He done flayed him to the ribs. His wife and children, they saw; she done fainted, Madame, and they let her lie in the dust where she fall. God sees these things and weeps. His tears be bad luck for those who does 'em."

"Then Fernando will have to explain to God why he does such things. What can I do, Fanta, nothing, for my place is in the home not in the fields."

"'It's them orders your husband say, Madame. A word from you to him be the end of all dat sufferin'."

"It is not my place to speak of things about which I know nothing."

"But, Madame…"

"And it is not your place to speak of this anymore. Is that understood?"

"Yes, Madame, but I ain't so sure God sees it like dat."

"Then God must do what he must do."

No sooner had Marianna uttered these words that she realized the blasphemy that she had loosed from her lips, a drear dirge that floated around the two women like a water moccasin in a pond circling a bather. If and when it would strike could be determined by no man.

A year later to the day, Marianna gave birth to a son and it seemed the sun would never set on Montroyal so filled with light were she and George.

Madame Rochambeau had never seen Marianna's baby and anxiously but happily made the journey to Montroyal when news of the birth reached her. Fanta brought her to Marianna's boudoir. The young mother was recovering slowly, and lay full-length in her soft white muslins and laces, upon her bed. The baby was beside her, upon her arm, where he had fallen asleep, at her breast. A high yellow slave woman sat beside a window fanning them. Madame Rochambeau bent her portly figure over Marianna and kissed her, holding her an instant tenderly in her arms. Then she turned to the child.

"This is not the baby!" she exclaimed, in startled tones.

"I knew you would be astonished," laughed Marianna, "at the way he has grown. The little rascal! Look at his legs, mother, and his hands and fingernails…real fingernails. Fanta had to cut them this morning. Isn't it true, Fanta?"

Fanta bowed her turbaned head majestically, "Yes, Madame."

"And the way he cries," Marianna went on, "is deafening. George heard him the other day as far away as Kizzy's cabin."

Madame Rochambeau had never removed her eyes from the child. She lifted him and walked with him over to the window that was lightest. She scanned the baby narrowly, then looked as searchingly as Fanta, whose face was turned to gaze across the fields.

"Yes, the child has grown," said Madame Rochambeau slowly, as she replaced him beside his mother. "What does George say?"

Marianna's face became suffused with a contented glow.

"Oh, George is the proudest father in the parish, I believe, chiefly because it is a boy, to bear his name; though he says not— that he would have loved a girl as well. But I know it isn't true. I know he says that to please me. And mamma," she added, drawing Madame Rochambeau's head down to her and speaking in a whisper, "he hasn't punished one of them—not one of them—since the baby is born. Even Toby, who pretended to have burnt his leg that he might rest from work—he only laughed, and said Toby was a great scamp. Oh, Mamma, I'm so happy, it frightens me."

What Marianna said was true. Marriage and later the birth of his son, had softened George Dumont's imperious and exacting nature greatly. This was what made the gentle Marianna so happy, for she loved him deeply. When he frowned she trembled, but she loved him the more. When he smiled, she asked no greater blessing of God. But George's dark, handsome face had not often been disfigured by frowns since the day he fell in love with her.

When the baby was about three months old, Marianna awoke one day to the conviction that there was something menacing in the air. It was at first too subtle to recognize. It had only been a disquieting suggestion; an air of mystery among the slaves; unexpected visits from far-off neighbors who could hardly account for their coming, then a strange and awful change in her husband's manner, which she dared not ask him to explain. When he spoke to her, it was with averted eyes from which the old love-light seemed to have gone out. He absented himself from home; and when there, avoided her presence and that of the child, without excuse. And the very spirit of Satan seemed suddenly to take hold of him in his dealings with the slaves. Marianna was miserable beyond words.

She sat in her room, one hot afternoon, in her peignoir, listlessly drawing through her fingers the strands of her long, silky brown hair that hung about her shoulders. The baby, half-naked, lay asleep upon her own great mahogany bed that was like a sumptuous throne, with its satin-lined half-canopy. One of Kizzy's little quadroon boys—half-naked too—stood cooling the child slowly with a fan of peacock feathers. Marianna's eyes had been fixed absently and sadly upon the baby, while she was striving to penetrate the threatening mist that she felt closing about her. She looked from her child to the boy who stood beside him and back again, over and over.

"Oh!" It was a cry that she could not help; which she was not conscious of having uttered. The blood stopped in her veins and a clammy moisture gathered upon her face.

She tried to speak to the little quadroon boy; but no sound would come, at first. When he heard his name uttered, he looked up, and his mistress was pointing to the door. He laid aside the great, soft fan, and obediently stole away, over the polished floor, on his bare tiptoes. She stayed motionless, with her gaze riveted upon the child.

George entered the room, and without acknowledging her, went to a table and began to search among some papers which covered it.

"George," she called to him. But he did not notice. "George," she said again. Then she rose and tottered towards him. "George!" she panted once more, clutching his arm, "Look at our child. What does it mean? Tell me."

He coldly but gently loosened her fingers from about his arm and thrust her hand away from him. "Tell me what it means!" she cried despairingly.

"It means," he answered lightly, "that the child is not white; it means that you are not white."

A quick conception of all that this accusation meant for her filled her with the courage to deny it. "It is a lie; it is not true, I am white. Look at my hair, it is brown; and my eyes are gray, true? I am white. I am white. I am white"

"As white as Fanta," he returned casually and went away leaving her alone with their child.

When she could hold a pen in her hand steadily, she sent a despairing letter to her mother. "My mother, they tell me I am not white. George has told me I am not white. For God's sake, tell them it is not true. You must know it is not true. I shall die. I must die. I cannot be so unhappy, and live."

The answer that came was as brief: "My own Marianna, come home to me; back to your mother who loves you. Come with your child."

When the letter reached Marianna she went with it to her husband's study, and laid it open upon the desk before which he sat. She stood like a granite statue in a cemetery.

In silence he ran his cold eyes over the written words. He said nothing. "Shall I go, George?" she asked in robotic tones.

"Yes, go."

"Do you want me to go?"

"Yes, I want you to go."

He thought Almighty God had dealt cruelly and unjustly with him; he cursed God. He realized he no longer loved Marianna because of the insult she had brought upon his home and his name. She turned away silently and walked slowly toward the door, hoping he would call her back.

"Good-by, George," she said as if from a far off place. He did not answer her.

Marianna went in search of her child. Fanta was pacing the somber boudoir with it. She took the little one from Fanta's arms with no word of explanation, and descending the steps, walked away, across the dewy lawn under the live-oak branches.

It was an October afternoon; the sun was just sinking. Out in the still fields the slaves were picking cotton, the sweat on their faces and hair catching the reddish light like sparkling drops of blood.

Marianna had not changed the thin white garment nor the silk slippers she wore. Her hair was uncovered and the sun's rays made a halo from its brown tresses. She did not take the broad, beaten road which led to town and the coach that would take her to her mother. Instead, she walked across a fallow field, where the stubble bruised her feet and snatched at her gown, shredding it. She disappeared among the reeds and moss-covered willows that grew thick along the banks of the deep, sluggish bayou as if absorbed into the Earth itself.

That December, Fanta sat in a rocker in Kizzy's cabin, nearest to the Christmas fire. Everyone gathered around as usual to hear her tell tales, but no one was prepared for what she divulged that night.

"I remember him so well," she said. "He was tall and straight as a ginkgo tree, skin white as buttermilk, hair like pitch. He wooed me in the old country but when I resisted, he took me anyway like the white devils do when they have a mind. I had this baby, it was his all right, pale as the full moon on a cold night, white as a bleached skull; now listen, I don't lie. I puts my mark on that baby boy's shoulder, on the back like my daddy from Africa told me to do as they did from the beginning of time, yes, a small, small brand from my daddy's ring heated in the fire, a lion face, look like a birthmark. The Ramvala, it came over me, inside me, crawled inside me and leaned on my heart. Next time, Master George Rochambeau take off his shirt, look at dat shoulder. Dat ain't no wart, nor bruise, nor mole, nor nothin' God coulda put there. It be the sign I put on him. I his mama; inside he black like me and a terrible curse will fall on anyone who breathes word of it, hear me. His daddy stole him from me, but I has the last word, the last word, and I says, damn them all to Hell."

(With a tip of the boater to Kate.)

Black Out

The power grid failed again early that morning and became a huge criss-cross of limp noodles just three days before Christmas. A wind from hell had survived its trek across Oklahoma, Missouri and Ohio with enough strength left to slaughter a few pine trees and Norway maples uprooting them from their frozen footings and sending them sprawling like prize fighters against the electric lines strung from pole to pole. Whole neighborhoods and even some small towns were taken back to the 1870s before there were plastic toggles on the walls of every structure that were the only barricade between modern man and the Mongol horde of nature's four seasons.

The wind got bored and moved on, driven out by the darkness that fell at a little after four in the afternoon, the gray blanket of sky unchanged for more than six weeks. Yes, winter was on us like a fat whore on a chamber pot. A pissing snow had been falling on and off and there nearly a foot of it on the ground, blown in careless drifts against the bases of our apple trees, the garage doors and a thousand other places that in warmer weather hardly seemed places at all. I could make out the church steeple sticking its ugly spire into the air, pointing at the empty sky like a finger ringing a doorbell in a house where no one had lived for centuries. Fuck it all, I thought.

At 2 A.M. I got out of bed to look out the window to see if any lights had come on anywhere. On some occasions, some neighbors had gotten power restored before us and nothing pissed me off more than that as if not only the universe but the goddamned electric company had conspired to have us last on their list. I sometimes wondered if I was just a paranoiac or truly the victim of some nefarious plan hatched by society or demons. It's easy to wonder when things go wrong so often and life seems like a bowl of crap that got spilled on you when you got yanked from your mama's womb. I don't put much faith in coincidence.

The blue darkness outside was steady and unbroken. I needed to wander the house a bit, check the small thermometer on the thermostat to see how close to frozen the pipes were. I had a thing about pipes freezing ever since my daddy died from heart failure due to thick globs of cholesterol breaking loose from his arteries

186

and clogging up his pipes to bursting. I didn't recall much else about him other than his death and maybe his face on winter nights lit by a cheap flashlight when the power went out then.

The usual sounds of creaking radiators and oak floors ticking as the heat dried them out had ceased and the only sound was my wife's irregular breathing over the high-pitched tinnitus whine in my ears. I don't know if I mentioned that I was a married. The snoring didn't bother me that much, not as much let's say as being victimized by the electricity. I really wanted background soundtrack music embedded in the wallpaper, deep cello tones and a drifting refrain of descent, sad but not sentimental. Instead, I knew that 2 A.M. or not, I had been bequeathed a black heart that beat an *a cappella* kettle drum rhythm in my house of the dead.

It was years ago that Kathryn had been diagnosed and the dreaded regiments of treatment appeared in full body armor on the nearest hill, rampaging through our lives leaving almost no two pieces touching. The civilization of our marriage at first, waged a battle of strategic defense, then retreat and survival and now defeat on his black horse cantered slowly through our bedroom the night I could no longer make love to her. That was six weeks ago.

The walk down the stairs was like descending into a swimming pool, the cold lapping at my feet, my legs, my crotch, the small of my back and finally the drowning depths. At the bottom I was submerged in the frigid liquid cold flowing in soft swells and currents around and through me. The shadowy hulks of furniture, the sarcophagi of sofa, chairs, sideboards and TV all abandoned to the flood, black in the blue light seeping through the windows from outside.

I pushed through the living room into the kitchen, the familiar white skeleton of the enamel-topped table glossy even in the blue grotto of the house. On it were the large manila envelopes holding the X-rays and their hapless blurs, the battle flags of the invasion. I pulled out a chair, its familiar rasp muted by the lulling swells. I sat and reconstructed in my mind the better times, the sun slants light the rooms, warm breezes lifting the curtains, the TV or radio singing to us. All the clichéd pieces, the pointillist pixels shimmering in the rising sea of cold in which I sat.

I looked at the window over the sink, a little altar to the goddess of dishwashing with its sacred pump bottles and baptizing liquids. The panes were frosted over to a frigid blur. On the sill were three sacrificial African violets which she adored and nurtured. They had finally succumbed as the cold had its way with them and now looked like three tarantulas, their hairy legs draped over the edges of the flower pots.

I got up and opened a drawer, removed a large carving knife, one of a set we had received as a wedding gift. Its worn handle was glad to be held. It seemed a harpoon now and led me through the slow currents and frozen eddies back up the stairs to the bedroom.

I stopped at the door and heard her rustle under the covers, her wheezing short gasps for air were a distant lighthouse bell leading me toward her. I stood by the bed. She looked up at me and the blade in my upraised hand and said, "I love you." I wanted to say, "I love you too, more than I thought possible," but the knife said it all and more.

The Education of Sebastian

I have home-schooled Sebastian from the time he was four. He's sixteen now and a fine lad, tall with delicate features, sensitive blue eyes and long dark brown hair. He's never seen MTV or listened to rock or rap and his friends, both male and female, are all home-schoolers as well. As a group, the parents of these children all have the same belief that it is contact with other children raised in lax, indulgent or negligent households that can create monsters out of children who are nurtured with good morals, a sense of decency and kindness and, foremost, a respect for their parents and other adults worthy of respect, each other, and life on planet earth in general. My success with Sebastian was a labor of love; he would be any parent's dream child with the possible exception of those fathers who lead vapid, superficial lives dependent on the vicarious athleticism of their victimized and brain-washed children. I am not justifying myself but explaining my motives and methods so that Sebastian will be understood and perhaps venerated by future generations, for he deserves it.

My wife, Kathryn, Sebastian's mother, went off her Prozac about a year ago and the calm undisturbed air within our home experienced its first prolonged turbulence. She had always been high-strung but Sebastian birth seemed to settle her down, although in retrospect, it might have simply taken the life out of her or some of it, anyway. In the hospital, after the unusually protracted delivery of nearly 14 hours, her eyes, for only a minute or two, went dead, looking at me as if focusing on a point several yards behind my head. I turned, thinking she might actually be seeing someone or something, but it was just the pale green glossy wall standing at attention at my back. I suppose the stare was the preface to her post-partum depression which settled in like Sebastian's invisible doppelganger. I was never one to countenance women's hormonal excuses, whether it was PMS, menopause or any of a dozen other pseudo-medical conditions that rationalize erratic female behavior but justify it as well to a suffering masculine world, as if the entire planet was to be governed by the secretions of ovaries. Regardless of my inadequacy in not recognizing the power of those secretions, Kathryn's mood swings, for lack of a more profound term, became

189

the obstacle course of my life and the boot camp of Sebastian's. It was only my fortuitous acquisition of Prozac and my careful surreptitious administration of it in Kathryn's morning tea that made life at our home if not stable, at least predictable. I promised myself that after she passed safely through her "change of life," the last hormonal cataclysm of modern marriage, that I would release her from the restraints of that magic elixir. I looked forward to meeting the woman I married again, particularly the one that was so voracious in the bedroom, for that small pill had transformed her into a sexual zombie and while she was compliant, she lacked interest having no more real sex drive than one of those inflatable gaping mouthed dolls. After a very short time, I lost interest myself, getting exhausted then bored from numerous vain attempts at kick-starting her libido. I felt then and still do that I had to take the chaff with the wheat and become reconciled to having a compliant housewife and mother to my son and a roommate of the opposite sex for myself in the hours after the dinner dishes had found their way into the dishwasher. It doomed Sebastian to being an only child but I felt that was the price that had to be paid for everyone's mental well-being.

Having spent most of my salaried life as a university professor in the humanities, it was easy and joyful to instruct Sebastian in the glories of art, literature and music. By the time he was fourteen, he had read most of Thomas Hardy, Charles Dickens, Edith Wharton the good plays of Shakespeare, the adventure novels of Jack London and all the other high spots of European and American literature. By the age of fifteen he could, within a few minutes of my turning on the CD player, identify the opus of Mozart, the symphony of Beethoven, the etudes of Chopin, the concertos of Rachmaninoff. He could tell Mussorgsky from Tchaikovsky, Ravel from Stravinsky. He became adept at the difference between Greek and Roman antiquities, Neo-Classicism, the Salon movement, Mannerism, Impressionism and even came to appreciate if not admire, the lackadaisical and techniqueless art of the moderns. His favorites in all things were very much like mine and if he particularly admired the work of and artist, writer or composer that I did not like, he eventually saw the error of his ways. He was quite independent. I let him down somewhat in the area of mathematics and the physical sciences, subjects that I did quite poorly in myself but he could balance a checkbook with some alacrity and could calculate the area of a room in a home or the MPG our car got. Physics, anatomy and geology, I left to video tapes and the Discovery Channel. It was biology that he excelled in, as I had, and we enjoyed field trips into a nearby state park to discuss evolution and the adaptability of a chaotic environment. I told him at length how humans were the only animals that could control their environment and even suggested, without admitting anything, that psychotropic drugs like Prozac were the ultimate fine-tuning of not only the environment but interpersonal relationships as well. His mind was a veritable sponge, parched in the desert of youth but now luxuriously quaffing at the abundant oasis of my lectures, discussions and assigned readings.

I taught him everything I knew about the opposite sex, dating, wooing and marrying. I anticipated the mystery and shock of nocturnal emissions, the often frantic desire to masturbate and how best to practice it without soiling sheets, bedding, bath towels or underwear. His smile was white and honest, his breath always fresh, his armpits deodorized, his anus carefully wiped. In fact, his worn underwear were indiscernible from ones in his dresser drawer. His room was meticulously kept. He learned to pick his nose and belch only when no one was about and in the event he had to pass gas in earshot of others, to devise what I called a covering sound like pulling a chair across a tiled floor, clearing his throat, or speaking loudly as a sort of noise camouflage. I knew these were all arts practiced by respected successful people and I was determined that Sebastian above all other things be successful.

Kathryn had taken on the disagreeable habit of infusing some of my lectures with her own often confused ideas especially on religious matters and she even had the audacity, one day while I was at the doctors for my annual physical, of attempting to teach Sebastian what she called manners and etiquette but which were really just a set of rules disguised to subliminally subject men to the whims of women. Such outdated and absurd practices as opening doors, pulling out chairs, paying for dinners and other anachronisms that perpetuated the notion that the gates of Heaven were located between the legs of females and that debasement and social servitude were required by the Gods that held the keys to those gates. It took me nearly a week to erase the effect of Kathryn's two hour "talk." It was almost the first time I wanted to do violence upon her, certainly the only time since my Sebastian drew breath. But in retrospect, ever the didact, I saw an opportunity to teach him one of the most important social lessons he would ever get.

I was well aware of how a relationship between a man and a woman could deteriorate into a hell on earth and that if Sebastian was going to pass on my genes and name, it was imperative for him to be able to navigate the waterspouts, typhoons, whirlpools and sea monsters that lay ahead of every man's journey through the ocean of marriage. Brutality, either mental or physical, was to be avoided at all costs because the new laws on domestic violence virtually guaranteed a prison sentence for any husband that physically reprimanded a wayward wife no matter how valid the provocation. Divorce was unacceptable as well because of the catastrophic economic consequences that so favored women as to render men financial eunuchs. So, I devised what I knew to be a fool-proof method for Sebastian to deal with feminine vicissitudes. But for the lesson to be effective, he had to experience first-hand the anguish a female could inflict upon the male. It was not difficult to orchestrate a suitable confrontation between Sebastian and my wife. It was in the nature of a laboratory session in his home school curriculum.

As we were living in Philadelphia all our lives, it was a simple matter to travel to the "right" part of that great putrid City of Brotherly Love at a particular hour of the evening to find a young woman who, for a reasonable sum, would show Sebastian the sexual act in the flesh, so to speak, and concretize my lecture on human reproductive behavior. It is true that he was younger than I had planned, for this lesson was not to reach the practical stage until his 18th birthday or thereabouts. Nonetheless, I had little doubt that he was ready and capable and Kathryn's behavior provided the catalyst for me to accelerate his learning of the solution to the larger issue of dealing with his frustrations as a man. This was a two-fold lesson of invaluable proportions.

It was a simple matter to time my son's liaison with the prostitute to coincide with Kathryn's weekly visit to her mother in King of Prussia. What I did alter, however, was her return, two hours earlier than usual and while I feigned needing to work at the university library, Kathryn came home as planned and discovered her son *in flagrante delicto* going at the pretty and streetwise Felicia, as I learned her name to be. Of course, Kathryn threw a fit and, hellion that she could be with the Prozac flushed from her system, cast the whore into the street with a stream of invective and then proceeded to berate and embarrass Sebastian for doing such shameful acts in the family home and so on and so forth. Try as he might to defend himself, Kathryn's throaty hysterical reprimands and onslaughts were more than he could take; the noble lad never implicated me, of course. I arrived in the knick of time, choreographed to the minute, to remove him from the heat of the fray and to take him up to his attic classroom, his mother assuming I would explain in detail all he had done wrong especially in regard to how men were supposed to respect women, etc., etc. and to administer a suitable punishment.

I sat with Sebastian in his classroom that I had furnished when he was old enough to sit at a desk. I had, as he grew, continued to provide a larger and larger chair and desk so that he always felt comfortable, never too small at a large desk to encourage the feeling that he was inadequate for the task at hand nor too small an accommodation that he might seem overpowering and therefore more capable than he actually was. This day, he was covered in perspiration after the incomplete union with Felicia and the run-in with Kathryn. He sat hoping to listen to me drone on about his assigned readings, the inadequacies of Jane Austen—for I had intentionally assigned him the tepid and dull Pride and Prejudice as an example of the superficiality of feminine priorities—but instead I simply placed a beautifully crafted cylinder about six inches long and one inch thick made of ebony with a mother-of-pearl inlay of a Japanese geisha in traditional dress holding a parasol. In fact, it looked exactly like an umbrella handle down to the silver button that modern umbrellas provide to release the spring-loaded mechanism of the canopy.

"What is that?" he said with considerable boyish enthusiasm. "It's beautiful."

"It's a weapon," I said.

"May I hold it?'

"Not yet."

I went on to explain as I held it up as if it were a test tube filled with an exotic potion that it was a *kijiri* or, in more common parlance, a stiletto.

"Before we go any further," I said softly, "how do you feel after being humiliated by your mother?"

"Father, I am so angry and frustrated, I don't know what to do. Must we talk about it?"

"Believe me, my son, it won't help," I said. "After a time, you will get over it, but it will stay in your system like the mercury found in tuna fish and, if you continue to eat, that is, if such episodes recur, it will like mercury, build up in your system until the critical point. Then it is too late to do anything and you will be either imprisoned or committed or both. I wish I could give you a simplistic solution like counting to ten or punching the heavy bag, but these do not work. The poison remains. That is where the *kijiri* comes in," I said as I lifted it again into the air, twirling it. This time I pressed the sterling button and the spike-like blade ejected with a quick click, crisp, metallic, catching the light from the setting sun and looking every bit a sorcerer's diminutive wand, its needle tip glistening.

"In 45 minutes," I said, "it will be rush hour and the sidewalks will be packed with people heading home, pouring out of office buildings. There will be many women who should have stayed home with their children but who prefer the workplace to being housekeepers because of their greed and insatiable libidos. I will take you to the northwest corner of Chestnut Street. You will wear a topcoat and carry my briefcase, looking to all the world like a fine young office worker. You will successfully endeavor to get into the flow of pedestrian traffic at its thickest heading southbound." His eyes followed mine as I spoke to him, hanging on to my every word and gesture as he was used to doing, his attention never wavering.

"Before the middle of the block, you will select a female target. Get as close as you can to her without being obvious. Carefully actuate the *kijiri* as I have shown you and with a quick jab, puncture her back to the hilt. Just as quickly, retract your stinger and keep walking. She will at first only feel an odd pinch, perhaps a shooting

194

pain. She will reach for her back and only when she sees her blood on her hand will she scream and probably collapse. You should be at least fifty feet ahead of her by the time a crowd gathers to see what has occurred. You will keep moving obliviously and I will meet you around the westbound corner. The penetration of your blade will transfer the poison in your system which your callous mother gave you. You will feel the release and a great calm will come over you. Thus, in the future, you will be able to cope with the inevitable stress that is the natural effluvia of male-female relationships."

"What is 'effluvia'?" he queried.

"Look it up. E f f l u v i a. And write the definition down when you are done. Now get dressed; we're running a tad late."

Within minutes he stood before me in his long navy wool over-coat, his hair casually caressing his forehead, his blue eyes clear, in-telligent, focused, determined to succeed at the task at hand. I gave the *kijiri* to him and he hugged me. It had been one of those days when a father feels he has accomplished something toward turning his son into a man. There is no greater gift a father can confer than the gift of knowledge and the guidance to use it.

"Let's get the car," I said. "Perhaps we'll stop at McDonald's on the way home."

"I'd like that, Daddy," he said.

Boots

My boat was drifting with the uncertain currents through the night, clouds obscuring the moon and stars as if a moldy quilt had been cast over the world by a careless innkeeper not realizing I was adrift and alone, oarless, rudderless and at the whim of the inky river. Black froth licked at the prow and pregnant thuds knocked at the hull as the boat glided, circling over submerged stones, the forgotten eggs of long-dead sea creatures. I held tightly to the sodden seat, prone and praying to any god that might listen to the prayers of a thief. My clothes had been tattered by the shredding wind and the only thing I owned untouched by the world's nefarious tricks were the beautiful bullhide boots that I had stolen from that damnable itinerant preacher. I regretted having to kill him, but he awoke just as I had snatched the boots from his bedside. What sin this might have been, seemed nothing to me compared to the sin that God had committed in sentencing me to a life of poverty and want.

The river calmed after a time and I could make out the silhouettes of reeds and cattails along the edge, black as if poisoned by the darkness and bent and broken like a giant had stumbled in the dark, his oafish hands breaking his fall near the shore. The slim current led me toward the bank and I leaned over and started paddling, feeling the nibbles of invisible fish on my hands. After a time, about a hundred yards downstream, I saw a fire glowing through the reeds, a cyclops eye of orange and red with jellyfish tendrils of smoke escaping to the sky. Three men sat near the fire, one standing and holding a rifle. I called out for help. They turned in unison toward me and immediately I had regretted my outburst. One called out to me and I thought I heard another say, "should I shoot him now?" but my mind was playing tricks on me, I was sure. A rope was tossed out and I thought for a moment to forgo its welcoming hand, but I was near starved and shivering uncontrollably. I grabbed it and was pulled to shore, fending my way through the brittle grasses that felt like skeleton arms and legs, sere and stiff, the smell of dead things in the air.

"Thank you," I said. "My name is Walter. Yours?"

"We have no names here. To name something is to control it.

And, anyway, what's it to you?" the tall one said. He was clearly the oldest, the other two looking no more than in their teens, but drawn and sallow, the dim light of the fire swallowed by the dark sockets of their sunken eyes. One of them held the rifle, his thumb caressing the stock rhythmically.

"Nothing really. Just being friendly."

"There ain't no friends out here either. What are you doing on the river in such a state?"

"I was upstream a few days' ride back when a storm hit. Lost my oars in the rapids from the cloudburst and had my rudder crushed on the rocks. Lucky I'm alive."

"Lucky, yeah." The tall man spoke like a Southerner, the others were voiceless but all three were thin as wraiths. The youngest had on a tattered shirt with sleeves unevenly short as if something had been chewing on them.

"Might I sit by the fire a spell. I'm soaked through to the core."

"Sure. Sit."

I sat uneasily feeling the warmth of the fire immediately. A light rain began to fall and spatter on the coals. A large skillet was balanced on a few rocks and in it were a few lumps of meat, black and dry, an indeterminate feast.

"Have a piece of meat. Hand him a plate," said the tall man to the boy standing to my left. "You could probably use something to eat if what you say is true."

"Well, thank you."

The boy whose hair I could now see was a knotted mass of red, went to the fire and with a long thin knife, stabbed a chunk of the flesh and placed it in a tin plate with a thud.

"It ain't pork," said the tall man.

"Beef then?" I said.

"No," he replied.

I tore off a piece and chewed its tasteless fibres, thick and dusty dry, my teeth gnashing it as best I could, flavorless, foreign, cooked through like a stone. One boy stood behind me, the other squatting, the rifle butt on the ground, the barrel held so that he could lean his face against it.

"Them is nice boots you got there," the tall man said. "Where'd you get 'em?"

"They were a gift. From my father," I said looking down.

"I don't think that's true," he said.

"I don't care what you think."

I looked at his boots and saw they were torn and held together with bits of string and bailing wire, a dirty toe peeking out between the two lips of a split in the leather.

"Them boots look like they too big for you," he said.

"I like 'em that way. Room to grow," I smiled without a response from any of the three who were quiet as pallbearers, the light tapping of the rain a somber drone.

"Where was you headin'?" he asked.

" 'Cross the river to Mecklenburg."

"What for?"

"A funeral. My father."

"The same what give you them boots, huh?"

"Listen," I said. "I appreciate your kindness, but I got to get going. Does that road lead back up north?"

"That road goes to hell, boy. Have some more meat. We're all done with her."

"No thanks. I am thankful to you, though."

After a time, he started removing his boots and when he had finished, he signaled to the boy behind me who took off his and put the man's on. The boy's boots were more tattered than the tall man's and a rank odor seeped out the top of them.

"Now you take those boots, mister, hear?"

I took off my boots and placed them neatly in front of me. The boy took them and handed them to the tall man who slipped them on. He stomped a few times, did a quick jig and said, "These is fine, right fine. I thank you."

I put on the boy's boots without saying a word, the boy with the rifle standing suddenly and looking shiftily between the tall man and me.

"Should I shoot 'im, Pa?" A minute that stretched into forever ended.

"No, I don't think so. He seems tame enough. Let's get goin'"

"But what about...?" the boy with the rifle said.

"I told you that fire would work. I don't need to wait no more. We done good enough. Pack up."

One boy picked up the dishes and the skillet, dumping the lump of meat into the dying fire where it caused a shower of sparks to fly up through the damp air. The rain had stopped. The boy behind me stroked the back of my head. "He's a pretty one, Pa," he said.

"Not tonight, boy. Best we get goin'."

The three of them slipped off into the darkness as if they were made of it, the night closing behind them. At my back, the dim edge of the sun peered beneath the cauldron lid of the sky.

My boat was drifting with the uncertain currents through the night, clouds obscuring the moon and stars as if a moldy quilt had been cast over the world by a careless innkeeper not realizing I was adrift and alone, oarless, rudderless and at the whim of the inky river. Black froth licked at the prow and pregnant thuds knocked at the hull as the boat glided, circling over submerged stones, the forgotten eggs of long-dead sea creatures. I held tightly to the sodden seat, prone and praying to any god that might listen to the prayers of a thief. My clothes had been tattered by the shredding wind and the only thing I owned untouched by the world's nefarious tricks were the beautiful bullhide boots that I had stolen from that damnable itinerant preacher. I regretted having to kill him, but he awoke just as I had snatched the boots from his bedside. What sin this might have been, seemed nothing to me compared to the sin that God had committed in sentencing me to a life of poverty and want.

The river calmed after a time and I could make out the silhouettes of reeds and cattails along the edge, black as if poisoned by the darkness and bent and broken like a giant had stumbled in the dark, his oafish hands breaking his fall near the shore. The slim current led me toward the bank and I leaned over and started paddling, feeling the nibbles of invisible fish on my hands. After a time, about a hundred yards downstream, I saw a fire glowing through the reeds, a cyclops eye of orange and red with jellyfish tendrils of smoke escaping to the sky. Three men sat near the fire, one standing and holding a rifle. I called out for help. They turned in unison toward me and immediately I had regretted my outburst. One called out to me and I thought I heard another say, "should I shoot him now?" but my mind was playing tricks on me, I was sure. A rope was tossed out and I thought for a moment to forgo its welcoming hand, but

I was near starved and shivering uncontrollably. I grabbed it and was pulled to shore, fending my way through the brittle grasses that felt like skeleton arms and legs, sere and stiff, the smell of dead things in the air.

"Thank you," I said. "My name is Walter. Yours?"

"We have no names here. To name something is to control it. And, anyway, what's it to you?" the tall one said. He was clearly the oldest, the other two looking no more than in their teens, but drawn and sallow, the dim light of the fire swallowed by the dark sockets of their sunken eyes. One of them held the rifle, his thumb caressing the stock rhythmically.

"Nothing really. Just being friendly."

"There ain't no friends out here either. What are you doing on the river in such a state?"

"I was upstream a few days' ride back when a storm hit. Lost my oars in the rapids from the cloudburst and had my rudder crushed on the rocks. Lucky I'm alive."

"Lucky, yeah." The tall man spoke like a Southerner, the others were voiceless but all three were thin as wraiths. The youngest had on a tattered shirt with sleeves unevenly short as if something had been chewing on them.

"Might I sit by the fire a spell. I'm soaked through to the core."

"Sure. Sit."

I sat uneasily feeling the warmth of the fire immediately. A light rain began to fall and spatter on the coals. A large skillet was balanced on a few rocks and in it were a few lumps of meat, black and dry, an indeterminate feast.

"Have a piece of meat. Hand him a plate," said the tall man to the boy standing to my left. "You could probably use something to eat if what you say is true."

"Well, thank you."

The boy whose hair I could now see was a knotted mass of red, went to the fire and with a long thin knife, stabbed a chunk of the flesh and placed it in a tin plate with a thud.

"It ain't pork," said the tall man.

"Beef then?" I said.

"No," he replied.

I tore off a piece and chewed its tasteless fibres, thick and dusty dry, my teeth gnashing it as best I could, flavorless, foreign, cooked through like a stone. One boy stood behind me, the other squatting, the rifle butt on the ground, the barrel held so that he could lean his face against it.

"Them is nice boots you got there," the tall man said. "Where'd you get 'em?"

"They were a gift. From my father," I said looking down.

"I don't think that's true," he said.

"I don't care what you think."

I looked at his boots and saw they were torn and held together with bits of string and bailing wire, a dirty toe peeking out between the two lips of a split in the leather.

"Them boots look like they too big for you," he said.

"I like 'em that way. Room to grow," I smiled without a response from any of the three who were quiet as pallbearers, the light tapping of the rain a somber drone.

"Where was you headin'?" he asked.

" 'Cross the river to Mecklenburg."

"What for?"

"A funeral. My father."

"The same what give you them boots, huh?"

"Listen," I said. "I appreciate your kindness, but I got to get going. Does that road lead back up north?"

"That road goes to hell, boy. Have some more meat. We're all done with her."

"No thanks. I am thankful to you, though."

After a time, he started removing his boots and when he had finished, he signaled to the boy behind me who took off his and put the man's on. The boy's boots were more tattered than the tall man's and a rank odor seeped out the top of them.

"Now you take those boots, mister, hear?"

I took off my boots and placed them neatly in front of me. The boy took them and handed them to the tall man who slipped them on. He stomped a few times, did a quick jig and said, "These is fine, right fine. I thank you."

I put on the boy's boots without saying a word, the boy with the rifle standing suddenly and looking shiftily between the tall man and me.

"Should I shoot 'im, Pa?" A minute that stretched into forever ended.

"No, I don't think so. He seems tame enough. Let's get goin'"

"But what about…?" the boy with the rifle said.

"I told you that fire would work. I don't need to wait no more. We done good enough. Pack up."

One boy picked up the dishes and the skillet, dumping the lump of meat into the dying fire where it caused a shower of sparks to fly up through the damp air. The rain had stopped. The boy behind me stroked the back of my head. "He's a pretty one, Pa," he said.

"Not tonight, boy. Best we get goin'."

The three of them slipped off into the darkness as if they were made of it, the night closing behind them. At my back, the dim edge of the sun peered beneath the cauldron lid of the sky.

Dear Officer O'Brien

Dear Officer O'Brien,

I hope this finds you well. I am feeling better since you arrested me and I want to apologize for giving you a hard time. As you know from my trial, I was very abused by my stepfather in ways no one should ever be abused. But I won't say anymore. I wrote this poem for your wife. Please read it to her. I look forward to meeting her one day as a sort of surprise visit which I have been planning for several years because I have so little else to think about—other than the crimes I did not commit. I do imagine how the real "perp" felt when he slipped his knife into those innocent women's private parts, the smell of terror and lust all mixed together like a sea breeze cocktail sipped on the beach in Miami. Have you and the Mrs, ever been there? I notice she has large breasts. You police fellows sure like big ones. Me too. Perhaps you have a daughter. I read in the paper that you did. Does she have a boyfriend yet? I hope not. I think that all women should remain pure until they meet the man most capable of introducing them to the sanctity of love. I truly believe I am that man. Why else would God have put me on the Earth? Riddle me this, Officer O'Brien. I bet you can't, Ha Ha. Please let your little girl, sweet and lovely as I am sure she is, read this poem or better yet, let her use it in the toilet—make a copy for her for her own private use and she can give it back to me when I visit. How delicious. I feel I will be released soon because my doctors have told the Board I am so much better. This letter is an example of how creative I can be. It's all a fiction like Edward Alan Poe would write. I love his poems, don't you? Here goes:

This thing, my life, all an agony, of Hell… of torture… And years of bludgeoning torment tiny nuisances. The disgust eyes, dirty frowns, and red fingers pointing at me. Feeling all the patheticness and humiliation. What time is right to abort the null existence and retire from sick lifeblood. And yet feelings—thwarted by sun's beams ready to attack, averted by smiling faces ready to rape—come, a wish to annihilate my self… If this wasn't true in my plaguing conscious. But Jesus Christ! Another day comes tomorrow, a shade better than the present, if I can imagine, a day anew like a newborn or an old-dying, when nothing is everything and everything is nothing and all is mere shutting of eyelids. Good Christ! Rip me apart, tear me to shrivels, eat me to help me see a better day's worth and salvage this decaying thing from myself.

With love and respect for a job well-done,
Peter-Peter-Pumpkin Eater.

Haircut

I am writing this with my back to the world for there are scant few if any who could understand me. To start at the beginning is good form but I should like you to see what lies in that garden near the yellow roses, but that shall have to wait.

I had put off my haircut for nearly three months, twice as long as habit persuaded, but it was a momentary foolish frugality, not something important that delayed me. My usual cutter was off and I was scheduled with a woman named Carolyn, 26 and perfect of form. Ordinarily, I would have had a queer named Jonathan, a flimsy fairy of a fop who was mewling, servile and efficient, but invisible to me as he blathered on with a too-thick tongue and chapped lips. But Carolyn was certainly different. She had full brunette hair—not lank, but rich and lustrous—an upturned nose, bright blue eyes and a trim, tight body with a round posterior and perky breasts. Yes, perky. What a delightful word. The way Jonathan sickeningly swished and swayed around the throne of my chair, Carolyn tangoed, making idle conversation with a velvet, throaty voice, brushing my shoulders with her breasts, my elbow with her ass, her scent slithering up my nostrils to some part of my brain that absorbed it and sent it into my blood like vandals on a subway car to my nether parts.

I could sense her interest in my wealth and success. She probably sensed my interest in her shape and youth. A fair exchange of superficialities. Neither of us knew the infinite variations of each others' personalities, but I aware, unlike her, that she was spiraling down to my center like light to a black hole.

Then there was the issue of my marriage. I had been married longer than Carolyn had been on Earth. But what is the point of such a long period of indenture if not to obtain some license? The bank account of my connubial status was showing a substantial positive balance despite some occasional withdrawals over the years. How many more opportunities like Carolyn would present themselves, the offering up of such a tender morsel laid out upon the table for me to taste, bite, chew and ingest? Thomas Aquinas once said that temptation is put before us by God as a test of our faith, a testimony to our goodness. But couldn't it also be a reward for a life well-led, a life so perfect in its outline that had the Deity poured forth His abundant light upon it, the shadow would be powerful enough, its umbra deep enough to warrant absolution from anything?

Had I not swallowed as Carolyn snip-snipped away at the locks around my left ear, I would have drooled onto the bright lavender cloak she so ceremoniously placed over me, gently snapped at my neck to protect me from my own hair. I imagined she viewed this garment as a table cloth, my head her meal to place where she needed it to be, a toothy, tonguey machine, the eater and the eaten inseparable, indiscernible, a jumble of lips, body fluids and apertures gaily confused and commingled.

There is little point in a detailed blow-by-blow of the drinks, the dinner, the small talk, the false earnestness, the heavy lightness of banter, the shifting, fluid, studied and subtle eye contact back and forth over *al dente* linguini, fluttering eyelashes over watery capuccini, the etc.'s and etc.'s of the waltz of seduction and seductiveness. Her apartment was predictably bourgeois: floral prints in nauseating abundance, the tacky taste of the underclass: a cheap scarf over a Wal-Mart lamp, a college days futon instead of a sofa, a mattress on the floor in the bedroom with faded pink sheets and half a dozen stuffed unicorns sappily waiting to watch the carnage. It was all embarrassingly predictable, beneath me really, except for the walk in the garden afterwards. The act itself was so mechanical that only the dessert would reveal my artistry.

I followed the glow of her cigarette tip like a comet trailing smoke through the solar system of that garden. I caught her in mid-sentence—something amateurishly philosophic about the light of the stars taking so long to reach our eyes—when the rock I held crushed her skull. I felt the warm spray of blood and cerebral fluid caress my face. What a grand finale to an otherwise photostatically reproducible evening. I could encase this moment forever, never having to daydream in the days and months and years to follow what she would be up to and with whom. The stress of that unrequited jealousy might haunt me indefinitely. But I had frozen the moment, stolen from time itself her face, her body and the love I had for her and could rest easy in it till the end of my days.

Terminator Love

My bedroom was dark, the ceiling the blue of dusk, the furniture deep gray. I had my headphones on and was listening to the love theme from *Terminator II*, my favorite part of the film. As the music rose and fell, I could envision the scene as clearly as if I were in the theater. Michael Biehn, the hero of all the Terminator movies, was bathing in a lake in the woods, his well-scarred body tan except for the cheeks of his rear end which were the color of mayonnaise. There was the Arnold Schwarzenegger Terminator hiding in the woods peeping through the limbs of some blue spruces, his red light eyes bright as Christmas ornaments on the Rockefeller Center tree. He watched Michael wash himself, particularly observing how the wan sunlight caught the peach fuzz coating on his ass, that beautiful mayo, cream-colored ass. Terminator's eyes narrowed and glowed fiercely staring at that double hemisphere of masculinity. He could take it no longer but strode out through the trees and, as if to show his peaceful intent, raised his hands in the air and said, "I come in peace, no pun intended." Michael slowly turned and said, "I knew you were there, big boy." Here, the violins and oboes made a lilting crescendo as Terminator grabbed Michael and nibbled the back of his neck. It was only a minute before his hydraulic reproduction pod penetrated those buns and when he orgasmed his machine oil into Michael, he blew him up from the inside, showering the serene lake with bits of blood, colon and stool in a most egregious fashion, startling a pair of mallards into flight and making the fish jump for a hundred yards in each direction. It was such a sad ending for our hero, but Terminator learned the dangers of man-love and would never be a threat to humanity again, not if he had anything to say about it. As the oboes and piccolos danced their sad dance in my headphones, Terminator took what was left of Michael and carried him to an old well nearby, tossing him in as a tympani thrummed away and the music ended with three cymbals crashing as the lifeless body fell down the shaft and landed in an antique wheelbarrow that some wayward youths had dropped down a few years earlier as a prank on a local pig farmer. Surely, no cinematic scene could have been more profound. I dabbed at my tears with the brittle end of my pillowcase and cursed my mother for insisting on starching my bed linens. Jesus, they were stiff as a priest's collar and crunched all night long as I moved to the inner rhythms of my sleep. I wish real life was more like the movies.

I had started seeing my ex-wife, Susan, again. Old loves die hard and while I had fallen in love with Robert, Sue never left my heart, my achy, breaky heart which creaked and groaned when I re-lived those moments with my childhood sweetheart. Unfortunately, Robert had discovered my liaisons with her by following me one day and seeing the two of us at a small café in the village. We were only talking, but it might as well have been a major doggie style sex party on the sidewalk. Robert is one of those "hold it in, then explode" types so I was not prepared when he cross-examined me that night as I lay in bed early complaining of a headache. He caught me in the lie and when I told him he should mind his own beeswax, he went temporarily insane. He smashed his fist down on a glass cocktail table that I had lovingly purchased at a designer close-out sale at Bloomies. The glass split into large triangular shards and he picked one up, entered the bedroom, and holding it like a dagger said, "I'm gonna cut your fuckin' heart out if I catch you cheating on me. Do you understand?" Well, of course I understood. I held the sheets tightly under my chin as if that over-starched 400 count Egyptian cotton could offer any sort of protection against a shard-wielding queen on a jealous rampage. Even his slight lisp had vanished like a blackbird in the night. The moments he spent looming over my prostrate form seemed like hours. I'd thought he would never leave. But eventually, the door to our apartment closed and I knew he had gone for a walk to cool down and contemplate how he could make up to me for being so violent. As I thought about it, I felt every inch like Michael Biehn bathing in the lake. Robert was my Terminator and I was filled with romantic notions of man love and how truly repulsed I was when I saw Susan's breasts in her tight fitting Gucci T-shirt. Those things are so gushy—yikes, nothing like a good hard set of pecks on a real man. Governor Arnold, where art thou? Art thou in the woods espying me? Robert? Robert, please return unto me. I'm just a die-hard romantic, I guess. I put on my headphones again and longingly listened to the love theme from *Godzilla*. Oh, sad Jurassic monster; come to me. Trumpet your tragic growls. I am here!

Time

I had been adopted by the Bensons when I was three months old. I didn't discover this until I was thirteen and it added much less angst to my puberty years than one would expect. They were good parents but I always sensed a certain distance that never quite mirrored itself in the eyes of my friends as they looked at their parents. I had made a real study of this parent-child relationship; it was a hobby of mine and very often my play-dates and sleep-overs—a common occurrence and quite de rigueur in the suburbs of Manhattan—were experimental proceedings more than social events. Not that I didn't like my friends. I did. I was accepted and acceptable and was neither a bully nor bullied but just one of many kids passing through the alimentary canal of a school system in an affluent American suburb. I had the advantage of having neither brother nor sister and. like anything else, it always seemed that perhaps I should have been better off with their company. But at ten or so, I determined that it was preferable to be an only child and better still to be an only adopted child.

From my graduation from high school until my thirtieth year, I have no episodes or longings, no love affairs or tragedies, no experimentations and no epiphanies to report that have not been reported a thousand times over. People need to realize that no matter how much they may think they are as phenomenal as a prize-winning rose in a garden, that there are ten million, million roses all about and the fact of dropping a petal or having particularly sharp thorns means not a whit. Should I feel myself so important as to immerse you in tales of sexual conquest, of great battles for great grades, of elections and betrothals, then I should only be making you feel more important than you are. We are indeed specks and anything that changes that belief is a fabrication, a bald-faced lie or an overt act of faith which is selfishly delusional. But it was in my thirtieth year that, after an unremarkably good run through the physics department at MIT that I received a job at a private research physics lab in the western mountains of Oregon, so near the border of Idaho as to be in both places at once merely by the form of my stride as I walked through its expensively marbled corridors.

"Welcome aboard, George," were the first words spoken to me

by Dr. Elbridge, a Harvard and Oxford fellow who had a theory about the nature of time and physicality. It would be onerous for me and boring for you to have me explain this theory in any but the most rudimentary fashion and I can say that it boiled down to a notion of time travel dependent on the motion of particles in the matter that makes up all things including human beings. It was on December first of last year that I volunteered to be the first person in reality to travel into the past and thus it happened that on that particular morning I arrived in New York City, Manhattan to be exact, at 7:37 A.M., December 9, 1986, almost a year before I was due to be born.

I arrived much as I had planned on arriving. Dr. Elbridge prepared well and I was dressed properly and had the proper currencies in my pocket and a well-rehearsed version of how and what I was to present myself as and to when I did arrive. I had memorized the streets of lower Manhattan, its hotels and restaurants and quite frankly, I felt no more strange there than I might have felt when getting off a plane in Brussels but with the distinct advantage of knowing the language better. Hardly a stranger in a strange land, I set out for the physics department at New York University to meet Dr Elbridge's father in order to tell him that his theory was not only correct but had been perfected and made practical by his eldest son, James, my employer. I made my way to the campus and in short order found the laboratory. The senior Dr. Elbridge was on leave, however, something we had not planned on and no one seemed to know when he'd be back. I was told to ask his assistant Mona Calibri, a Ph.D. student, as to his whereabouts and schedule.

I knocked at her door, a black shiny enameled mahogany slab at the top of an imposing staircase on the front of a Victorian brownstone in Washington Square. The sun was setting, long shadows criss-crossed the park and people hurried here and there, their shoulders hunched to their ears as the cold December wind blew off the Hudson in unrelenting gusts.

"Who is it?" the speaker by the door enquired.

"I'm George Benson. I'm a friend of Dr. Elbridge. I've heard you can tell me where he is. It's important."

"How important is that?" she said.

"Very."

The buzzer unlocked the door and I was suddenly in a dimly lit interior, the smell of coffee, cooking and steam heat heavy in the air. At the top of the thickly carpeted stairway, a twenty-something woman stood, hands on her hips, in front of a partially opened door.

"I'm Mona," she said. "Come on up."

Mona's apartment, one of four or five in the building, was much as I would have expected. It was neat and filled with patterned, over-stuffed furniture, a stereo with a pile of cassettes (something I hadn't seen since I was a kid) and a large TV set, the kind that weighed a hundred pounds but only had an 18 inch screen. The computer she used had a smaller capacity than my cell phone. She had been watching a speech by Ronald Reagan who was still talk-ing when I walked in. There was a large poster of Einstein sticking his tongue out and a Harvard banner pinned to the wall.

"One of the students over at the lab said you'd know where to find Doc Elbridge," I said.

"Doc Elbridge? I never heard anyone call him that. You from upstate?" she said with a slight smile.

"No. Actually I'm from the coast. Do you know when he'll be back? I've got to catch my flight home tomorrow and it's important I see him."

"I wouldn't count on either event," she said pointing to the TV screen. Crawling under Reagan's wrinkled visage was news of an impending blizzard that would shut down every airport in the northeast. Not that I was taking a plane.

"Oh, that's bad luck," I said. "Guess I'll have to take a train."

"Don't think that will work either," she said. "Would you like a cup of coffee?"

"Sure. But what's the rest of the bad news?"

"He won't be back until Monday. Took his son with him to the Chicago Science Fair."

How could my Dr. Elbridge not have remembered? I thought. Absent-minded professor syndrome? I guess there are a lot of things people don't remember.

"Oh, crap, that really is my bad luck."

"Well, you could stay on," she said. "Getting a room won't be hard. You might even make an arrangement with the U. I assume you're a grad student?" she added handing me the mug, steam rising from it.

"Yeah. At Stanford. I was planning on tonight of course. I've got a reservation at the Penta."

"Well la-de-da. The Penta? Guess you've got a very nice stipend or very rich parents or both."

I never knew anyone who said 'la-de-da.' I could imagine what she'd say if she knew I wasn't going to be born for another eight or nine months. La-de-da this, I thought.

"You're right. I am a grad student but I'm working under a substantial federal grant with Dr. El…..Dr. Elmore." That was close.

"What's the project?" she asked, suddenly warming up to me as she sat on the sofa and brought her knees up to her chin. I felt a connection of sorts. I couldn't say what it was but it felt like the dreaded love at first sight condition that I always thought was total BS and a disease I would never be subject to. She was suddenly beautiful, the deep brown almost black eyes, the curve of her lips and the sheen of her brown hair. Beautiful and familiar at the same time.

The details may or may not be significant, but the afternoon and evening flew by; dinner, drinks, the whole thing was perfection. I didn't need the hotel reservation and when I woke up the next morning Mona was beside me, more beautiful than when I met her. The snow was falling in heavy clumps and there was at least six inches on the window sill. I could hear the distant rumble and metallic scrapes of the city snow plows. I had not even attempted to resolve the failure of my mission and I realized that I'd be yanked back to my real time in less than an hour.

I slipped noiselessly out of bed and went to her desk. I found a pen and a piece of paper and scribbled one of my Dr. Elbridge's formulas onto it. I added the words, "You're right, Dad." It was not enough information to change anything but it was enough to convince Mona's Dr. Elbridge that this was a note from another time. For good measure, I added, "George Bush, Senior, will be the next president. And then a guy from Arkansas." I know it wasn't the most brilliant seer-saying I could come up with but Mona was stirring and my time was limited. She lifted her head and said, "Leaving me a note?'

"No. Its's for Elbridge. Can I ask you to give it to him?" I put it in an envelop and sealed it, putting his name on the front.

"Can't wait a few days, huh?'

"No, I am so sorry." I got back in bed and we made love again and I told her… well, it's not important.

She got up to shower and we said our good-byes.

"I'll take you to Penn Station, so you can get a train to Chicago. You'll be there by tomorrow morning, catch a flight and make it to the coast by Monday. Will that do?" she asked.

"Don't worry about me," I said. "Just remember that I love you and I'll be back soon."

"Sure," she said.

By the time she got out of the bathroom, I was gone and back in my time. I had forgotten the detail of unlocking her door from the inside but it was too late to fix that. Hopefully, she wouldn't notice.

Of course, the experiment was a success and I debriefed Dr. Elbridge about almost the whole thing. I underwent a battery of medical testing and they discovered an inoperable malignant tumor deep within my brain. It hadn't been there just two days before and there is no tumor that grows that fast unless something unusual is afoot. I think my journey qualified as the cause.

That afternoon, I received a phone call from my mother.

"George," she said in her calm modulated voice. "Your father is dead. It happened last night. They did all they could. I was there with him. When are you coming home?

That was very much my mother. She knew that if she had not gotten out all the important information in one paragraph, she'd break down and stumble through her sadness like a person lost in a jungle, tripping over emotions, memories lashing her face, a tropical storm of tears raining down on her and drowning out her ability to speak. My father had been sick a long time and so none of this was a surprise, but the news took the air out of me anyway. There's no preparing for the horror of reality no matter how much time you have to hide from it.

"I'll be home tomorrow morning, Mom," I said. "I'll be there for breakfast. OK?"

"Of course. I'll be waiting."

I arrived as promised and let me tell you there was more emotion going on than I thought was possible for me. Maybe it was my own condition that was at the bottom of it, but knowing I wouldn't see my next birthday was almost as painful as figuring out how to tell my mother. It was almost New Year's Eve and my birthday was in August. It was a long nine months I'd be spending and not a good nine months. I knew enough to know the tumor was inoperable, that I'd go through some gruesome and painful chemo-therapy and the debilitating radiation treatments that would make me bald and listless, fatigued and useless. I might even decide to forego any of it and just let nature take its course even if I had already messed with Mother Nature by traveling through time. Yet, I think, it might have been worth it. That trip gave me Mona and awoke in me feelings I thought I'd never have. Forgive me the cheesy philosophizing. I'm entitled. I'm a dead man walking.

The next morning, after making the arrangements for dad's funeral, I sat with my mother and we talked. I told her nothing about my condition; at this point it was useless to go into it. She looked so tired and haggard. I couldn't add to her sorrows. The truth would out soon enough and it could wait.

She got up from the table, left the room and came back with a large accordion folder filled with papers.

"Your father wanted you to have this after he died. I was going to wait until after I died to have it delivered to you but I see now that that is foolish. I might be able to help."

"Help? With what?"

"These are your adoption documents. We thought you might want to track down your birth parents but I think that will be impossible. Your mother died giving birth to you. The medical report is in there along with her autopsy." She handed me the file. "And there is nothing about your biological father. I'm afraid it was a one-night stand, as they used to call it. I'm sorry, son, but there you have it. After you've had time to look through these papers, I'll answer any questions you might have. You were the light of our lives and we loved you beyond words."

I didn't know what to say but I could feel the gates opening inside me. The last thing I would have been interested in discovering were the facts of my birth. What good would it do? I started tucking in some of the papers whose corners had stared to protrude. This could wait, I thought. One document would not slide in. A small photograph was stapled to the corner of a printed form. It was my biological mother's autopsy. Without knowing why, I lifted that document out of its burial place and looked at it. It was the Coroner's Report from New York University Hospital where my mother had died on August 14, 1987, my birthday. The photograph of her face told me everything. Underneath that sad, tired beautiful visage, the name "Mona Calibri" was neatly typed.

Path of the Hurricane

a Ten-Minute Play Thinking of Shakespeare

Office of the Commandant of a Nazi Concentration Camp. The commandant is seated at his desk staring out a grimy window. An aide-de-camp enters.

AIDE
Sieg Heil, mein Commandant. I bring word from the Eastern front.

COMMANDANT
I dread the sound of it.

AIDE
And so you should; so should we all who serve the Fatherland for the red horde from foul Russia, most despicable of all who breathe has this day encamped but 20 kilometers to the east of here, this very spot.

COMMANDANT
Is there any word word from your pallid tongue that might give us hope? Are there no regiments under the crooked cross to defend us?

AIDE
Nein, mein commandant. The Russians spread their filth over the fatherland like the locusts that covered impotent Pharaoh and cover all they see with the red of their putrid souls and the blood of lost defenders.

COMMANDANT
Then it is surely near done. Tell the guards to exert greater vigor in their task, fire up the furnaces ever higher and swing the scythe of righteous cause the quicker for the wheat we thus cut down is poisoned. Now go.

AIDE
Sieg heil!

He exits

A female inmate enters, his housemaid, stands at the door sheepishly and awaits his command. He looks at her in disgust and waives her in.

COMMANDANT
So Frau Juden, you are like the hands of one our fine German clocks, never failing to be on time.

INMATE
Yes, my lord.

She begins to clean.

COMMANDANT
You know for six months you have been here every day and I have never seen your eyes. Look at me.

INMATE
I fear you and was ordered never to look you in the face.

COMMANDANT
I tell you now.

He slams his fist on the desk.

COMMANDANT
Look at me!

She does; trembling.

COMMANDANT
Your dark eyes have more than fear in them for like two muzzles of an unloaded gun, they take aim at my heart.

She looks away.

INMATE
This is not my intention, commandant, for what you saw were the black pits of hopeless fear.

COMMANDANT
Hopeless?

INMATE
Yes, for I know from this dreadful place of eternal night, no one goes free except to meet God.

COMMANDANT
Then we gladden him. Is this not all the work of your god whom you say knows and controls all things? Did he not also condemn you to the wasteland for forty years?

INMATE
He did, but he left us hope.

COMMANDANT
What good hope but that it gives false promise of an escape from a place where no escape is possible? Hope is the irksome, impotent demon that truly makes you suffer the longer for if you had no hope, then you would die the quicker, your heart realizing the futility of beating.

INMATE
But I have a daughter here. Can I not hope for her sake? She is but 11 years old and knows little of the world. In her innocence she accepts what lot is given her, if that be pain and fear, then she looks to me for succor. In the night I tell her tales of green places, of loving people, of bird songs and cool waters. With this I fill her soul if not her stomach so that she may face the day thinking of calm tomorrows. When I fed your own children their breakfast of eggs and toast and honey, I hoped that someday she may have the bits and crumbs from that glad table in a place where the sky does not bleed, Thus, I go on . My hope is for her, not myself, for within I am the walking dead.

COMMANDANT
I will tell you this for, swine that you are, you are faithful in my service. Hug your daughter doubly tonight for it shall be both your last.

She falls to her knees, groveling.

INMATE
Tell me this is not so, please tell me!

COMMANDANT
And make a liar of myself? Our time is nearly done, the war lost. Soon we will all be in the dirt together. We are all doomed, but my duty is complete for you and yours under these boots are crushed, sad grapes, withered and sere, foul, left too long on desiccated vines, abandoned by your vintner. No wine, but dry sorrow shall emit, empty prayers to an empty sky.

INMATE
But your god surely watches and weeps, hopes that you have a mote of mercy left in you?

COMMANDANT
That most beloved monster in Berlin is my god and such gospel as he did spew touched my soul which now I know is made hard with the task I have been given of necessity. With him, I have cast my lot, sworn my allegiance. I shall not break my oath.

INMATE
But if all is lost as you now say and your cause ends by means of God or man, should you not spare those you can and in some way cleanse your soul?

COMMANDANT
My soul is gone, taken by the sluggish fiend of certainty for nothing so weakens firm resolve as a soul.
INMATE
Still, can you not do some act...release us or at least turn your head

and have that thorny gate left unlocked, unmanned that it will seem we did escape by churlish happenstance? Surely, some god somewhere will see and speak for you at the foot of the Almighty.

COMMANDANT
Defective Jewess! You do not see! Shall I, who for five years have sent a million to that black shower, now change course and in so doing say to all the world, "I did sin!" My task was just, my duty righteous, that mass death was its symptom, blame me not. Your God who lifted your rabble from servitude in Old Egypt, did nothing here. Does he not, therefore, condone. If I cease now as you sake, and let even one of you go free, then I have branded myself, "murderer" and thus annihilated my life. My children who will most certainly survive me, shall have shame for their only garment.

She stands up and looks him full in the face.

INMATE
Murderer you are! Foul and detestable fiend! The shredded wind that blows from this deathly hell-hole shall wail your name for eternity. "Monster," it shall howl and you shall be hunted down and devoured, hung like rotten fruit upon a blighted bough. Like wolf cubs who have lost the safety of their ravenous pack, your children and theirs shall be marked, forever damned and live their miserable stained lives in shameful ignominy, friendless, hopeless, cursing you and your loins.

She spits at him. He raises his hand to strike her but all his energy has evaporated. He becomes limp and sits in his chair, his eyes downward.

COMMANDANT
Go, say your farewells. Think not of the wrongs you believe I do but of yourself, your brethren and of your fragile child without stain who, like a reed alone stands in the path of the hurricane.

She turns and leaves, head bowed. He removes a pistol from his desk drawer.

END

Don Paulo

Don Paulo sat in his wicker chair and gazed out at the oily iridescent Mediterranean. The August heat sat on the coast like a fat woman on a chamber pot. There was no breeze to churn the milky sky, the air thick as butter. Small waves like flaps of skin rubbed against the gritty shoreline a hundred yards below where Don Paulo sat.

Even his chair did not help to cool him. Shaped like the tail of a peacock erect and displayed out, it was supposed to catch the slightest breeze from the water. Today, the sea was breathless. In the spring and autumn, when the wind shifted to an offshore flow, the back of the chair protected him from its onslaught, from its intrusion and would feel protected as if by a large hand from the wind that had spent many days or even weeks blowing the sand and soil from all over Spain and finally freeing itself into the uncluttered expanse of the green Mediterranean, Don Paulo's chair its last minute resistance. But it was still August and the heat had not lost its will to smother.

Moored out to sea not a kilometer from where he sat was the two-masted frigate from the Vatican, its white and gold flag of the Papal Legation and the red and black pennant of the Inquisition limply draped in the thick air like wet laundry. The ship rocked slowly to and fro on the weak swells, the salt water tasting its barnacled hull. Don Paulo squinting in the glare could make out what seemed like floating coconuts scattered near the prow. It was the crew that had taken to swimming to fight off the fist of August. Feeble shouts could be discerned even where Don Paulo sat, as the men called to each other or laughed or cursed or mocked.

Don Paulo's house sat on the cliff overlooking the sea. The grass, stiff and sometimes sharp as razors was dry and brittle with only a smattering of green here and there where water had puddled in last month's rain. The only boundary between the lawn and the drop to the shore below was a thicket of shore roses, their leaves yellow and speckled brown, pregnant red rose hips like cherries, the residue of its white profusion from June. A large section of the hedge, however, had been swallowed up by the last storm as the driving rain and wind collapsed the sandy soil in chunks down to the beach. Looking up from the long strand below, one could see the fringe of shore roses running the length of the cliff and in the middle, the vacant space. It was a sheer drop from the lawn to the great boulders below that were white as skulls, the chalk of the hillside exposed by centuries of intolerant weather and before that of eons of the raging Mediterranean boiling against its shore before men crawled out of the tall grass of the veldt and made their way to Italy.

Don Paulo's wife, Margheritta, had died twenty years earlier giving birth to the twins, Rafael and Maria. As a physician, he attended his wife's pregnancy and when she died, as so many did in childbirth, he felt doubly guilty for making her pregnant with twins and for not being able to save her life when the terrible bleeding started and did not stop until she was as white as the rocks on the shore.

At first, Don Paulo despised the two infants who were the cause of his loss. He had loved her beyond reason and he could only vent his frustration and anger and remorse on the most blameless of all the parties to the tragedy. Also, his faith, weak from as far back as he could remember, virtually disappeared altogether. He viewed God as an indifferent stranger needing to be cajoled by prayer, illogical ritual and money. As a physician, the only one in Verdura, he knew every resident and was familiar with the struggles each had with the two masters Jesus so clearly spoke of when he said that men cannot serve both God and Caesar. It was no coincidence to Don Paulo that the throne of the incestuous insane Caesars would be inhabited by the Popes of Mother Church. God of course, was still in his Heaven, but the two masters remained even if the name of one of them had changed from Caesar to Pope. He knew how the tithe bled the people dry and how the incessant feast days and days of obligation took men from their trades. Days lost attending to the rituals and needs of the Church were days that were lost forever and from which no money could be earned to pay the bills. Tales still abounded behind closed doors and in low voices of how families had only narrowly evaded starvation when the Archbishop of Pescara ordered the construction of the Cathedral of Santa Croce in the piazza in Verdura, how many daughters of workmen had to take to the streets to provide ducats for food for their families. The devout and everyone else perhaps not so devout, were forced to provide cheap or free labor to its construction and, on top of that, that same Archbishop ordered that it be built on the site of the town's only school, assuring the bewildered townspeople that faith was much more important that reading, writing and arithmetic although when the tithe came due everyone was expected to be a mathematical genius and calculate to the half lire what was owed His Holiness Pope Alexander VI in Rome.

As a silent act of rebellion, Don Paulo had Margheritta buried in the meadow behind their home overlooking the sea. Father Lodanno, the parish priest, at first frowned upon this and so enquired why the husband of "a true Catholic, if there ever was one," in his words, would be buried in unconsecrated ground. Don Paulo responded, "Father, it was her wish to be buried in view of the sea which she so loved."

"Perhaps this was just a passing thought," the priest replied. "She could not have desired to be so far from the church, surely."

"As we cannot ask her, I think it is best that I honor her wishes. Besides, I truly doubt that she would have wanted to be in the middle of Verdura, away from all she loved, with only a view of the cobbler, the butcher shop and the home of the Castigo's, a family she never got along with. And the dust from the roads around the cathedral; well, everyone knows the headstones get buried every summer."

"But it is hallowed ground, my son, and you know…"

"I know what she wanted and that is what will be. Thank you, Father, for your concerns."

Father Lodanno was not so easily outwitted, though, and so, he appeared the day the grave was being dug to sprinkle holy water on the soil. He said fifteen minutes worth of prayers and rang a small bell. Then he declared the grave to be in hallowed ground. Don Paulo had to stew with this particular move in the chess game of his life and it was only after the service and many shed tears, for Margheritta was beloved in the town, that that night he went out under a nearly full moon and dug another grave as far from the original as possible, disinterring Margheritta's coffin with the help of Augusto, the caretaker, who crossed himself so many times during the procedure that it took two hours longer than it should have. Dawn broke as they were filling in the new grave and making the old one look undisturbed.

"There, my beloved, forgive the extra journey. But look how beautiful the sea is from here. Now you know how much I love you," he said as he stood looking out watching the clouds tumble in the morning breeze like children playing.

After a time, Don Paulo saw the foolishness and futility of such an act and buried in the new grave, along with the body of his beloved wife, his hatred of his innocent babes and the futility of small revenges